Praise for Shar

"Fans of *Jane Eyre* will go feral for this mysterious, historical fantasy retelling of their favorite classic read."
—*The Everygirl* on *Salt & Broom*

"Readers of Brontë's original will appreciate this character-driven, romance-filled mystery."
—*Booklist* on *Salt & Broom*

"Fisher's loose retelling brings a gothic fairy tale vibe to the classic and adds some twists that will keep even those familiar with the original guessing."
—*Publishers Weekly* on *Salt & Broom*

"A pleasant, atmospheric romp that fantasy or romance fans will enjoy. There's no need to be familiar with Brontë's novel to enjoy this one."
—*Library Journal* on *Salt & Broom*

"Fisher has a fantastic voice—crisp, magical, and crystal clear."
—Darynda Jones, *New York Times* and *USA Today* bestselling author

"Magical and brilliant! A fast-paced romp that expertly weaves two different worlds into an adventure not to be missed. Sharon Lynn Fisher crafts clever dialogue and creates characters to fall in love with."
—Lorraine Heath, *New York Times* and *USA Today* bestselling author, on *The Absinthe Earl*

"The environment is lush and imaginative, with everyone appearing to hide their own seductive, dark secrets. It's a world that comes alive with mysterious, foggy moors, dangerous peat bogs, and gorgeous green hills . . . Irish mythology and folklore are where Fisher's writing shines."
—*Kirkus Reviews* on *The Absinthe Earl*

"This is quite a wonderfully dizzying mash-up of a historical setting, time travel of a sorts, and the fae. If you're a reader drawn to historical fantasy and magical Regencies, definitely give this series a try."

—*Book Riot* on the Faery Rehistory series

"This is a really fun sci-fi romance . . . Very cool setup and characters that I couldn't put down . . . The twist at the beginning will really hook you in!"

—Felicia Day, actress and producer, on *Ghost Planet*

Grimm
CURIOSITIES

Grimm
CURIOSITIES

SHARON LYNN
FISHER

47NORTH

Text copyright © 2024 by Sharon Lynn Fisher
All rights reserved.

Published by 47North, Seattle

www.apub.com

Amazon, the Amazon logo, and 47North are trademarks of Amazon.com, Inc., or its affiliates.

ISBN-13: 9781662515712 (paperback)
ISBN-13: 9781662515705 (digital)

Cover design by Alison Impey
Cover illustration by Colin Verdi

Printed in the United States of America

For Dad, who knew how to tell a story

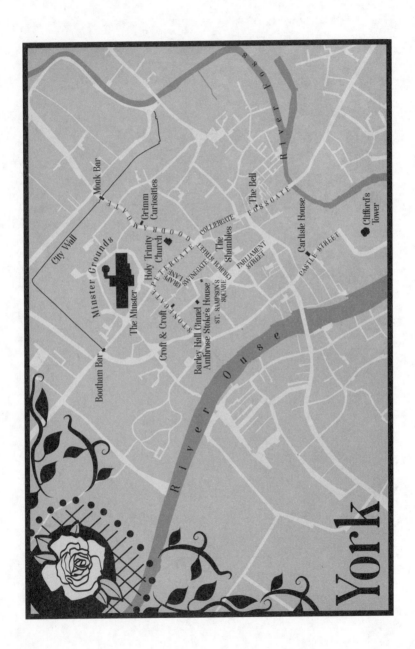

York

Author's Note

Before you begin this journey, it will be helpful to know a few fiddly York words.

BAR. Place-names that end with *bar* (such as Monk Bar) are city gates. This is due to the lingering influence of the language of the Norse people who once lived there. In York, these gates are set in the old medieval wall, which is built on top of an original Viking wall. All of them once had portcullises (Monk Bar still does) and were fortified with barbicans.

GATE. Words that end with *gate* (such as Goodramgate, where the Grimms have their home and shop) are streets. Also from Old Norse influence.

GINNEL. Essentially a narrow alleyway between walls or buildings. They serve as pedestrian shortcuts between streets. *Snicket* is another name for a pedestrian alleyway.

THE SHAMBLES. A neighborhood of York dating back to at least medieval times. Historically the Shambles housed the shops and homes of the city's butchers. Now it's a tourist's delight. (It's worth looking up some photos!)

Bonus word:

SNICKELWAY. A term coined by author Mark W. Jones, who wrote a book about York's little passages. The term combines the words *ginnel*, *snicket*, and *alleyway*. It's modern, so I haven't used it, but it's too charming not to mention.

He sprang to his sleigh, to his team gave a whistle,

And away they all flew like the down of a thistle.

—*Clement Clarke Moore,*
"A Visit from St. Nicholas," 1823

Curiosity

They say York is the most haunted city in England, but I'm probably the only person in it named after a ghost. My mother called me Lizzy for the little girl whose spirit once haunted this house, and from the day of my birth, Mama never saw Lizzy again. So I suppose Mama knew what she was about.

We live above our shop—Grimm Curiosities—on Goodramgate. Until three years ago, my papa, Herbert Grimm, ran the business. His passion was old castaway things, the curiouser the better. I'd never seen him look so lovingly at Mama as he once did at a seventeenth-century Dutch boxwood pipe whose bowl was carved to look like the head of an old woodsman.

But Papa also had a merciless sweet tooth, and in the end, it took him from us (or so we were told by his physician). In one fell swoop we lost his knack for finding treasures along with nearly all his business connections. Mama and I kept on as best we could—combing the papers for estate sale and auction notices—but not many dealers or auctioneers were eager to trade with women, even Grimm women. We were advised to sell the shop.

Neither of us could bear the thought. Grimm's was a part of Papa, and therefore a part of our family. The shop, with all its wonders, had been as much my home as the rooms abovestairs. So instead of selling it, we curtained off one corner, and Mama went into business as a medium. Which means people paid her to speak to the dead.

Mama had at first been uncertain about it, worrying what the citizens of York would think of us. I assured her that her work as a medium would dovetail nicely with the charmingly eerie ambience the shop already possessed. People up from London—or down from the dales or moors—would consult her on a lark, hoping for a story to tell their friends.

The gamble paid off beyond anything we could have imagined. In a matter of months, "Madam Grimm" was more successful than Papa's curiosities had ever been. People came from as far as Edinburgh and Dublin to consult her. But only some of them came on a lark, and even the ones who did often got more than they bargained for. Mama was not peddling parlor tricks; she had a very real gift.

And that being the case, the work took a toll. Those high times lasted all of a year, before, on the twenty-third of December 1850, Mama spoke to her last ghost—and then never spoke again. Since then, she'd spent her days in our rooms above the shop, staring out the window at the buildings across the way and the people strolling by on the cobbled street below.

The money she'd earned had gone to pay off debtors and past-due rent, and for a time helped to keep us above water. But now we'd fallen behind on rent again, and our landlady had given us until the first of the year to catch up. Moreover, we counted on December to get us through the first, thin months of the new year, when sales were slower.

Much was riding on this Christmas season.

"Mama?" I knocked on her door before carrying in her tea and toast. I set the tray on the table beside her chair.

"Oh!" I said, glancing out the window. "How pretty." Large snowflakes, like bits of lace, drifted down over rooftops and sooty chimneys in the pearly predawn light. Happy exclamations rose from the street below. "Look, Mama, the first snow of the season."

2

Earlier in the year, I would have said her expression didn't change. But by studying her closely in the long, quiet days since then, I had learned to detect minute changes in her features. There was the barest flicker of a smile, though it touched only her pale-blue eyes. It was the hope I held on to.

"I'll go down and open the shop now," I said. "The snow should put people in the mood for Christmas shopping. Knock your heel against the floor if you need me."

Like every other morning, I waited for a reply that I knew would not come. I touched her shoulder. "Eat, Mama."

Her gaze drifted from window to teacup, and I watched her lift it to her lips. She was in there somewhere, I knew it. After that first horrible week of her affliction, she recovered the ability to feed herself, though she wouldn't unless I reminded her. Dr. Stuart said it was shock. He said she'd come out of it in time. But for some months now, he had been urging me to commit her to the asylum on the outskirts of town. I couldn't help feeling that if I did, she would never come home. What's more, there were alarming rumors about the place.

I knew, too, that the physician was both skeptical and disapproving of Mama's gift. He felt she should have been discouraged from believing in it, and that her work as a medium was an indulgence that had disordered her mind. He hinted that he blamed Papa for not rooting out her "peculiarity" while he was alive. But Papa had loved peculiarity even more than he'd loved his pudding.

Sighing quietly, I left Mama to her breakfast and started downstairs. As a child I'd been afraid to go into the shop when it was dark. Besides antique furnishings, books, and jewelry, there were bones, skulls, snakeskins, and mounted animal heads. We had a ghastly eighteenth-century cabinet—enormous, black-lacquered, and highly flourished—that I'd feared was concealing a ghoul who would burst out and drag me into some nightmare baroque landscape, never to be seen or heard from again.

Growing up in a place like this did wonders for the development of imagination.

Holding the lamp before me, I stepped carefully and managed not to fall on the stairs, trip over the bear rug, or overturn the toy display. I lit the shop's lamps first and then crossed to the front windows, lighting the candles lining the sills, around which I'd arranged glass Christmas tree ornaments and holly sprigs. After shoveling coal from the bucket into the stove, taking care not to soil my dress, I unlocked the door and stepped out into the brisk winter air.

Lacy snowflakes continued floating down, and the mood in the street—busier than this time yesterday—was elated. I tilted my head back and closed my eyes, catching a few flakes on my cheeks and lashes. The icy kisses made me smile.

I took my watch from my apron pocket. Nearly half past eight—opening time on these dark December mornings. Still, I had a few minutes, so I walked to the pastry shop just up the street.

"Good morning, Miss Lizzy!" called Mrs. Finch brightly, though she was counting out change for a customer. The aroma of holiday spices enfolded me deliciously.

"Good morning, Mrs. Finch."

The customer, a lady about Mama's age in a dark-green dress, thanked Mrs. Finch and left the shop. Mrs. Finch wiped her hands on her spotless apron. Her round cheeks were pink from the ovens, and her curly copper hair hid beneath a crisp white cap.

"Brisk business today, I expect, with the snow," she said. "Long as it doesn't come down too thick."

"Yes, I hope so!"

"What can I get for you this fine morning?"

I surveyed the case before me. "Do you have any Christmas cake?"

"Indeed, I do." She opened the case and took out a cake topped with glazed fruit. "Anything else, love?"

"That's all, but would you be able to slice it up for me? I thought it might be festive for our customers today."

"That's a nice touch," she agreed, setting the cake on the counter and slicing it deftly before placing it in a box. She reached again into the case and pulled out a small ginger cake, shaped like a star and dusted with icing sugar. "Now take this for your mama, too."

"Oh, no, I—"

"Now, I won't hear it." She nestled the confection in with the slices of Christmas cake. "You take it to her with my compliments. A shilling for the Christmas cake."

"You're very kind," I said earnestly, opening my coin purse. Gingerbread was Mama's favorite.

"There was a time when the mister and me weren't so welcome on this street, Miss Lizzy. Your mother and father were always good to us, and I'm not likely to forget it."

The Finches were Irish immigrants, and the citizens of York could be cruel.

My throat tightened, causing my voice to wobble slightly as I replied, "Well, I thank you, and Mama will be so pleased. Good day, Mrs. Finch."

"Good day to you, love."

As I slipped outside, a mother and daughter entered the shop, chatting enthusiastically about the wintry weather. The sound of their laughter followed me back down the street, and my chest began to ache.

Come, Lizzy, this is hardly helpful.

The sadness had stolen upon me, as it often did. But today was not the day for it.

Back inside our shop, I set the ginger cake aside for Mama's tea. Then I laid out the Christmas cake slices on a platter and placed it on a round tea table, along with forks and a stack of small plates. I took a few holly sprigs from the window displays and arranged them around the platter. *A personal touch will make the sale,* Papa had always said. It was the only reason I could justify a shilling spent on cake.

One of the slices had broken apart while I was arranging, and I had just popped a piece of it into my mouth when the bells hanging from the front door handle jingled.

A man stepped inside and I straightened, swallowing the half-chewed cake as he removed his hat. The dusting of snowflakes on his fine, dark cape coat quickly melted. He was a tall gentleman with neatly trimmed black hair, golden-brown skin, dark eyes, and a day's worth of stubble shading the strong angle of his jaw.

I drew my shoulders back, belatedly hoping no coal dust smudged my hands or face. Clearing the last of the cake from my throat, I said, "Welcome to Grimm's, sir."

Looking startled, he hesitated near the door. Perhaps he'd wandered into the wrong shop.

"Is there something I can help you find?"

"I—yes, perhaps." He turned his hat in his hands and glanced about the shop before his gaze came to rest again on me. He seemed to really *see* me this time, pausing to look me over in a curious yet inoffensive way. My cheeks warmed. "I came for Madam Grimm," he said. "Are you she?"

Oh. It had been some months since anyone came into the shop hoping to consult Mama. The people I'd had to turn away had not always been gracious.

I took a step toward him. "I am *Miss* Grimm," I said peaceably. "I believe you may be referring to my mother."

"Ah," he said, his gaze searching the back of the shop.

"If you have come hoping to speak to a medium, I'm very sorry to tell you she is no longer offering that service. I hope you've not come a great distance."

"Ah," he repeated, his tone sinking rather than lifting this time. He cleared his throat. "Do you think she might be willing to make an exception?"

"I—I'm afraid it's impossible, sir."

"I will pay twice the normal fee, if—"

"I tell you, it is *impossible.*"

"Ah."

I winced. "Forgive me. It's just that my mother is ill and has been for some time. I'm afraid the money will make no difference."

He let out a sigh and shook his head. "No, I beg you'll forgive *me.* I'm sorry to have pressed you."

I studied him more closely, and though he was a handsome and apparently healthy man, perhaps four or five years older than me, I discovered signs of sleeplessness in his face—recesses under his eyes and pronounced wells below his cheekbones. I was familiar with these signs from my own mirror. "Can I offer you a cup of tea?"

His eyebrows lifted, and I wondered what I was thinking. His air of sadness had stirred my sympathy, and I suppose I felt guilty about disappointing him, but I had a business to run. As if in answer to this thought, the door jingled again, and a lady and gentleman entered.

"It's kind of you, but no," he said. I was both relieved and disappointed. "Perhaps I'll just have a look around."

"Please do," I said. "I'll be with you again in a moment."

I turned to greet the new arrivals. Mr. and Mrs. Lackland wanted a gift for a wealthy aunt, and I managed to interest them in a taxidermy peacock, not particularly old but very fine—and disturbingly lifelike. I had acquired it at an estate sale with the help of Mrs. Finch's son dressed in one of Papa's suits, which Mama had altered in the time before her illness. I thought I had the Lacklands sold, but on the point of decision, Mr. Lackland suggested they do a little more shopping first, and they left. My heart sank. Sale of that garish, glass-eyed creature would have neatly caught us up on our rent. Had I named too high a price?

"That must be frustrating."

I glanced up to find the gentleman from earlier watching me, and my face grew hot. Had my frustration *shown?*

"All part of the job," I said, forcing a smile.

"Hmm," he replied, obviously not buying it. He seemed to have recovered from the earlier disappointment, and I couldn't help feeling curious about why he had wished to consult Mama.

"I'm sorry I was unable to help you, Mr. . . . ?"

"Carlisle," he said, eyes moving over a mahogany curiosity cabinet. "No need to apologize. It was a rather desperate plan anyway."

Carlisle. There was a baron by that name with a town house in York. Might this be him? Or perhaps his son? His clothing was certainly fine enough. Besides the coat, his boots were sleek and gleaming, as was his silk top hat.

"Are you a relation of the people at Carlisle House?" *Subtle, Lizzy.*

His eyes returned to me briefly. "Lord Carlisle is my father."

Heavens. I knew Papa had regularly sold to various gentlemen—and ladies—of consequence, but I had never met any of them. What was the Christian name of the baron's son? I felt like I'd seen it recently in the newspaper.

Antony.

Mr. Carlisle moved to the toy display, picking up a wooden doll crafted in the previous century. She had golden curls and wore a perfectly preserved rose-and-gold gown. Glancing at me, he held up the doll.

"I wish to purchase this."

"Of course, sir." I propelled myself forward. "She's very pretty, isn't she?"

"Indeed," he said somberly. "How much?"

I normally suggested an inflated price, assuming the customer would counter with a lower one. But I had a feeling this gentleman wouldn't dicker, and I had no wish to take advantage of him. "Ten shillings?"

He nodded, and I said, "I'll just wrap her up for you." He'd removed his gloves, and our fingers brushed as he handed the doll to me, causing an unexpected ripple of warmth.

Moving behind the counter, I asked lightly, "Is this a gift? If so, I'll tie it up with ribbon." Of course there was no real need to ask a grown man buying a doll whether the purchase was a gift, but my curiosity had finally gotten the better of me.

"Yes," he said, "thank you."

I lined a box with tissue paper and gently inserted the doll. Then I tied it up with red ribbon. I placed the package on the counter, and Mr. Carlisle placed a sovereign beside it, the bright coin clicking under his thumb.

"Just a moment," I said. "I believe I can make change."

"No need," he replied, picking up his purchase.

I stared at the coin—*two weeks' rent* gleaming there in the lamplight. Bemused, I smiled at him and said, "I thank you, sir. Whomever she is, I hope the doll brings her a happy Christmas."

My smile faded away as I saw that his eyes shone with tears. "As do I. Merry Christmas, Miss Grimm."

The Collector

When the door closed behind him, my eyes again found the sovereign, with its lovely profile of the queen. Though only a dent in our ten-week deficit, it felt like a tiny circle of hope. *May it bode well for the season.*

Finally picking up the coin, I warmed it in my palm and thought about Mr. Carlisle, wondering what weighed on him so. I read the papers regularly, but mostly with an eye for acquiring goods for the shop. I tried to recall details about the baron and his family.

Then it came to me—some months back, I'd read that Lady Carlisle had died. The article caught my eye because I'd previously read about a foundation the lady endowed to feed, clothe, shelter, and educate the young women who supported themselves and sometimes their families by working on the streets of our city. Mama and I were alone in the world, and I often worried about what might happen to us if the shop failed. In truth, *often* didn't come close. The thought had grown into a shadowy thing always lurking at the edges of my mind.

Lady Carlisle's death could explain both her son's sadness and the reason he wished to consult Madam Grimm. Though his mother's death had likely not imperiled him as Papa's had us, I knew how desolating the untimely loss of a parent could be, and my heart ached for him.

The shop bells rang, and I slipped the sovereign into a pocket as three young women entered, finely dressed and laughing.

"Welcome to Grimm's," I called, walking out from behind the counter. "Please let me know if I can help you find anything."

The lady in front nodded in reply, and they began to browse. The youngest of the three, an auburn-haired girl whose blue-and-green tartan dress peeked out from under her fur-trimmed pelisse, helped herself to a slice of Christmas cake.

"He's devastatingly handsome, is he not?" said one of the browsing ladies in a low voice as she and her companion examined our collection of geodes.

"I suppose he is. Though rather morose."

"Well, his mother has just died, Isabel," scolded the other lady, "and they say his sister hasn't spoken a word since."

I glanced up from the antique Neapolitan nativity figures I'd been rearranging to give the ladies privacy.

"Yes, poor thing," said Isabel, letting out a sympathetic sigh. "They say it's an affliction of the mind."

The ladies moved on to the stuffed and mounted beasts, and I heard a muffled shriek and giggle as they discovered the peacock.

They *must* be referring to Mr. Carlisle. Probably they had passed him in the street. And the sister—whom I presumed he'd bought the doll for—had stopped speaking, just like Mama.

My heart thumped away in my chest. I strained my ears as I went back to the crèche, hoping the ladies would go on with their discussion, but they had taken up more mundane topics, such as whether an Aunt Violet might like a collection of pinned butterflies. I was about to go and offer encouragement, when the younger lady approached me with her plate of cake.

"Did Lord Carlisle's son come into your shop?" she asked, smiling shyly. On closer inspection I saw she was young indeed, likely not long out in society.

I glanced at the other two ladies, who had gone quiet.

"Why, yes, he did, in fact."

"And did he buy anything?" she whispered.

I weighed my response carefully. Though it would reflect poorly on Grimm's were I to share a customer's private business, it could be immensely helpful for word to get out that the baron's son had made a purchase here.

Finally I said, "Yes, but I'm afraid it's not my place to say what."

She stepped closer. "What was he like? Is he kind?"

The other ladies, though still browsing, had not resumed their conversation. "We spoke only briefly, but yes, he seemed an amiable gentleman."

A warm flush spread over her features. "The baroness has always given a charity ball before leaving town for Christmas. This year would have been my first to go, and I've so looked forward to meeting all the elegant ladies and gentlemen." Her smile faded. "But I don't imagine there will be festivities. Not so soon after—"

"Cecile," Isabel said rather stiffly, "come, cousin, and see if you think Papa might like this pipe."

"Excuse me," said the girl self-consciously. She set her empty plate on the tea table and joined the others.

As for me, it was high time I forgot the baron's son and remembered my job, so I went over to assist the ladies in their shopping. In the end, they bought the butterflies and a geode, but not the pipe. Yet all in all, a success.

No sooner had I wished them good day than several more people filed in, and business remained brisk until teatime. There were no purchases to equal Mr. Carlisle's, but the handful of smaller coins more than made up for the Christmas cake.

I closed the shop and took up a tray for Mama. Most days we ate an early tea instead of luncheon and then had supper, our most substantial meal, after closing for the evening.

"You're in for a treat today," I said as I breezed into her room. "I'm afraid we're doing pickled herring again, but Mrs. Finch has sent *ginger cake* with her compliments. She remembers it's your favorite. I thought it very kind of her."

I watched for any subtle reaction to this mention of her old friend. She continued to stare out the window, and I touched her shoulder.

"Eat, Mama. Then maybe we'll have time to go out before I open the shop again. It would be nice to see the snow, wouldn't it?"

Dr. Stuart encouraged fresh air and exercise, and thankfully Mama was biddable enough to accompany me when I asked. I tried to get out with her every day, but between running the shop, preparing our meals, and helping Mama wash and dress . . . Well, I did what I could and felt it was never enough.

Her gaze moved from the window to the tray, and she picked up the star-shaped cake. A fat glazed cherry rested in its center. I couldn't help smiling as she raised it to her lips. *She still knows what she likes,* I thought. And that, too, gave me hope.

When she finished, I helped her on with her cape and guided her downstairs. Twilight would come in an hour or so, but for now people still strolled the bricked street and I thought we would have time to follow the curve of Goodramgate in the direction of Monk Bar, a very old defensive tower at one entrance to the city. The snow had stopped, but like Mama's ginger star, everything had been dusted with white, brightening this tail end of the day.

I hooked my arm through Mama's, urging her along. As always, she went without complaint, but she took no interest in the scene around us. People were happy. They carried towers of packages tied up with red and gold ribbons. Children tracked about joyfully in the scant snow, like it was the most magical thing they'd ever seen. On one corner we passed a group of carolers, bundled up tightly against the cold and gripping candlesticks, puffs of fog escaping their parted lips along with festive song. I bought chestnuts from a man roasting them on the street, and we burned our fingers and tongues on the smoky, caramelized meats.

"Miss Grimm?"

We had just turned and started back to the shop when a gentleman approached. I felt a flicker of recognition—and pleasure.

"Mr. Carlisle!"

He smiled, with less of the tinge of sadness than in the shop. "This is a pleasant surprise." He balanced his small stack of packages in one hand and tipped his hat to Mama. "Good evening, ma'am."

"Mama, this is Mr. Carlisle, son of Lord Carlisle." Fixing my eyes on him, I said, "Please forgive Mama for not greeting you. She hears and understands, but she does not speak."

The gentleman's eyes widened as his gaze came back to me. For a moment he lost his voice. Could what I'd overheard earlier about his sister be true?

"What a remarkable coincidence," he said at last. "That is—forgive me—but how long has she been so?"

"Her affliction came on suddenly, about a year ago. Which is why she no longer offers—"

Suddenly Mama's hand shot out, grabbing Mr. Carlisle's arm.

"Mama!" I cried, reaching to free him. But her fingers curled tightly. "I'm so sorry," I said, flushed and flustered, still working to pry her fingers open.

"Wait," he breathed.

I looked at him, then at Mama. She stared fixedly into his face. Her eyes were wide and shone with tears. Then her mouth began to work as if she were trying to speak to him.

"What is it, Mama?" I cried, caught between alarm and elation. I hadn't seen her this animated since before her long silence. People on the footway were circling wide around us as they passed, staring. Out of the corner of my eye, I glimpsed the couple I'd tried to sell the peacock to hurrying by.

Abruptly she let him go. She sank back a step, and her gaze drifted down.

I leaned close to her, gently taking her hand. "Mama?"

No response.

Glancing at Mr. Carlisle, I felt a tear slip onto my cheek. "I'm so sorry, sir," I said, quickly drying it with the back of my glove. "She's never done anything like that before."

I saw compassion in his eyes, but also keen interest.

"Miss Grimm, I confess I'm quite overcome myself. My sister also recently lost the ability to speak, shortly after my mother died. Not only silent, but never interacting with anyone. Her physician has offered no explanation beyond shock. I wonder if—" He considered a moment. "I wonder whether you and I might benefit from sharing our stories with one another."

My heart leaped at the suggestion. I hadn't expected to see him again, much less dared to hope that he and I might have an opportunity to discuss our mutual troubles. And Mama had tried to *speak* with him; perhaps she might do so again.

"Indeed, sir, I would like that very much."

Eagerness and relief lit his expression. "When would be a convenient time?"

As far as I was concerned, the sooner the better. "I always close the shop for tea. If you like, you could come around three o'clock tomorrow? Or if that—"

"You may expect me then. I'm grateful to you, Miss Grimm."

I felt confusingly elated. Perhaps due to the change in Mama, and the possibility I might at last learn something that would help her. Not to mention the variety that welcoming a guest would bring to our routines. *And not just any guest.*

Mr. Carlisle glanced up the street. "The light has gone while we've been talking. May I escort you back to your shop?"

The lamplighters had been out when we first met him, and the neighborhood had grown quieter since then. The pubs and shops along our way were still open, rectangles of light beaming through windowpanes onto the street. I felt safe enough, yet I worried what would happen if Mama were overcome by another fit. But I suppose more than that I was enjoying his company and was happy to have it for a little longer.

"If it's not too much trouble, sir, I thank you."

He began to offer his arm to Mama, but then thought better of it, offering it to me instead. As I rested my gloved hand in the crook of his elbow, small wings fluttered in my chest. Grasping Mama's arm lightly with my other hand, I said to her, "We'll be home soon."

We got underway, Mr. Carlisle stepping along the edge of the street while Mama and I walked on the footway. "I wonder whether the snow will continue," he said.

My thoughts were awhirl over the various developments—not least among them, the fact I was promenading through the streets of York with a baron's son. It felt like stealing a moment from another world, one I glimpsed only occasionally from the shop window or on my strolls with Mama. I was grateful for Mr. Carlisle's introduction of an easily managed topic.

"I hope it will," I replied. "The snow lifts one's spirits, I think."

He smiled, and it both narrowed and brightened his eyes. "I agree. Night falls so early. It would be a dark time of year, indeed, were it not for the festive mood in the streets. I wonder how people bore it in ancient times."

"Well, I believe there have always been celebrations around this time."

He glanced down at me. "Truly?"

His keen interest warmed my cold cheeks. "The Norsemen who settled York would have celebrated Yule, anticipating the return of the light. They would have feasted much as we do, and there would have been great fires through the night."

"I had no idea. I guess I think of Norsemen as always banging their swords together."

I smiled. "I can't say with surety that there would not have also been sword-banging."

He laughed, and then he leaned slightly closer. "Take care; the footway is uneven here."

Something had disturbed the flags just ahead of us. We slowed, and I guided Mama around the spot.

"Are you a student of history, then?" he asked.

Though somewhat befuddled by his gallant behavior, I managed to reply, "Not really. The shop has always had a fine collection of old books, though. When I was a girl, I used to read them while my father worked."

"And do you still love old books?"

"I suppose I do. But I rarely have time for actually reading them."

Frowning, he struck a more somber note. "You manage the shop alone."

"I do now. For a while after Papa died, Mama and I worked together."

"It seems you have a great deal on your shoulders, Miss Grimm."

I smiled, not wanting him to view me as an object of pity. "Well, we all have our burdens, I think."

"True. Though for some of us, the burden is lighter than perhaps we deserve."

Raising my eyebrows, I said, "I hope you're not referring to yourself, sir. Your mother having recently passed, and now this affliction of your sister's."

"I do at least have the luxury of time to grieve."

This was quite true, and there was no point in saying otherwise. Yet my heart ached for him, understanding his grief perhaps better than most people could.

"Here we are," he said as we drew up in front of the shop's overhanging, half-timber facade. The building was one of the oldest on the street, believed to have been built in the fifteenth century. Which explained its tipsy appearance, uneven floors, and general creakiness.

"I thank you, sir," I replied, releasing his arm.

"I will see you tomorrow at three?"

"Yes," I said, noting another excited flutter, "we shall expect you."

He lifted his hat. "Good evening, Miss Grimm, Mrs. Grimm."

Adjusting his grip on his packages, he continued down the street.

I watched him going until Mama drew my attention with a sniffle. I unlocked the shop and let her inside. When I'd removed our capes and bonnets, I took her up and settled her in her room before returning to the kitchen behind the shop to put cabbage and potatoes on to boil for our supper. Then I went back out front and flipped our window sign to OPEN.

I had little time to think about Mr. Carlisle and our agreed-upon meeting, because the teatime lull had ended. Snow was falling again, and I waited upon a steady stream of shoppers, making one modest sale and several smaller ones.

At a quarter past eight, I closed the door behind my last customer and moved to tidy up after the Christmas cake, which had been devoured down to the last crumb.

"Excuse me, miss?"

Jumping at the unexpected voice, I turned to find I'd overlooked a customer—a gentleman in the back corner near the stove, where my mother had conducted her readings. I'd left the armchair her customers had used and added a side table, lamp, and bookcase, creating a nook for browsing through books. The gentleman sat in the armchair with a small volume across one knee. As I went to assist him, he rose from the chair. A handsome man, probably around forty, he was fair with round, heavy-lidded eyes. He had a broad, square jaw and curling dark hair shot through with silver.

He smiled and held up the book he'd been reading: *Glamour* by A. A. It brought with it a shock of memory. The volume was one of a set by this author, all on mystical and mythical subjects, and as a child I'd read them all. Though they were short, they'd not been written for children, so my memory of the information they contained was spotty. But I'd spent many happy hours examining the beautiful illustrations. This one, as I recalled, was full of fairies.

"Have you more titles by this author?" asked the gentleman.

As I moved closer, my gaze caught on an odd stick he had tucked under his arm. At first I had taken it for a riding crop, but it was thicker, and I thought made of stone rather than wood. The stick had caught my eye because its tip was ornamented with a stag figure mounted atop a metal ring. Beneath the ring, faces had been carved around the shaft. Though Papa would know better than I, the object seemed to me not only antique, but ancient. An artifact of some kind.

I met the man's gaze. His eyes were keen and prominent—glassy, I would almost have said, yet not vacant. More like . . . serenely attentive. *Like he is quietly reading my thoughts.* Unsettling, yet also somehow alluring.

"I believe we do, sir," I replied. "This was the only one on the shelf?"

"It was."

I frowned, recalling that I'd seen this book recently without it fully registering. I'd found it on the counter one morning after opening. A customer had come in at the same moment, and I'd hurriedly shelved it.

"We have quite a few books boxed away in the back. I can make a search if you'd like to return another day?"

The corners of his mouth dipped minutely. He raised the book. "How much for this one?"

I stared at the plum-colored cloth cover with its silver medallion depicting a fairy. Knowing what treasures hid inside, I suddenly found myself loath to part with it.

I blurted the first figure that came into my head. "One pound, sir."

Certainly an inflated price for a book that was not antique. Locally published, as I recalled, they might very well be available from every bookseller in the city.

His eyes registered shock. But then he smiled. "I see you know the value of your merchandise. One pound it is."

Mechanically I walked to the counter, my delight over the sale only slightly diminished by nostalgic regret over loss of the book. Which was foolish in light of another two weeks' rent!

He placed his purchase on the counter. Reaching into his pocket, he produced a sovereign and dropped it into my palm, where it felt weighty and solid. The book had been here so many years that this felt like a sovereign of pure profit. How many books in the series? At least a dozen that I recalled. My heart skipped. If they were still here somewhere, we would get a respite from our money troubles.

"Shall I wrap it for you, sir?"

"No need." He reached again into a pocket, then held out a card to me. "Please do let me know if you find any more. I'll buy them all."

I swallowed. "Certainly. Have a good evening, sir."

"You as well, Miss Grimm."

As he strode toward the door, I held the card close to the lamp on the counter.

AMBROSE STOKE
COLLECTOR OF ANTIQUITIES
9 ST. SAMPSON'S SQUARE
YORK

It was all I could do not to fly immediately to the back room in search of the other books.

"Mr. Stoke, Is It?"

Mr. Antony Carlisle

It wasn't strictly necessary for me to pass by the Grimms' shop again, though I had decided to dine at my club and it was in approximately the same direction. I noticed Miss Grimm just closing and stopped a few yards from the door, not wishing her to see me walking by and get the impression I was watching her—despite the fact I was literally doing that. After she changed the shop sign to CLOSED, she suddenly turned the pale oval of her face from the window. Seeing her moving away, I stepped closer.

She'd gone to speak to a man still inside. The fellow faced my direction, and I got a quick look at him above her halo of crinkling golden hair before I propelled myself onward.

Ambrose Stoke. His father had been Sir Arthur Stoke, a friend of my father's who had inherited and expanded a successful Yorkshire brewing business. Sir Arthur had two sons, and both were members of my club.

Because of the association between our families, I knew Ambrose, the elder son, had declined to inherit the family business for some reason, instead taking up residence in an old house in St. Sampson's Square, near the Shambles butcher quarter. After the old knight's passing, his younger son took over Stoke Brewery.

Ambrose was a devilishly good-looking fellow, middle-aged but never married, and decidedly odd. Now that I thought about it, he was a collector of some kind, which explained his being in Miss Grimm's shop.

Not that any explanation was owed.

But I thought about the young woman I'd just met, and for the first time it occurred to me how perilous was her situation. With the mother unfit to serve as chaperone, it was hardly proper for her to be alone in the shop with gentlemen like myself and Stoke. She was safe enough from me, and likely Stoke as well, oddness notwithstanding; his was an old and respected Yorkshire family. But any fellow might walk in off the street. I had a mind to go back and, once Stoke had gone, make sure she'd locked the door behind him.

Because apparently I've taken leave of my senses.

I supposed it was my mother's influence. She'd always had a care for the poor, and especially for women and girls who made their living on the seedier streets of York. In the slum dwellings of areas like Bedern and Walmgate, where families lived in squalid conditions, quietly starved, and rarely felt the warmth of the sun on their faces. My mother's physician said it was likely her charity work that had exposed her to typhoid fever.

Though I hardly knew Miss Grimm, I would not like to see harm come to her—no more than I would to any young woman so alone in the world. Also, the unique personal pain we shared had interested me in her welfare. The idea of an unfortunate *encounter* in her shop was itself enough to make me shudder, but such an event could also drastically—irrevocably—diminish her station.

Perhaps at our meeting tomorrow I would learn something of her situation that might reassure me. Perhaps she had a protector I was unaware of.

"Mr. Carlisle?"

I stopped and turned. Stoke was striding toward me. Something about the way the man moved bothered me—always deliberate, yet soft and smooth. He never seemed to be in a hurry. *Like a great, prowling cat.*

I felt the unfairness of this judgment and offered a friendly smile. "Mr. Stoke, is it?"

Though the two of us had met when I was a boy and now frequented the same club, we weren't at all acquainted as grown men. He and his father had fallen out over the family business, and I never saw him at Carlisle House after that.

Mr. Stoke returned my smile, eyes bright in the lamplight. "Indeed. I recognized you and thought we might have the same destination. And if so that we might as well walk there together, if it suits you."

"Certainly. Come along and I'll buy you a drink." Perhaps I might discover what business he had with Miss Grimm.

As if it's any business of mine.

Nostalgia

Locking the door behind Mr. Stoke, I went to the kitchen and filled bowls with cabbage and potatoes, sprinkling a few grains of salt over the top. The plain fare would have appalled Papa, but we often ate this way now, as much due to the many demands on my time as to the state of our finances. The stew would warm and fill our bellies, though.

Mama and I always ate the last meal of the day together, and I carried the steaming tray upstairs to the sitting room between my bedchamber and hers.

Usually I made some attempt at conversation, though it was really just talking to myself, but this evening I was preoccupied with the day's events. The unexpected acquaintance with one of York's most prominent citizens, of course, and also the meeting with Mr. Stoke. These events taken together with the brisk business in the shop and Mama's first attempt to speak in a year—well, the day had been a rousing success. But there were loose ends I kept picking at in my mind.

Was there some connection between Mama's affliction and that of Mr. Carlisle's sister? It seemed unlikely there was any *direct* connection, though perhaps they both owed to grief in some way. Yet Mama had fixed on him, and I couldn't imagine why.

And what of Mr. Stoke? What was it about A. A.'s books that made him willing to pay a small fortune for them? Were they in fact rare? If he returned for the others, perhaps I would ask him.

When we finished our meal, I helped Mama dress for bed and saw her safely tucked under the bedclothes. On impulse, before blowing out her candle, I said, "We had an eventful day, did we not? We may now say we know a baron's son. I thought Mr. Carlisle very agreeable."

I'd hoped mentioning him might revive her again, but I was disappointed. Showing no sign of having heard me, she rolled onto her side, facing the wall. I sighed and blew out the candle. "Good night, Mama."

I carried the dishes down to the kitchen and washed them. When Papa was alive, we'd kept a maid of all work to assist Mama. What had seemed no more than modest necessity at the time now felt like a great, out-of-reach luxury.

As I finished my chores, I thought about how much of the day's earnings I could spare toward making our guest comfortable and welcome. Really every penny of it should go to our landlady, but I could hardly serve Lord Carlisle's son a tea of day-old bread and pickled herring. Then my overtaxed brain recalled that a small fortune in books might be hiding in the storeroom. I dried my hands and carried the lamp across the short corridor, in front of the staircase, that connected kitchen and storeroom.

Inside was a higgledy-piggledy mess that had changed little since Papa died. Odds and ends of furniture, crates of books, mismatched dishes, mangy stuffed creatures, and a surplus of cobwebs and shadows. I went around and lit half a dozen candles, illuminating the legions of dust motes I disturbed with every step and breath.

Moving to the book crates, I set the lamp on a battered giltwood console table with a sinister-looking cupid head nesting in the center of the carved flourishes and flowers. Then I took off my apron and spread it over a box so I could sit without soiling my dress. Mama and I each possessed a single fine dress we wore for special occasions and for when we helped Papa in the shop. Once Mama was no longer able to work, I alternated between our two dresses so that when one needed washing, I had another. Though I tried to be careful, every movement I made in here sent up a fresh cloud of dust, and I would likely have to switch from my dark-rose silk to Mama's moss tomorrow.

Gingerly I began to dig through the crates. Luckily the A. A. books had a distinct design. Small enough to be comfortably carried in one hand, each volume had a solid-color cloth cover with a silver medallion at the center. The medallions bore illustrations relevant to each book's topic. The title and author initials appeared only along the spine.

My eyes had begun to water from the dust by the time I found what I was looking for, though not by the book covers. A box end stamped with the words *Ginnel Press* stuck out from under a nearby tablecloth. A ginnel was a narrow alley connecting two streets, and Papa had taken me exploring through all of York's ginnels when I was a child. Therefore, the publisher's name had lodged in my memory; I recalled thinking the books had somehow come from one of these curious passageways.

I dragged the box free and lifted the lid. Inside was a beloved piece of my childhood that I hadn't thought about in many years. A dozen books? This was more like twice that. How had *Glamour* ended up in the shop while the rest hid in here? Papa must have missed it in packing up the box.

I took a deep breath. Twenty-four pounds—a whole year's rent.

If I can bring myself to sell them. Papa had taught me to read using those books. Yet I couldn't afford to be sentimental over such a valuable piece of childhood nostalgia.

I slipped my fingers in among the slim volumes and pulled out one with a gray cover—*The Wild Hunt*. The illustrations in this one had produced nightmares, yet I'd returned to it every Christmas. My father's parents came from Bavaria, and when I was a child, my grandfather told me stories of the Wild Hunt, which was said to take place during yuletide. He spoke of a neighbor who claimed to have seen the raucous host charging across the sky on the longest night of the year. Another man told Opa he was *swept up* in it on St. Nicholas Eve while returning home from a pint with friends. He was set down just before dawn ten miles from his home. (Oma had given the opinion that this story likely involved more than one pint.)

I opened the book to a two-page illustration of a host of ghosts, witches, and Anglo-Saxon brutes—haggard, murderous, and well armored. The latter rode great stags or spirited steeds while the rest trailed behind in a kind of frenzied, tumbling fashion. My grandfather spoke of the Wild Hunt being led by Woden, an old god of war and the dead, and his two ravens. I recalled the book mentioning other folkloric figures who might lead it, along with stories about aerial hosts from other cultures.

Replacing the book, I drew out another of my favorites: *Doorways*. This book was about magical passages to other lands and other worlds. Some doorways were simply pairs of ivy-wrapped columns or standing stones, while others were made of wood with handles and knockers. One illustration depicted the carved wooden archway of a very old ginnel near the Shambles in York. There was a wardrobe, too, ordinary as it could be except the doors were thrown open to reveal a craggy cliff with an ancient stone fort overlooking the sea. The book closed with these words: *While some doorways are more magical or purposeful than others, any sort of door may take you to any world, so long as you believe it will. Which is far more difficult than it might sound.* To this last line I could attest.

As I was about to slide the book back into the box, I noticed a folded slip of paper in its slot. It had perhaps fallen out of *Doorways*, or been inserted between the book and one of its neighbors. I fished the slip out and opened it, immediately recognizing my father's handwriting.

DO NOT SELL

My heart jumped as if I'd been shouted at. Here was the reason for these books being boxed up in the back; Papa had meant to keep them!

Or maybe just this one? No, it wasn't like my father to break up a set of anything. *Glamour* must indeed have been overlooked. *And now I've sold it.*

Even as my stomach knotted with regret, I reasoned with myself. Papa was no longer here. He would feel differently now, knowing how much the money would mean to Mama and me. *They're only books.*

I ran my fingers over the spines. *Ghosts & Spirits. Ireland's Merrow. The Werewolf. Iceland's Hidden Folk. Witches of Wales. The Krampus*—another of Opa's stories. Only books, and I hadn't thought about them in years. Yet seeing them again had transported me back to the hours I'd spent with Papa in the shop. Sitting on his lap, pointing at words on the page, asking him what they were.

I heaved a sigh, causing a nearby candle to gutter.

Sleep on it, Lizzy.

Replacing the lid, I blew out the candles and went upstairs.

If I thought the light of morning would have me shaking my head at last night's uncertainty, I was mistaken. I awoke Saturday to a headful of questions. Had the Ginnel books been somehow important to Papa? Maybe they'd been gifts and never intended for shop inventory. As far as I knew, he'd never sold one. Had he kept them because *I* had been fond of them? And who was the note written for? Papa had an excellent memory when it came to inventory. I could only imagine he'd meant the note for Mama and me, as we often helped him in the shop. He didn't want them sold by mistake. He might have even been thinking of his death; his condition had been known for some time. It had come far sooner than any of us expected, despite the fact Dr. Stuart had warned the diabetes could weaken his heart.

How I wished I could ask Mama about this! Then it occurred to me there was no reason I shouldn't. I could read her sometimes by small changes in her countenance, and yesterday she had briefly reanimated. *It can't hurt to try.*

When I'd dressed, I went down and made porridge. Before taking Mama's to her room, I returned to the storeroom and retrieved a butter-yellow volume whose medallion featured an illustration of a lantern—*Will-o'-the-Wisp.* I placed the book on the tray and went upstairs.

She was sitting up in bed, staring out at the snow drifting softly down. I was glad to see her awake, and I was glad to see the snow. Though if it began to pile up, it would have the opposite effect of yesterday.

"Good morning, Mama," I said, setting the tray down before going to help her dress.

When I'd settled her in her usual spot, I poured her tea and picked up the book.

"I know it's cold, and I will see to the fire," I said, "but I need to ask you something. Papa has a whole set of books like this one downstairs in a box. A man came in yesterday asking for them, and he is willing to pay a good deal of money. But there was a note in the box, written by Papa, that said 'do not sell.' Do you know why Papa might have wished to keep them?"

Her eyes remained on the breakfast tray. "Mama, will you look?" I said, unable to keep a note of impatience from my voice.

She did raise her gaze to the book then, but she only eyed it blandly.

"Do you know anything about these books? Were they important to Papa?"

No change. Sighing, I set the book down. "Do you know a man called Ambrose Stoke?"

Her eyes widened, and my breath caught as they shifted to my face. "You *do*," I said. "He was perhaps a customer?"

Her mouth opened, and for one shining moment, I thought she would speak. But like yesterday, her lips tried to form words, while no sound came out. After a few moments she closed her mouth and turned back to the window, fingers knotting in her lap.

While I had no answer to my question, I had evidence that yesterday wasn't simply an anomaly. Both Mr. Carlisle and Mr. Stoke had interested Mama enough for her to try to speak, and this was a distinct improvement in her condition. Though without knowing why, I could really draw no conclusions from it about *anything*.

The weight of all this settled over my shoulders. There were days I felt so *tired*.

"All right, Mama," I said, trying to keep the disappointment from my voice. "Eat your breakfast. Mr. Carlisle is coming to tea today, so we shall treat ourselves. That will give you something to look forward to."

Her head turned, gaze settling lightly upon me, her eyes a little brighter—I wasn't sure whether in anticipation of tea itself or the visitor. Then she bent her head to her porridge, and I went to build up the fires and open the shop.

I had decided to work until afternoon and then do some shopping before our guest's arrival. The timing wasn't ideal for reducing shop hours, but I wasn't about to put the gentleman off until the new year and risk losing this opportunity.

I deliberated some over where to host Mr. Carlisle. The shop would not do, so really there was no choice but the upstairs sitting room, though he was bound to find it dull and confining. Had I not been so surprised by his proposal that we meet again, I might have thought to suggest the tearoom across from the Minster.

The Christmas shoppers braved the snow again today, and I kept busy. Having earned four weeks' rent yesterday, I found myself less anxious in the cases where browsing did not lead to sales. In what seemed like no time, the shop's grandfather clock struck half past one. I went to turn the sign, but before I got there, the bells on the door jingled and in walked Mr. Stoke.

"Hello again, sir. I'm sorry to say I must close early today, and I haven't had a free moment to look for the books." It was a bald lie that took me by surprise. I hadn't yet made up my mind what to do, and his sudden reappearance had flustered me.

Shaking his head, he replied, "Not at all, Miss Grimm. In my excitement at finding the book, I'm afraid I wasn't very forthcoming with you yesterday evening. I failed to introduce myself, which wasn't right, and I've come only to rectify that."

I lifted my eyebrows. "You did give me your card, sir."

"Yes. But I knew your father, and I should have said so. I also should have said that I was sorry for your loss. It must be difficult for your mother and yourself, left to manage things here on your own."

These belated sentiments puzzled me, but he did appear genuine. "Indeed, it has not always been easy. You were a friend of my father's, then?"

His eyes swept slowly around the shop. "More associate than friend, I suppose, though I always thought your father a kind and decent man. He had a good eye for antiquities, which I very much appreciated."

"I thank you, sir. I must admit you've aroused my curiosity about the A. A. books," I ventured. "I know little about them and find them rather mysterious. I enjoyed reading them as a child, though."

He brightened. "Did you? Then we have it in common. My mother gave me the collection on St. Nicholas Day when I was ten, and I devoured them. My interest in them did not wane even as I grew older and went off to school, much to my father's dismay. Far too unserious a subject matter for a brewer's son."

"You were not allowed to keep them, then?" I guessed.

He gave me a pained smile. "Alas, no. But my father, too, is gone, and my mother as well. My brother has the family business in hand, and I am a bachelor with plenty of time to follow my own interests. I suppose at my age one grows nostalgic."

How curious to have discovered this connection to a man who, until yesterday, had been utterly unknown to me. And this had happened *twice* in the same day. Moreover, Mr. Stoke's story had made me sympathize with him, just as Mr. Carlisle's had. And both men had for some reason captured Mama's interest like nothing in the last year.

"What happened to your books," I said, "if you don't mind me asking?"

"Consigned to the flames, I'm afraid," he replied with a forced lightness. "My father's butler noticed them in my trunks when I returned home from school for Christmas the year my mother died."

"I'm so sorry, Mr. Stoke." What a dreadful man his father must have been, to burn gifts from his son's mother after her death. Was this not fate? A message from the heavens that I should let go of the books? Had my father been the one to hear the tale of Mr. Stoke's loss, would he not have been moved to give them up? As the gentleman had observed, my father was a kind man.

"Have you found no more of the books?" I asked. "Other than the one you bought yesterday, I mean."

He shook his head. "I'm afraid not. I tried several times to find the publisher without success—despite the fact they are in York."

"Ginnel Press, was it?"

"They are as elusive as A. A. himself. Or *her*self."

"Perhaps they, too, are mythical."

It was a poor joke, but he laughed anyway. "Perhaps."

"And you've checked the booksellers? They would have far more selection than we do, of course." The longer I went on like this—like I didn't know very well I had the entire collection, save one, in our storeroom—the worse I felt. Not only that, I might seem to be encouraging him to look elsewhere for the books, which I wasn't sure I wanted him to do.

Papa's note had complicated a decision that shouldn't at all be complicated.

"More than once," he said, "and I believe I have worn out my welcome, which I may soon do here as well." He smiled, and I felt another pang. "I don't think many of the books were printed. Perhaps they didn't sell well. Or perhaps they were *all* sold and the publisher has since closed its doors. There is no publication date given, but at this point they would be at least three decades old."

This could explain why my father wished to hold on to them; he was obsessed with anything unusual or rare. Which reminded me of one question I had yet to ask.

"Did you ever happen to ask my father about the books?"

He nodded and glanced down. "I did in fact, some years before he passed. He was reluctant to part with them, which I can understand, and I don't know what may have happened to them in the intervening years. It could be that he changed his mind and did at last sell them, or it could be that, as you say, they are moldering in a box somewhere. I thought I would try again in case there was a chance."

The way his smile fixed on me gave me a shiver. Did he suspect that I'd lied to him? *Guilty conscience, Lizzy.*

At last he put on his hat. "Well, I shall take my leave, Miss Grimm, and let you enjoy your respite. If there is ever anything I can do for you or your mother, anything that might ease your burden in any way, you have my card, and I hope you will let me know. And I hope you won't take offense at the offer."

"No indeed, it is very kind of you, Mr. Stoke. I thank you." He seemed in earnest, and I was touched, though of course unlikely to seek the aid of a man I barely knew. "And I'll send word about the books."

"There's no hurry, but I do appreciate it."

He bowed and left the shop. As he passed the front window, I thought about the foolishness of my indecision.

When Mr. Carlisle has come and gone, I shall choose my course and be done with it.

Finally, I turned the sign, locked the door, and went up to check on Mama and tell her I was leaving for a while. Then I donned my bonnet and cape and hurried out to do the shopping.

I allowed myself to spend like it was a feast day, buying a small cured ham in the Shambles, Stilton and pears from the market, and another Christmas cake from Mrs. Finch. It wouldn't be all that Mr.

Carlisle was used to, but at least we wouldn't embarrass ourselves. If we had to skimp at Christmas to make up for the splurge, so be it. It was only Mama and me anyway.

Back at home, I tidied the sitting room and made a simple table centerpiece from a fresh candle and a small wreath of ivy and holly I'd bought from a costermonger. I'd also purchased some oranges, and I arranged them in a bowl on a table near the stairs, where I thought they might scent the room as we walked by. On impulse, I dug a fingernail into the skin of one orange and rubbed the fingertip against each side of my neck—something I'd sometimes seen my mother do just before Papa came upstairs for tea.

Stationing myself in front of a window to watch for our guest, I noticed finger smudges on the glass and used a corner of my apron to rub them away.

"I wonder what he will think of us, Mama," I murmured.

Before I could turn to check that she was still tidy, I saw him, his long strides carrying him quickly down the street. I tugged my apron over my head and hurried to my room, tossing it across the foot of the bed. Then I took a moment to smooth my hair, breathe, and collect myself.

This is about helping Mama. No reason for all this fuss.

Immaterial that our visitor was also a "devastatingly handsome" gentleman of rank.

Descending the stairs, I heard him tapping on the shop door.

Coincidence

"Good afternoon, Miss Grimm," said Mr. Carlisle with a bright smile.

Flushing with pleasure to see him again, I stepped back from the door. "Please come in, sir."

I relocked the door behind him, and he removed his hat and coat. Taking them from him, I inhaled the scents of evergreen, citrus, and spice. Maybe a little brandy, too. It gave me a mental picture of what Carlisle House must look like inside, all decked out for the season.

I laid the coat over a chair and set the hat on top. My heartbeat had gone quick and light.

"Thank you," he said. It occurred to me for the first time how quietly deep his voice was. And standing closer to him near the windows revealed that his eyes were the color of burnt sugar.

"I have tea ready upstairs, if you'd like to follow me." My own voice sounded unnaturally high—from a nervousness I hoped he wouldn't notice.

I turned to thread my way back through the shop, and he replied, "I hope it's no hardship having me here. I know you must be very busy. Especially this time of year."

"No hardship, sir." I started up the stairs. "On the contrary, we hardly ever have callers, and your visit shall be a welcome break in our routine."

"That is kind of you. But I wouldn't want any . . . any consideration of rank to make you feel you couldn't avoid my company."

I stopped and turned without thinking, missing a heartbeat as his upward momentum brought him quite close. "I assure you that we are very happy to have you, Mr. Carlisle. With that said, if it is no longer convenient for *you*, we would certainly—"

"Not at all." He sank down one step, giving me more room but bringing our eyes almost level. "I confess that yesterday I was so eager to talk with you about your mother's affliction I gave no thought at all to how it might inconvenience you, and I only wished to remedy that error."

He, too, looked uncertain—flustered, even—and I smiled. "We are pleased to welcome you to our home. Though I'm afraid we are rather poor and plain here, so you must prepare yourself for that."

His face relaxed. "By the state of your shop, I suspect your home to be neat and comfortable, and I don't know what more anyone could wish for."

This was most gracious of him, and I inclined my head. "Let us go up, then."

When we reached the sitting room, I said, "You remember Mama, Mr. Carlisle."

"Good afternoon, Mrs. Grimm." He nodded, and after a slight pause moved into the room, no doubt remembering that he couldn't expect a reply. He was very gentlemanly in all his manners.

I watched Mama closely for a reaction to our guest but was disappointed. She didn't acknowledge him in any way. "If the two of you will keep each other company a moment," I said, "I shall go down for our tea."

He turned. "May I help you, Miss Grimm?"

"Thank you, sir, I can manage."

I'd already arranged all the food on the dining table, along with a bottle of beer for Mr. Carlisle, should he want something other than tea. I had only to bring up the teapot and cups. Still, when I returned with the tray, he came and took it from me, carrying it to the table.

I set out the cups and poured, and Mr. Carlisle came to my chair, sliding it out so I could sit down, as Papa had always done for Mama. His attention to all these details touched and surprised me, as I imagined they were managed by servants in his own home.

We were arranged on three sides of our four-person table, with our guest having the best view of the windows (though from here there wasn't much to see but the building across the street). I had placed the food and teapot at the center of the table, with the decoration behind it at the fourth place, as the table was small. I couldn't help wondering what Papa would think of having such a distinguished guest in our home. He was always curious about everybody and would have asked Mr. Carlisle a hundred questions, baron's son or no.

"As I predicted, you have a charming home," said Mr. Carlisle.

"I thank you. It suits Mama and me very well." My gaze swept the room as I tried to see it from his perspective. The shop was dark, richly textured, and atmospheric, and Mama and Papa had created a contrast to that in our home. Our furnishings were worn, even threadbare and scuffed in places, rather like the house itself, but Papa had exquisite taste, and our chairs and sofa were inviting and comfortable. Much of our more interesting bric-a-brac had been moved to shop inventory after he died, but paintings of soft country landscapes done by my Oma—bluebell meadows, stone bridges, and frothy becks—adorned the walls. Mama and our former maid had further brightened the room by sewing floral-patterned cushions and throws. At the back of the room, a folding screen concealed another, narrower stairway, this one leading to an attic room that had been used by Oma and Opa but was mostly empty now.

"Might I inquire when you lost your father?" asked Mr. Carlisle.

I reached for the pitcher and tipped milk into my tea. "It has been three years now."

"I'm very sorry. You must miss him."

"I do indeed, very much."

We were a subdued party, with Mama not engaging in conversation and me almost too nervous to speak.

"Mr. Carlisle, if you will hand Mama's plate to me, I will serve her."

"No, I insist," he said. "Tell me what she would like."

"That's kind of you. A little of everything, then, not skimping on the cake." On Dr. Stuart's advice, we had tried to keep sweets out of the house after Papa's diagnosis (though I knew very well he continued to pay regular visits to Mrs. Finch). Since his death, we hadn't often allowed ourselves the luxury. But Mama, too, had a sweet tooth, and I could see it still brought her joy, so I liked to indulge her when I could.

Our guest placed two slices on her plate. The corners of her lips quivered.

Once he'd served Mama, I urged him to serve himself, and then I took a thin slice of ham, a little Stilton, and a slice of bread. My appetite was normally quite healthy, but it had fled upon Mr. Carlisle's arrival. I also poured some beer into a glass for him, setting the bottle next to it. His eyes moved to the label.

"Stoke Brewery," he said. "I had a drink with Ambrose Stoke last night."

I eyed him with interest. "Oh, indeed?"

"Yes, he's a member of my club, and our fathers were friends. I never really spoke with him before last night, though. Seems a pleasant fellow." He lifted the glass and sipped the golden liquid.

"Here is another coincidence, then," I said. "For I, too, became acquainted with Mr. Stoke last night. He came into my shop looking for books."

"In fact he mentioned stopping in your shop, but not that you were a stranger to him before that."

"A complete stranger. Though when he came back today, he said he had known my father."

His eyes darted to me before he raised knife and fork, cutting into the ham. "Came back?"

I nodded. "He felt he'd been rude yesterday evening in not mentioning knowing my father. He's quite keen on purchasing some books of Papa's." Inside I cringed, realizing I'd just admitted—to a friend of Mr. Stoke's—that the books were in my possession.

My guest frowned. "You're reluctant to sell them?"

I stared, the implication of this statement being somewhat startling. "Forgive me for asking, but he told you that?"

He shook his head. "Your look suggested it to me. I beg your pardon."

If Mr. Carlisle had read me so easily, what must Mr. Stoke have seen? I let out a quiet sigh, and his eyes came to my face, fork halted halfway to his mouth.

"Well, you're not wrong," I said, "but I'm afraid I haven't admitted to Mr. Stoke that I *have* the books."

His expression contained a spark of amusement. "Your secret is safe with me."

I laughed and felt a swelling of gratitude—along with a tickle of warmth. "It's rather a silly secret. The books are all perfectly preserved in a box in the storeroom, and he is willing to pay a handsome sum. Far more than they're worth. There should be no trouble over it at all. And yet . . ."

He sipped his beer and said, "The books mean something to you."

I wasn't used to anyone taking such an interest in me, certainly not someone like Mr. Carlisle. Though it unsettled me to find that I was not at all mysterious to a keen observer, I had to admit that I *enjoyed* his interest, along with the warmth and friendliness of his manner.

"I read them as a child," I replied. "But it's more than that. There is a note in the box, written by Papa, that says 'do not sell.'"

"Aha," he said, brows lifting. "That is indeed a wrinkle."

"I'm not a grasping sort of person, but it *is* a great deal of money. It's just Mama and me here."

He nodded grimly. "And it falls to *you* to provide for the both of you. I'm sorry you face such a decision."

Again he had correctly interpreted my vague explanation. I gave a small shrug and sipped my tea. "I don't mean to complain. And I'm not usually so indecisive. He told me a very sad story about how he once owned a set of the books and lost them, and I feel like that should have been an end to my ambivalence."

"Yet it wasn't."

I sighed. "Apparently not. Today he mentioned that he tried to buy the books from Papa as well, and Papa refused. Which isn't surprising, after finding the note."

Mr. Carlisle frowned. "Seems he ought to have mentioned that right up front."

"Perhaps. I took it that his enthusiasm for the books had caused him to forget his manners, or at least he said something like that."

My guest looked unconvinced. "But if he was so eager for the books, why would he have waited three years after your father's death before approaching you?"

A fair question. I fiddled with the handle of my teacup. "Out of consideration for our grief?"

"It seems a long interval for that. But then, he's rather an odd fellow. Never married, my father once said, because the old things he collects mean more to him than a woman ever could." He drained the last sip of beer from his glass, and his gaze came to rest on me. "What will you do, Miss Grimm?"

I shook my head. "I keep hoping a decision will come to me. Perhaps another night of sleeping on it. But none of this is what you came here to discuss. Shall we move on to that topic?"

"Certainly, if you're ready."

I lifted the teapot and refilled all our cups. "Would you tell me about your sister? Then perhaps I'll settle Mama in her favorite chair, and I can share our story with you." Her gaze had drifted to the windows, where the falling snowflakes were just visible in the twilight. "Tea, Mama," I said softly. Her head slowly turned, and she picked up her cup.

Mr. Carlisle had drained his cup already, but he raised his hand when I started to pour another. "Thank you, Miss Grimm. Everything was delicious."

"I'm happy to hear it, sir. Please, finish the beer if you like. Mama and I rarely drink it."

He poured the rest of the bottle into his glass, and I got up to add coal to the stove.

"Allow me to do that," he said, quickly rising and coming to take the shovel.

I watched him refill the grate, and for reasons unclear to me, it brought me a sense of peace I hadn't felt in years. I didn't mind doing all the things Papa used to do—some of them I quite enjoyed—but having the gentleman here, eager to help me, an attentive and sympathetic listener . . . I suppose it was comforting to lean on someone else, if only for an hour or two.

As the coals caught, a soothing popping and crackling filled the room, and we both returned to the table.

"As I mentioned yesterday," began Mr. Carlisle gravely, "my sister, Sophia, has fallen into much the same state as your mother. It happened about a week after my mother died."

"I see," I said gently. "Are there any details about that day you'd feel comfortable sharing? Anything she may have been doing at the time, or how she seemed right before? She must have been devastated by the loss of her mother."

"Indeed she was," he said, fingers threading together in his lap. "She always had my mother's joyful energy, but that light went out when Mother died. I suppose it was to be expected." His frown deepened. "This was something more, though. A maid went in to open the curtains one morning and found Sophia awake and staring. No one could get her to speak or even look at them after that. One odd detail surfaced in the days that followed. The night before it happened, Sophia's governess had overheard her holding a conversation when no one else was in the room."

"Talking in her sleep?"

He shook his head, more in uncertainty than denial. "Miss Clyde said it sounded like she was talking to my mother. Which didn't really worry us at the time. She was far too young to lose her mama."

"This will sound strange, but . . ." I hesitated.

"What is it?"

"Well, did anyone think she might *actually* be talking to Lady Carlisle? My mother receives—*received*—messages from the dead. She always has. She named me after a ghost in this very building."

This brought a quiet smile to his lips. "May I ask your Christian name?"

My heart pulsed. "Lizzy. *Eliza*, officially, though I have no memory of anyone ever calling me that."

His smile broadened. "It suits you." But the smile was lost as he continued, "It *was*, in fact, whispered among the servants that my mother's spirit might still be with us. To my dismay, at first. I didn't believe in it, and it only caused me pain to hear of it. As much as I missed her, I preferred to think of her someplace happy and peaceful, not haunting Carlisle House."

"Of course," I said softly. His gaze lifted to my face, and I saw the rawness of his grief. Lady Carlisle's death had happened so recently, and it was obvious how much she'd meant to him. "Did a physician evaluate Sophia?" I asked.

He nodded. "He could find nothing wrong with her physically. He believed Sophia was avoiding accepting our mother's death and advised us not to say anything that might seem to encourage her in any delusion. I was of much the same mind at the time."

"What does he say about her condition now?"

His expression was weary and flat. "That she is in shock, and that it will pass."

I frowned. "Perhaps we have the same physician."

He looked at Mama. "Your mother's been like this for a year now?"

Her attention was again fixed on the window. Dusk had deepened to dark, but the diffused yellow glow of the streetlamps reached us from below.

"Yes. If you'll excuse me a moment, I'll take her to her room and make her comfortable." It wasn't the only reason. For all she seemed lost to the world, I knew she could still hear me sometimes, and I thought it might upset her to listen to me recounting the history of her illness.

"Of course." He stood up, glancing at Mama. "Thank you for your hospitality, Mrs. Grimm."

I went to her and took her hand, murmuring, "Come, Mama."

When she was settled in her chair with a blanket over her lap, I returned to the sitting room, leaving her door open for propriety's sake. Since her illness, I often dealt with men alone in my job, both in the shop and outside it. Of course Mama was always with me at home, but most of the neighborhood knew something of her condition by now. I'd had to give up worrying what people might think of me, but I wanted Mr. Carlisle to know I did have a care for my reputation.

"It feels so late," I said, joining him again. "I never really grow used to these short days."

"Are you tired, Miss Grimm? If so, we can certainly continue our discussion another time."

Was I tired? I had no idea how to answer that question. I was never *not* tired. Yet I had no desire to abbreviate his visit. "Let us continue, if you're willing."

"I am indeed," he said, finishing his beer. "I'm eager to hear your story."

I angled my chair slightly toward him and sat down again. "Well, as you know, Mama worked for a while as a medium. The regular business of the shop is in some ways challenging for a woman. Men are not always willing to trade with us, which makes it difficult to acquire stock."

He frowned. "That is unfortunate, though I'm sorry to say it doesn't surprise me."

"I suppose I was naive, but it did surprise *me*. I thought my father's associates would want to help his family. Instead, it was suggested we should sell the shop and I should find a husband to support Mama and myself. One man, older than my father, hinted that he would be willing to marry me with the shop as dowry. He became quite offended when I did not take up the hint."

Mr. Carlisle's frown deepened. "Sadly, that does not surprise me, either. So your mother's work as a medium was your own plan for saving your family business?"

I nodded. "We had meant for Mama's work to supplement our income. We put an ad for 'spirit communication' into the papers, thinking people might come out of curiosity."

"And did they?"

"They did, and I think at first it *was* mostly out of curiosity. But I soon learned that people can become quite desperate when they have unfinished business with a loved one who passes. Mama very quickly established a name for herself. People came to our shop from all over the country. We even had a gentleman from Dublin. Soon the *shop* was secondary income to Madam Grimm. But being so close to other people's grief all the time, to say nothing of conversing with the dead—it took a toll on her."

"I can only imagine."

"Sometimes people became angry, too, if Mama couldn't help them. She might be unable to find the spirit they sought, or the spirit might be unwilling to communicate. We would in those cases return their money, of course, but Mama felt it as keenly as they did, like she'd failed them. At any rate, we were doing well enough that I suggested she cut back to two or three days per week so she would have time to rest and recover between. She agreed, but her very next customer turned out to be her last."

Mr. Carlisle's brown eyes were soft with sympathy. "I confess you have me on the edge of my seat, but I can see that talking of this pains you."

I realized my eyes had dampened. "I'm all right," I said, pressing a fingertip to the outer corner of each. "It's only that I've talked of this to no one but Dr. Stuart, and you're a very kind listener." I always felt it keenly—the fact I had no one in the world to talk to about my burdens and my grief. Yet I thought I'd never felt it *so* keenly as now, with Mr. Carlisle here to temporarily fill the void.

"Not at all," he said quietly. "I'm very sorry for your pain."

"And I for yours, sir." I cleared my throat. "The only part of my tale that remains is that Mama's last customer—a man from the moors who had just lost his wife in childbirth—came out from Mama's nook in the shop to tell me something was wrong. I found her struck silent and senseless, much like now, only worse. From what I could gather, Mama seemed to have made contact with the woman, and spoke a few words to her, but then suddenly her eyes glazed and her expression went blank. I sent a neighbor for the physician, but he could find nothing wrong with her. He told me she would improve with quiet and bed rest."

"But she did not."

"She did to a point," I said. "After a week she began responding to my suggestions that she eat, and eventually she complied when I wanted to dress her or take her for walks."

He nodded. "It has been the same with Sophia."

"It does sound as if our experience has been uncannily similar. Visits from the physician, assurances that it was shock and would pass. Some judgment. In our case, over what Mama had been doing, how it would 'unsettle anyone's mind,' and how I'd been wrong to encourage her."

Then I recalled something from his earlier story. "You said that when your sister was first afflicted, you agreed with the physician that she shouldn't be encouraged in any 'delusion'—I assume with regard to communication with her mother. Your feelings about spirit communication changed at some point, as you came here hoping to communicate with Lady Carlisle yourself."

He took a deep breath. "I confess I've grown desperate over these months of Sophia's condition remaining unchanged. My father intends to take her to London in the new year. He will consult physicians there, and I am very much afraid they will recommend she be placed in an asylum." Fixing his eyes on my face, he said, "Such horrible stories come out of those places, Miss Grimm."

"Yes. Dr. Stuart has recommended the same. Even if we had the money, I doubt I could bring myself to do it. I don't believe people are cured there." My eyes drifted to Mama in the other room. "That gives us something like three weeks, then."

"Three weeks?"

I met his puzzled gaze. "Until the new year. Three weeks to see if we can figure out this mystery on our own. I, for one, believe it is a spiritual rather than a mental affliction, and as such we are no less qualified than the physicians to cure it."

A smile spread over his face. "I begin to see how you manage it all."

Belatedly my cheeks warmed at my emphatic—and rather presumptuous—speech. "What do you mean?"

"Running the shop, taking care of your mother and your home. Your mind is very organized. And determined."

What a contrast he was to the men I met with on shop business! No patronizing commentary, no disapproval. He was in fact praising me for the very qualities many men would find distasteful in a woman. I imagined his mother was to be credited for his attitudes. Yet he couldn't have taken a lesson he himself did not believe in.

"It's really you who have inspired me anew to look for an answer," I replied. "I had begun to fear nothing could be done. I think there must be some connection between your sister and my mama, don't you? There seems too much coincidence in it for it to actually *be* coincidence."

"We're in agreement about that." I could see the relief in his eyes, and I, too, felt greatly relieved. I was no longer alone in this.

Yet the Lizzy he had referred to—the Lizzy who worked tirelessly taking care of Mama and the shop—now spoke in my mind: *He is a*

stranger whose station in life is far above your own. You are nothing to him.
He may very likely change his mind and give in to his father's wishes.

To which the Lizzy who still held on to hope replied, *It will cost*
me nothing to try.

Only that wasn't really true. It would cost me time and effort, precious commodities in my world.

"I was wondering whether your mother had any more spells like
the one yesterday?" asked Mr. Carlisle.

I hesitated as my mind came back to the moment; then I remembered this morning. "Yes, in fact she did. I showed her one of the books
in the set that Mr. Stoke wants to buy. I asked her whether she knew
why they were important to Papa. Which may seem a strange thing to
do, but I am always trying to reach her, and sometimes I can detect a
reaction. She didn't respond to the book, but she did to my mentioning
Mr. Stoke. She tried to speak again, but it was the same as yesterday."

He frowned. "And this has happened only these two times since
she was first afflicted?"

"That's right."

He gave me a significant look. "Maybe too much coincidence to
be coincidence."

Studying him, I nodded. "Tell me what you're thinking."

He gazed into the fire. "I'm not sure. But *something* caused her to
make an effort at communication twice. It doesn't seem unreasonable
to think it might have been the *same* something in both cases. Are there
similarities in the situations?"

I considered this. "Yesterday it came on suddenly, when she met
you. Then today when I mentioned Mr. Stoke. You and Mr. Stoke know
each other, and I met you both for the first time yesterday. Beyond that,
I can think of no connection." Besides the fact both gentlemen were
unmarried, rather charming, and pleasing to the eye, which was wholly
immaterial.

He sat back in his chair. "Could it simply be that she's beginning
to wake from this long sleep?"

I glanced again to her bedroom, and my heart sped up. "It is tempting to hope so," I said unsteadily.

"Indeed, for both of us."

Our eyes met, and we sat suspended for a moment in a kind of kinship. Of grief and worry and frustration, but also of hope. There was something more, too—something outside our circumstances.

A spark of curiosity.

Then he shifted in his seat, and I read in the movement the beginning of his leave-taking. My disappointment took me by surprise.

But he settled again, flattening his palms atop his legs. "Continue to watch her closely, Miss Grimm. In the meantime, what about these books?"

"Do you mean Mr. Stoke's books?"

"The ones your father did not want to sell to him, yes. There is some mystery there, would you agree?"

"I would. Several mysteries, in fact. Why did my father want to keep them? Who wrote them? Where is the publisher? Why are there no other copies?"

"Well, although I can't imagine any connection between *this* mystery and our primary one, we do know Mr. Stoke is of interest to your mother for some reason. Besides that, the books have a connection to your father, and I don't think we can rule out the possibility your father's death might relate in some way to your mother's condition, just as my sister's may be related to our mother's death. Do you think it worth taking a closer look at the books, and maybe even trying to find out who wrote and published them? Even if it doesn't connect, it might help you decide whether to sell them."

"It seems a good place to start," I agreed. Then I smiled. "Your mind is very organized, Mr. Carlisle."

He grinned. "A rather recent development, I'm afraid."

"Yes?"

"I may have lacked focus in my earlier years. In fact, my father told me so on several occasions, once when I was sent home from Eton for playing a prank that injured one of my instructors."

"Oh dear! What has changed?"

Sobering, he replied, "My mother's work changed me, I suppose. Lack of focus is a luxury many do not have. I had opportunities most people don't, and they came to me by birthright rather than hard work."

"You are right. But surely a boy cannot be blamed for taking the life he's always known for granted."

"Perhaps not," he replied, inclining his head. "But a man can. I'm grateful to my mother for giving me a better understanding of the world." He shrugged wearily. "Even if, in my father's view, it has made me soft."

It was lovely to see his devotion to his mother, and his obvious respect for her desire to help others. Many besides his father would consider both unmanly. Yet another similarity between Mr. Carlisle and Mr. Stoke—paternal disapproval.

"I have read about Lady Carlisle in the papers," I said. "I think she must have been a remarkable woman."

"I believe she was. She would have admired *you*, I think."

I felt the color stealing into my cheeks. "Me?"

"Your competence and self-sufficiency. The way you care for your mother."

"It's very kind of you to say so. Most days I end up feeling there were many things I should have done better."

"I think the most competent people are also often the most critical of themselves."

Our gazes held again, and in those fluttering heartbeats of silence, the grandfather clock downstairs struck half past four. My guest rose from his chair. *It had to come.*

"I should let you get on with your evening, Miss Grimm. Shall I return another day so we may look at the books?"

I stood up, smoothing my skirt. "Yes, certainly. Though, if you like, we could divide and conquer. I can send half the books with you, and we could each go through our half before our next meeting."

"That seems an excellent plan, if you would trust them to me."

"I have another thought, as well. You must say if it makes you uncomfortable."

"I approve of all your thoughts so far."

I smiled, feeling a twinge of pleasure. "Well, I was thinking that if your sister is well enough to leave home, you might bring her with you the next time you come. We could see what she and Mama make of each other, if anything. What do you think?"

His brow furrowed as he considered.

"It won't offend me if you think it ill advised. I wouldn't wish to place Miss Carlisle in any danger."

"On the contrary, I think it's another excellent idea. The exercise and change of scenery will do her good. I'll see if I can manage it for our next meeting."

"Very well. The books are in the shop storeroom. Shall we go down?"

Mr. Carlisle took the lamp from the table near the stairs, where it rested next to the oranges, its warmth slowly releasing their sweet scent. Together we went down to the shop.

"You must excuse the state of this room," I said when we reached the door. "All Papa's efforts at tidiness and organization were exhausted on the shop, I'm afraid, and I haven't had the time to do much about it."

I opened the door and he raised the lamp, casting light and long shadows through the room. "If I were a ghost," he said, "I believe I could be quite happy here."

I laughed. "I did warn you. The books are just over—oh heavens!"

The box had overturned, upsetting the lid and spilling half of its contents onto the floor.

I knelt beside them. "What on earth?"

"Perhaps it fell from the table?"

"Impossible, since it was beneath. How very odd." I righted the box and counted out eleven volumes from the floor. There was an old medical bag on the table, and I stood up and placed them inside. Then I scanned the room, looking for I knew not what.

Noticing, Mr. Carlisle held up the lamp again. "Do you suspect an oversize rodent?"

Again I laughed, though my voice had a nervous edge. "I hardly know what to think, but I suppose it doesn't signify."

I snapped the bag closed, and Mr. Carlisle took hold of the handle.

Unlike Mama, I had never seen or heard a ghost. But because of her, I did believe in them. However, there was a perfectly earthly possibility for what had occurred. As far as I knew, Mama never left her bedroom without me, but her behavior had been odd the last couple of days. *Odder.* The book I'd shown her at breakfast hadn't seemed to register, yet I might have been wrong about that. Could she have come down here while I was out shopping?

"There are twenty-two books?" asked Mr. Carlisle.

"Hmm?"

He lifted the bag slightly. "Twice eleven."

"Ah. I believe there are two dozen. But I sold one to Mr. Stoke. It had somehow made its way into the shop, and that is what began this whole dilemma."

He raised an eyebrow. "I would say that either your books are ambulatory—in which case you must double whatever you intended to charge Mr. Stoke for them—or ghost-Lizzy is playing tricks on you."

I shivered. "Mama said she went away after I was born, but I'm beginning to wonder."

We made our way out to the shop entrance, and he handed me the lamp.

"When do we meet again?" he asked.

Pleased to see him as eager as I was for our next meeting, I said, "Would Monday be convenient? Or Tuesday, if you need more time."

"We won't be holding our annual charity ball this year, so it seems I have nothing *but* time, at least until the new year. Monday it is."

I smiled. "Until then."

"One thing, Miss Grimm—I don't want you laying out any more feasts. I intend to arrive on your doorstep with provisions."

"Oh, please don't go to any trouble—"

"I insist on going to some trouble, as you have."

Relieved, I gave a nod of acceptance. While I was eager to have him here again, and there was nothing more important than helping Mama, I couldn't continue such expenditures.

He lifted his hat. "Thank you again, and good evening."

"Good evening, Mr. Carlisle. Please take care in the snow; the footway may be slick." He didn't have far to go. York was a mere village in comparison to London, and Carlisle House was an easy half mile from the shop.

I watched after him as he tracked through the couple of inches' accumulation of white powder. An unfamiliar emotion tugged at me. *Longing*, I realized. How soothing his presence and companionship had been.

It was a perilous pleasure to dwell on.

Closing and locking the door, I surveyed the dark interior of the shop—glass eyes of mounted deer heads gleaming in the lamplight, that ridiculous peacock, and the cabinet that had so terrified me. I'd thought my childhood fears had all been replaced by adult ones, but now that my visitor and his humorous commentary had departed, I felt an uneasiness pricking the back of my neck.

What *had* overturned that box? Might my ghostly namesake have returned? Mama believed little Lizzy had gone on to her final rest, but none of us really knew what came after, not even Mama. She had told me once that spirits were evasive on such questions, and she seemed to think it unwise and even disrespectful to ask.

Sighing, I walked back through the shop, breathing easier when I reached the stairs. As I set my foot on the bottommost step, I felt something there and stepped down.

Bending to look, I drew my breath in sharply.

A *Ginnel book* lay on the step.

Ginnel

I straightened and turned, holding the lamp high. "Who's there?"

No answer but the ticking of the grandfather clock.

"You have my attention." My voice trembled. "Please show yourself."

I glanced to the right, at the door to the storeroom. I had closed it behind us, I was certain—yet it stood half-open. My breaths came quick and light as I went and pushed it open the rest of the way. "Mama?"

Feeling air against my face, I peered into the shadows at the edges of the room. There were no windows or other doors to let in a draft, yet cobwebs hanging from a centuries-old iron chandelier wafted slightly toward me.

"Is anyone there?" I called, my voice faint and reedy. My skin had gone clammy, prickling with unease. *Had* my ghostly namesake returned?

No reply came. No movement answered beyond the light breaths of air.

Slowly I walked back to the stairway. Heart thumping, I picked up the book. *The Krampus*—red cover, black lettering, silver medallion depicting a bundle of switches. This book had frightened me as a child, more even than *The Wild Hunt*, so I remembered it quite well. Krampus was a kind of opposing figure to Sankt Nikolaus—St. Nicholas, the patron saint of children. Yet the two often appeared together. A goblin-like creature with long, curved horns, Krampus was said to punish naughty children while St. Nicholas gave treats to the good ones.

Upstairs, I took the book straight to Mama. "What do you know about this?"

My question didn't rouse her.

"*Mama.*"

Her head slowly turned.

"Someone left this book on the stairs. It wasn't me, and it wasn't Mr. Carlisle. Also, someone overturned the box of Ginnel books in the storeroom. Do you know anything about that?"

Her hands gripped the arms of her chair, and I could see they were trembling. But her gaze remained fixed and expressionless.

"Mama, *please.*" A sob escaped my lips, and I sank to my knees before her. "I can't keep on like this. I feel so alone, and so frightened. What's going to happen to us?"

A tear slid slowly down her cheek. I dropped my head in her lap, weeping quietly into her skirts. After a few moments I felt her hand come to rest on my back, and then I was sobbing in earnest. I couldn't recall the last time she'd voluntarily touched me.

It felt good for once to let the storm blow through me, rattling all my doors and windows and threatening to take off the roof. Gradually it blew itself out. Mama's hand fell away, and I sat up. Though her eyes and wet cheeks shone in the candlelight, her gaze remained distant. I wiped my face, picked up the book, and got to my feet. Laying my hand on her shoulder, I said, "Try to come back to me, Mama."

I went to the sitting room and added more coal to the fire before going back downstairs to open the shop again. Happy voices reached me from the street outside, soothing my jangled nerves. I stepped out the door for a few breaths of cold air, and to be closer to the merriment and falling snow.

Business was slow that evening, though it seemed like the whole town was out enjoying the wintry weather. Only a handful of customers had come through by half past seven, and I decided to lock up a little early.

I went to the kitchen and made up two plates of pickled beetroot, bread and Stilton left from tea, and a small bunch of bruised watercress I'd bought earlier from a shivering flower girl in the street. She had wrenched my heart with her blue lips and threadbare wrap, and the cress, kept somewhat fresh in a glass on a windowsill, I guessed, would likely be the last we'd eat until spring. She'd asked a ha'penny, and I'd given her the two pennies left in my coin purse. Her grateful smile and "Bless you, miss" only made me wish I could have done more.

After supper, I made tea and picked up *The Krampus* again. Bundling myself in a shawl, I sank into the chair by the sitting room window. I ran my fingers over the red cloth cover, still in excellent condition, and the embossed medallion. I opened the book to the first page, stamped with the publisher's name and emblem—a curving cobble path lined by buildings. Beneath it were the words *York, England.*

I thought about the name, Ginnel Press. York had many ginnels like the one depicted on the emblem. They were of varying lengths, often crooked, and they could be unsafe, as they made good hiding places for the criminally minded. It was a fitting name for an elusive publisher, as well as for one that published books about shadowy and elusive beings. I wondered whether the name might be literal, too. Was the publisher's office accessed from a ginnel? It could explain why I'd never noticed it. Mr. Stoke struck me as the type of person who would have thought of that and made a search.

The book's second page contained an illustration that transported me to childhood. A horned beast with a sack of children on its back was gobbling up a *boy* like a gingerbread figure. The first time I'd looked at it, I'd gone crying to Papa, who had assured me Krampus was a story adults told children to get them to behave. But I had only to read a few pages of the book to discover it treated its subject matter quite seriously. Krampus had originated from the snowcapped Austrian Alps. He was the shadow of St. Nicholas; together they represented the light and dark in our natures. Not all of God's children were worthy of God's gifts all the time, the book reasoned, and Krampus was there to remind them to keep to the light.

The severity of punishment meted out by Krampus depended on the severity of the misdeed, according to A. A., the mildest being a switching with birch twigs. More serious offenses might result in imprisonment in the creature's mountain cave, shown as filled with bones of victims and past meals, along with many strange objects that had the look of monstrous toys.

Letting out a deep breath, I set the book aside. I couldn't see any relevancy to the questions Mr. Carlisle and I were seeking to answer, though it had seemed to make sense as a starting point. And as for whether I should part with the books—it felt ever likelier I would have no choice.

With my mood turning prickly, I went down to the kitchen and poured a splash of sherry from the last of four bottles that had been given to us by a grateful customer of Mama's. I'd been rather stingy with the gift, allowing us each small glasses on feast days or times when my worries wouldn't settle on their own. Courage thus fortified, I went back to the storeroom for the rest of the books.

Though I found the box still upright, the lid had been removed and was nowhere in sight. My heart hammered against my ribs as I bent to lift the box. Then I saw two of the books on the floor—*Doorways* and *Ghosts & Spirits*. Swallowing dryly, I picked them up. The room had gone so cold I could see my breath.

"Whoever you are," I challenged shakily, "it seems you have plenty of time on your hands. I would be very happy to put you to work at something useful."

What if it's Papa?

The thought hit me so forcefully I gasped. What if he'd come back to warn me against selling the books? It hardly seemed a message important enough to return from the grave, however extreme Papa's love for such things might have been.

I felt another breath-like movement of air, against the back of my neck this time. My courage failed me. Leaving the box behind, I hurried out of the room and up the stairs.

Moving almost in a trance, I stacked *Doorways* and *Ghosts & Spirits* atop *The Krampus* and then went to settle Mama for the night. I tried to continue my reading after that, but I could not focus. Something supernatural was going on in our shop, that seemed certain. *Could* it be Papa? If only I could speak to him. But I didn't have Mama's gift. Even if I did, I had fresh evidence from Mr. Carlisle that communication with the spirit world could be perilous. Were I to end up like Mama . . . I shuddered to think what would happen to us.

"I must take a page from Papa's book instead."

When Papa was investigating the origin of some mysterious object in his collection, he didn't rush. He had a shop to manage, and he was head of a family. He didn't let himself get discouraged when he met a blank wall; it was all part of the intrigue, and Papa loved it. He kept patiently tugging at threads, in his own good time, until the mystery unraveled.

Three weeks wasn't a lot of time, especially with Christmas in the middle of it, but I, too, was now head of a business and a family and must pace myself.

So rather than read, I stared at the books and thought about their author. Not only who he was, but how he had come by his information. Other books, probably. Though perhaps like me his parents or grandparents had told him stories. The topics of these books were drawn from various cultures—Bavarian monsters, Irish fairies, Norse elves. Maybe not passed-down knowledge, then. The author was educated. A folklorist or professor. A traveler, even. Someone Papa would have admired—likely envied—and perhaps that explained his attachment to the collection.

The author could be anyone. Surely I had no greater hope of discovering him than did Mr. Stoke. A. A. (anonymous author?) might not be from York. Or from England. He might not be alive.

The publisher, at least, was here, and they must know *something* about the author. It was the publisher I must find, if indeed they still existed. Mr. Stoke would likely have checked the ginnels. He would have asked the booksellers, and probably the other publishers in York. Who might he not have thought to ask?

Someone small.

Ginnel would have had to hire a printer. There were several of those on Stonegate. The books would have been printed decades ago, but it was worth trying.

The grandfather clock struck half past nine. Our supper dishes still sat on the dining table; I had put off clearing up as long as I could. I loaded the tray with plates, cups, and a candle and made my way carefully downstairs, feeling each step with a toe before lowering my weight onto it. I encountered no more stray books.

As I washed our dishes, I made up my mind not to be afraid of this spirit—or whatever manner of creature it was—if I could help it. There had been no serious mischief, and it might very well be trying to communicate something important. Mama had said her medium work was most successful when the departed had some message for the living.

I'd already begun to think of the spirit as Papa, and to believe he did want me to keep the books. But without knowing why, I wasn't sure it was a good enough reason for turning down Mr. Stoke's money. Though the overdue rent was the most pressing, it wasn't the extent of our deficit. There was the need to put away money for the early part of the new year, and the fact we couldn't acquire more items for the shop without funds. Each time we sold something, I rearranged things or brought out something from the back, but that would work for only so long before the displays began to look sparse. Papa had sold many things on consignment, but few of those sellers had agreed to continue working with us after his death.

If only Papa had been as concerned about securing his family's future as he had been about these books.

No more incidents occurred as I finished my chores and dressed for bed. I lay for a long time staring at the candle on my bedside table, trying to settle my thoughts so I could rest. Despite the fact our money worries were never far from my mind, today had been like a holiday in some ways. Entertaining a guest and treating ourselves a little. Having a person to talk with who had nothing to do with shop business or debts. Mr. Carlisle had been earnest, interesting, sympathetic . . . nothing I would have expected from the son of a baron. Mama and I had been treated far more shabbily by some members of our own class.

I'd already begun to anticipate Mr. Carlisle's next visit, and I knew it would brighten the hours until then. The worried, frugal, cautious creature that had rooted into my mind when Papa died disapproved of this frivolity, but I decided right then that my Christmas gift to myself would be a break from listening to that sad-violin voice. Just until the new year.

That resolution, be it ever so short-lived, did lift a bit of the weight, and I blew out the candle and closed my eyes.

Sunday morning brought a change—fog, and streets made sloppy and treacherous by the melting snow. The walk to Holy Trinity Church was mercifully short, though still enough to soil our dress hems.

Papa had not been especially devout, but we'd regularly attended Sunday morning services since I was a child. He deemed it a wholesome activity that was also good for business, as he almost always met with at least one customer or associate after the service. Though Papa was in trade and therefore not considered a gentleman, he was sometimes invited by one to the Yorkshire Club while Mama and I went home to prepare Sunday dinner.

We'd continued attending church after he died, without enjoying the same business benefits, while also enduring stares and whispers—first because of Papa's death, then because of Madam Grimm, and now because of Mama's affliction. I avoided our neighbors and acquaintances after the service, as they always asked the same questions—to which I had no new answers—or gave well-meaning, tedious advice. But it was a lovely little church, originally built some six hundred years ago, and I found it restful listening to the preces and the choir. It was really the only waking time I felt I could be still.

When Mama and I returned home, I opened the shop for a few hours. Sunday business hours were frowned upon by some, of course, but you could always find bakeries, greengrocers, and public houses open. Printers, too, I hoped.

Few people were out and about today, however. There was nothing festive about fog, after all, and I imagined people huddling around their stoves with books and newspapers while awaiting their Sunday dinner. I busied myself merging the doll and stuffed-bird displays for reasons I couldn't have explained, though I was pleased with the result. Then I moved a large bowl of "mermaid scales," as Papa had called them, to the counter, where they'd gleam in the lamplight. They were pretty things that I'd loved to stack and sort as a child, paper-thin disks of a substance like mother-of-pearl in shades of either green and brown or turquoise and silver.

As the day wore on, the fog thickened, and the lamplighters were at it by teatime, when I closed the shop. I considered taking Mama with me for the exercise, but it was a cold, damp afternoon, and I'd be much quicker on my own. I didn't really like leaving her alone, but I liked dragging her along on my errands in uncomfortable weather even less, and I knew very well I'd find her in exactly the same location and position upon my return. So I shoveled fresh coal into the stove, checked that the screen was securely in place, and lit the lamp in her bedroom before departing.

Most destinations inside York's medieval wall could be reached on foot in a quarter hour or less. The nearest printshops were on Stonegate, an easy distance from our shop if I headed toward the center of town and turned right onto Petergate. However, I could also continue straight onto Church Street and take Swinegate instead. Where Swinegate ended, a ginnel that was a combination of tunnel and narrow alleyway led at last to Stonegate, and to a printshop with a carved and painted devil figure peering down at passersby.

I knew about this alternate route because my father had once taken me through it. And I recalled this vividly because he told me it was to be an adventure for just the two of us; I was not to tell Mama. A street called Grape Lane intersected Swinegate where the ginnel began. Some years later, I overheard our maid refer to a "lady of Grape Lane." Some years after *that*, when Papa began giving me newspapers to read, I came to understand Grape Lane had once been a place of business for the women forced to earn their living on the streets. That type of activity had moved outward to slum areas many years ago, and the street name had been changed to Grape Lane from something far less innocuous. But I supposed the ginnel had been tainted by this history, and Papa didn't want Mama to know he'd taken me there.

I wasn't sure it was advisable for me to venture there alone. Considering how convenient it was to my plan for visiting the printshop, I also wasn't sure I would be able to resist the temptation.

When I reached the intersection where the choice must be made, I opted to stay with the main streets and save the ginnel for fairer weather, when there would be more people about. On days like this, when the fog shifted and swirled in the street, and the others I passed kept their heads down and their winter wraps drawn close—when the clopping of horses echoed such that I had no idea which direction the rider was coming from until he'd popped out and startled me—it was easy to see how York had come by its reputation as the most haunted city in England. Roman legions had gone to battle with the earliest Britons here, leaving traces of their city beneath ours. Norsemen had raided and eventually settled here. William the Conqueror had brutally subdued York's mixed Anglo-Saxon and Viking population. And many people had been executed for their religious practices.

When I thought of the city's history, I couldn't help but remember Papa and his love of stories, both fanciful and factual.

At last, I came to the red devil, a brightly painted wooden sentinel perched on one corner of the printshop's facade, right next to the entrance to the ginnel I had decided not to take. When Papa had pointed him out to me, he'd said that printers of old were haunted by their own variety of demon that caused typographical errors. Though modern printshops might not put much stock in the idea, according to Papa it was only because the blame had shifted; printing apprentices were now known as "printer's devils."

The building itself was a fine old jettied and timber-frame house with a street-level shop window, much like our own. The plaster on this old house had been embellished with flower disks and curling vines. Above the door hung a small sign with black lettering—CROFT & CROFT. It seemed as good a place as any to start.

Through the shop window, I could see they were indeed open. Oily yellow lamplight illuminated the dark, rigid lines of the presses along with the young men who moved among them like ants, black-waistcoated with shirtsleeves folded back.

I took a deep breath, working up my courage, and opened the door.

The men didn't even look up as I walked in, and they were so hard at work I couldn't imagine them slowing down enough for me to speak to one. The shop had four presses. Some of the workers were arranging letters in trays. One man used a roller to apply ink to the letters. Others pulled levers on the presses to lower a flat iron panel down onto large ivory sheets of paper.

"Can I help you, miss?"

I flinched at the sudden, rather loud voice behind me. Turning, I found a man standing with arms crossed, eyeing me speculatively. Only—on second look, not a man, but a woman wearing black trousers and waistcoat, her ginger hair tucked up into a bowler hat. A pair of spectacles rested on the bridge of her nose.

"Yes—um—thank you. I wanted to ask you about . . ."

I trailed off as she began shaking her head. The constant dialogue kept up by the workers—barked orders, questions, and replies—drowned out my voice. Uncrossing her arms, the woman pointed to a staircase near the back of the shop. She started toward it, and I followed.

The room at the top of the stairs presented quite a contrast to the scene below. A large mahogany desk dominated the space, which was lined with bookshelves and wood paneling. A welcoming fire burned in the grate, a well-padded armchair and small tea table resting nearby. A portrait of a man with a white beard and cane hung behind the desk.

Instead of going to the desk, the woman waved me to the armchair and stood with her hands clasped behind her.

When I was seated, she said, "My name is Croft. What can I do for you?"

I raised my eyebrows. "Of Croft & Croft?" I realized it must have sounded foolish, but I had not expected one of the Crofts to be a woman.

"Not precisely," she replied. "The first Croft was my grandfather. The second was my father. There was also my brother, Philip, who didn't live long enough to order a new sign. By the time I took things over, I couldn't see the point of spending a guinea on such a thing." She frowned. "If you came here expecting to deal with one of *those* Crofts—"

"No," I said hastily. "Not at all." I shifted in my seat, annoyingly nervous. I took another deep breath and said, "I'm Lizzy Grimm."

A smile spread over her face. "Of Grimm Curiosities?"

"That was my father, but I run the shop now."

She dipped her head. "I'm very pleased to meet you, Miss Grimm."

"And I you, Miss Croft."

"What may Croft & Croft do for the proprietress of Grimm Curiosities today?" She wasn't mocking me. Her tone was respectful and earnest.

"I'm afraid I have no printing business at the moment, but if I ever do, you will have it. I'm in search of a piece of information, and I hoped you might be able to help me."

Her forehead furrowed, ginger brows drawing down. "Go on."

"I'm trying to discover who published a series of books. Ultimately, I'm trying to discover their author. He was anonymous, you see, and the books—"

"Is this about Ginnel Press?"

I stared at her, my jaw hanging open.

"Pardon the interruption," she continued, "but there was a fellow here a few months back asking about them."

My hopes flattened. "A Mr. Stoke, I'm guessing," I said with a weary smile.

"Exactly the one. I'm afraid I sent him away disappointed."

I nodded and began to rise. "I'm sorry to have wasted your time, Miss Croft."

She held up a hand. "Now, wait a minute. Why don't you tell me exactly what you want to know and why."

I studied her, afraid to let hope revive. Also reluctant to tell her my business. But what was the point of coming here if I wasn't going to give it my best effort?

"The books are on folktales and mythology," I said, "written by an author who goes by A. A. and published by Ginnel Press. I have a set in my shop, and Mr. Stoke would like to buy them. I'd ask that this go no further, as I haven't yet told him I have the books. My father did not want them sold, but we could use the money, so I'm trying to learn more about them."

She stood lightly thumping her thumb against her chin. I held my breath, listening to the popping of the coal fire.

"Here is the thing, Miss Grimm," she said at last. "*We* are Ginnel Press."

"*You* are?" I stared.

"Well, more precisely, we invented Ginnel Press. There really is no such thing."

I frowned. "I don't understand."

"I don't much either, I'm afraid." She straightened, folding her arms over her chest. "All I can tell you is that there is a box in our storage room stuffed with papers relating to Ginnel Press. When I took over the business, I looked through them enough to determine that an author called A. A. came to us some forty years ago—when my grandfather was still running the shop—wanting to hire us to print a series of books he had written. There's a single invoice—for two sets of the books. A note on top of the stack of papers says that it is all confidential, proprietary Croft & Croft information. I can't imagine why all the secrecy over forty-eight books, but there it is. I elected not to disclose this information to Mr. Stoke."

"I see." Though I didn't, really. Why would she tell me and not him? Regardless, at last I knew *something*. The books were indeed rare—though also more mysterious than before. "May I ask why you've told me?"

She met my gaze, her eyes bright. "Because frankly Mr. Stoke felt a little full of himself, and he didn't give me much of a reason for why he wanted the information. You, on the other hand, have given me a very good reason. I think women running family businesses must help each other if they can, and I honestly don't give a fig about four-decades-old confidential documents."

I laughed. "Well, I thank you, Miss Croft. And I will respect the confidentiality of what you've told me. Do you think there's any possibility the author's true name might also be found in your grandfather's old papers? I'd be happy to know *anything* that might help with my decision."

She chewed at her bottom lip. "Tell you what, come back in a couple of days. In the meantime, I'll give them a more thorough look-through."

I rose from the chair. "I am in your debt, Miss Croft."

She grinned. "Just remember us for any printing needs, as you've promised—clandestine or otherwise."

"I certainly will."

She started down, and I followed, my mind turning over all she'd told me. Only two sets! I wondered how Papa and Mr. Stoke's mother had come by theirs. It seemed they must have been available for purchase at some point. Perhaps the author had died, and they'd both purchased them at an estate sale. Or could it be Papa and Lady Stoke were both somehow connected with the author?

I would have loved to talk more with Miss Croft, and not just because I was anxious to know the truth about A. A. I couldn't help wondering whether she'd faced the same kinds of challenges Mama and I had, and what she'd done about them. Was that the reason she dressed in men's clothing? I'd do the same without hesitation if I thought it might make a difference.

We reached the shop, and my heart gave a leap as the front door opened and in walked Mr. Carlisle.

"Would You Like to Join Me in a Small Adventure?"

Antony

"Miss Grimm!" My voice wmas all but swallowed up in the shop bustle.

Recognizing me, she smiled and came over to the door and did something I wasn't prepared for—rose onto her toes to bring her face closer to mine, so she might be heard. I think it surprised her, too, as the color in her cheeks deepened.

"Have you business here, Mr. Carlisle?" she asked.

"I do, in fact. I won't be long, though, if it would be convenient for you to wait a moment?" I hadn't expected we'd speak until tomorrow, but it was just as well not to put off what I must tell her.

"Certainly, I'll just step outside."

As she left, Miss Croft called for the shopmen to take a break.

"An unexpected honor, Mr. Carlisle," she said, joining me. "What can we do for you today, sir?"

I took from my coat pocket the paper I'd been given. "Invitations," I said. "I had no hand in them and will be quite useless should you have any questions. However, I believe the lady has been very thorough."

She unfolded and looked over the sheet. "So the charity ball is going forward after all."

"It is. My father has enlisted Miss Isabel Stoke, whose grandfather was a dear friend of his, to help us pull things together in time."

To my thinking, a suspiciously odd and sudden decision that likely had very little to do with continuing my mother's charitable legacy and a lot to do with my father trying to maneuver me toward a marriage of his choosing. Not only that, it was deucedly inconvenient, as I had intended to spend as much time before Christmas as possible at Grimm Curiosities.

"I see," Miss Croft replied, though for some reason she looked almost as unsettled as I felt. "Mr. Carlisle, I was very sorry to hear about your mother. She was a kind woman, and our family has always considered it a great privilege to serve her and *her* family."

I acknowledged this with a nod. My mother was, in fact, the reason we still did business with Croft & Croft. Many customers had deserted them when Miss Croft took over the enterprise. I'm sure my father would have been among them, but luckily such matters as printers were far beneath his notice.

"I expect you'll want these right away, the date being only a week from now?"

It was the reason my father had insisted I put in the order myself. My mother rarely took advantage of our rank, but my father viewed it as our birthright. "Yes, as soon as you can manage it. If it's too much—"

"No indeed, it's a small job. We shall fit you in, sir. If you'd like to send someone round for them . . ." She took out her watch. "Let us say at seven o'clock?"

"Excellent, Miss Croft. I thank you." Though I was less than enthusiastic about the ball, I did appreciate her effort.

When I left the shop, I found Miss Grimm outside, patiently waiting in front of the window.

"What a pleasant surprise meeting you here," she said.

"I was about to say the same. To what do I owe the pleasure?"

"That will require a little explanation. But it is relevant to our endeavors."

"May I walk you home, then, if that's where you're going, and hear all about it?"

"You may. Would you like to join me in a small adventure?" By the light escaping the shop window, I caught a glint of mischief in her eyes, and it went right to my heart.

"Very much, Miss Grimm. Lead on."

She took my proffered arm, but we walked only a couple of yards before halting in front of the ginnel that cut through to Church Street. The daylight gone now, a streetlamp burned just inside the passage. Fog and shadows gave the opening a somewhat sinister appearance, especially with the imp grinning down at us from the printshop.

"My father led me through here when I was a child to show me the red devil," she said, pointing at the fellow. "Today I thought I might retrace those steps in case it would shed any light on our mysterious publisher, Ginnel Press. But with the early nightfall and thick fog, I thought better of it. Now that you are here—"

"You thought we might go together. Very sensible." I was alarmed she'd even considered doing such a thing on her own, but of course I had no business saying so.

"Considering what I've just learned from Miss Croft," she said, "it's really no longer necessary, but I'm afraid I'm still feeling the urge. Nostalgia, perhaps."

I knew that I must speak to her of the new demands on my time, but our unexpected meeting, and my desire to walk and talk with her, made me loath to spoil the moment. "May I ask what you've learned?" I said, taking up her hint.

"It was told to me in confidence," she replied, lowering her voice and moving closer. "You must promise the information will go no further."

I put a hand over my heart, touched by her faith in me. Not to mention the trust that allowed her to feel safe in my company. "You have my word."

"*Well,*" she began conspiratorially, "Croft & Croft *is* Ginnel Press. Forty years ago, Miss Croft's grandfather was approached by an author who wished to print his own books. Croft printed two sets of the series under a fictitious publisher name."

"What excellent instincts you have, Miss Grimm!"

"Excellent *luck*, really," she said with a laugh.

"I won't hear it, for you had the idea to come here." She really was remarkably resourceful. "Was Miss Croft able to give you the author's name?"

She shook her head. "But there may be answers in the old records, and she intends to look deeper into it. I'm to come back in two days. I also learned that *Mr. Stoke* recently came to Miss Croft seeking the same information."

"He did, did he?" I didn't like hearing this. I couldn't help feeling there'd been something slightly shady in his dealings with Miss Grimm. But perhaps I'd been prejudiced by my father's disapproval of him. "I suppose it's not surprising after what you've told me about him. So she's given him the same information?"

"She hasn't! She wasn't persuaded that Mr. Stoke had a legitimate need for it."

"Good for Miss Croft. And he shan't ever hear it from me, so the secret is safe."

Her soft smile inflicted a pang of guilt. I tried to think how to phrase my news in a way that wouldn't make her suspect I had lost interest in our endeavor. My desperation to help Sophia—whom I had failed by not being more present after our mother's death—had now grown to include Miss Grimm and her mother, who seemed like they might be balancing on the edge of ruin.

Before I could speak, she said, "Are you ready for our adventure?"

"I am indeed."

We couldn't walk abreast into the narrow alley, so I gestured for her to lead the way. I immediately regretted it, as I'd forgotten the ginnel soon opened into a small, square courtyard—an excellent place for a cutpurse (or worse) to lie in wait for victims on a foggy winter evening. But we arrived there without incident, and my companion paused. The footway continued on the other side, another lamp marking its entrance.

This space was empty but for a staircase leading to the upper floor of the building on our left, where a candle burned in a window. Other than that, no indoor lights shone from the structures around us. It was rather a desolate spot.

"Do you know the history of this ginnel?" asked Miss Grimm.

"I don't, but I'm guessing you do."

Her eyes followed the lines of the buildings while mine followed the lines of the delicate bones of her face. Her features were soft, her complexion fresh as a gardenia but with a delicate rosy tinge in the apples of her cheeks. We lacked the light to see them properly, but I had observed the previous day that her eyes were a uniform, dark China blue, like the surface of the sea on a still, cloudy day. I also knew that under her bonnet hid cider-gold hair with a rebellious nature. She might have been a doll in her shop, were it not for the variability of her expressions.

"These structures on either side of the passage were once a part of the same large house," she said. "Barley Hall was originally a priory, but later the church leased it to wealthy families. At some point it was divided, and the corridor converted to this ginnel. We might very well be standing in the parlor."

"I had no idea. You seem to know a great deal about our city."

She smiled. "Papa loved York and collected facts about it just like he collected everything else. He was full of curiosity, and his enthusiasm was contagious. He injected a little magic into everything he did."

I envied the fondness in her tone. My own father was a decent man. He treated servants kindly and had been indulgent with my mother and sister. But the two of us were at odds from the time I was old enough for school. I supposed that was the way of it with fathers and sons, especially eldest ones. So many expectations, they must naturally clash with a young man's desire to go his own way. Even now, my father rarely trusted me to do the right thing. For good reason—we often had different ideas about what that was.

"I find that quite wonderful, Miss Grimm." Our eyes met, and she glanced down. I thought perhaps there'd been more warmth in my look and tone than was entirely proper. "Shall we continue on our way?" I asked more lightly.

She raised her eyes, but before she could answer, her expression froze. The shy smile slipped away as she shifted her head slightly, peering around me. "There's a man watching us, Mr. Carlisle," she whispered.

Quickly I turned, peering through fog into shadow. "Who's there?" I called out.

No answer came, and I continued to scan the small courtyard. "Where, exactly, Miss Grimm?"

"In the corner there, next to the stairs."

Still I could see nothing, and I thought perhaps her eyes were better than mine. "Go back to the printer," I said, pressing her arm to get her going that direction. "I'll be right behind you."

We started toward Stonegate, but before we left the courtyard, I paused and looked once more.

My companion gasped, drawing my eye. "I was mistaken, Mr. Carlisle," she said shortly. "Let us go."

Briskly she walked on toward Stonegate. "Miss Grimm!"

At the printer she turned toward Petergate, and I had to increase my stride to catch up with her. "Miss Grimm, what—"

"If you'll give me a moment, sir," she said quietly, avoiding my gaze.

"As many as you like, only tell me whether you're all right."

She eyed me apologetically. "I will be. Let us walk on to the shop."

Her manner alarmed me, but she soon slowed her pace, and the rigid lines of her figure began to soften.

"Forgive me, Mr. Carlisle," she said at last. "I had a shock."

"So I gathered," I replied, relieved that she seemed herself again. "Can you tell me about it?"

We stopped under a streetlamp. She took a breath, pushing her hands deeper into her muff. "I did indeed see a strange man in the courtyard. He wore a domed hat—a helmet, I now believe—and held an axe. He bore a large disk on his back, a shield, I think." She met my gaze. "He looked like a warrior of old."

This was quite a detailed description, yet I'd seen not even a vague hint of the man. "Might it have been a trick of the shadows?" I regretted this as soon as I said it; it was just the sort of patronizing remark I had heard both my father and our physician make to my mother and sister.

Miss Grimm frowned and shook her head. "I know you didn't see him, but he looked as real to me as you do now. I thought he meant us harm." She paused for another breath. "Then he turned and walked through the wall."

"He went into the building?"

"Yes, but not through a door. He *walked through the wall*."

Finally, I understood. "You saw a spirit!"

She eyed me uneasily. "I believe so. My mother has always had that ability, as did her grandmother. I thought that I had not inherited it."

"I gather this is not a welcome development."

In a strained voice she said, "You've seen Mama."

Of course. There were more frightening things than spirits. "Yes," I said. Had her hands not been captured by a roll of brown worsted, I doubt I'd have been able to stop myself from reaching for one of them.

Then one of the captives emerged, swiping a tear from her cheek as she turned to walk on. I placed my hand on her arm.

"Miss Grimm."

She looked at me, eyes gleaming.

"We are in this together," I said gently, "are we not?"

The tension in her face eased away. "Yes."

"We will get to the bottom of this, I promise you. Whatever it takes."

Father and his schemes can go to the devil.

Relentless as the Dawn

He put out his arm again, and I took it gratefully, relieved to steady myself against someone more rooted in the physical world than I felt at the moment. If he had any doubts about what I'd seen—any concerns about the state of my mind—he kept them to himself. I sensed that he believed me, and that soothed me like nothing else could have.

We soon reached the shop. I unlocked the door, trying for a lighter tone as I said, "Tomorrow will still be convenient for you?"

He hesitated, a shadow crossing his face, and I got the feeling he was about to back out of our engagement. But then he smiled and said, "I'm looking forward to it. Good evening, Miss Grimm."

As I pushed open the door, a letter fell onto the threshold. He bent to pick it up and handed it to me.

"Thank you, sir. Good evening."

I'd been gone longer than I'd intended, and I went straight upstairs, calling, "I'm home, Mama."

I was relieved to find her exactly where I'd expected to. "I'm sorry to have left you alone for so long," I said, spreading a blanket over her lap. She didn't acknowledge my arrival, but I continued, "I'll see to the fire and get started on dinner. Tomorrow we're to have Mr. Carlisle for tea again. Perhaps his sister, too."

Papa had been particular about Sunday dinners, favoring roasts that we could continue serving in some form for the early part of the week. While the roast tradition had departed with our maid, I generally tried to make the meal special in some way—particularly now that the ones during the rest of the week tended to be makeshift. But this week's splurge had come in the form of yesterday's tea.

I had a store of root vegetables and herbs in the pantry, which could be cooked with the ham bone and perhaps some suet dumplings. It would be simple, hot, and hearty. Only after I'd put the vegetables on to boil and taken a pot of tea upstairs did I remember the letter. Picking up the folded paper from the table, I bent close to the lamp and read:

> Dear Mrs. Grimm,
> As you know we're almost to Christmas, and I'm afraid I must have at least four weeks' rent immediately. The fact is, others are behind as well, but none so much as you, and I must have something to put Christmas dinner on the table with. Your husband was a good man and always paid promptly, so I've tried to be patient, but I'm afraid I must now insist.
> Yours respectfully,
> Mrs. Thomas Schofield

Four weeks! I sank down in the nearest chair with a sigh. That would eat up all I'd earned from the purchases of Mr. Carlisle and Mr. Stoke. Thank goodness for both gentlemen, else I'd have no hope of paying! What would Mrs. Schofield have done in that case? Cast us out into the street?

There was nothing for it but to turn over the money. That left us very little for the next week, at the end of which rent would come due again, relentless as the dawn. The worst of it was that the two pounds would come nowhere near resolving our debt. When would she demand the rest?

I got up and walked determinedly down to the storeroom.

Setting the lamp on a table, I went straight to the books. Surprisingly, there had been no antics since the previous day; the volumes remained neatly stacked in their box.

"It can't be helped, Papa," I said stiffly, digging through them. "I still don't really understand what these mean to you, but you can no longer help us, and we must help ourselves. I love you dearly"—my voice broke here—"and I always will. But you mustn't bother me about this anymore."

Choking on the constriction in my throat, I paused to collect myself, covering my face with my hands. There was a slight motion in the box as the books I'd disturbed resettled. I opened my eyes and found *Ireland's Merrow* sitting on top.

Quickly I glanced around the room. "Papa? Are you there?"

For some reason my newly discovered "gift" had chosen to show me an axe-wielding Norseman rather than the one person who could actually help me.

I looked down at the book.

So be it.

I picked up *Ireland's Merrow* and carried it out to the shop counter, then went to the kitchen to finish Sunday dinner.

My heart thumped with a dreadful anticipation as I went down on Monday morning. I more than half expected to find the book gone, returned to its fellows. But there it still lay, on the counter where I'd placed it.

"Thank you, Papa," I breathed as I unlocked the front door.

I stepped outside for a few minutes to watch the day brighten. The fog had cleared, but the clouds hung heavy and low, so *brighten* was a relative term. The air felt sharper, and I thought more snow might be on the way.

A rider passed in the street, his mount's hooves clopping against the cobbles, warm puffs of breath steaming the air. I stepped back toward the shop door as a gentleman approached down the footway, tipping his hat with a "Morning, miss" as he strode past.

With last night's letter from the landlady, I'd all but forgotten Mr. Carlisle's visit today. I only hoped Mrs. Schofield would make *her* call before then, as it was bound to be awkward.

"Good morning to you, Miss Grimm." Another gentleman had approached, this time Mr. Stoke. He tipped his hat, making no move to enter the shop, and I thought he must be on his way elsewhere.

"Good morning, sir." My resolve after the visit to the storeroom held firm, and I decided there was no time like the present. "It's opportune you've come this way, as I have found another of your books."

His brows lifted. "Indeed? How splendid."

"If you're not otherwise engaged, I can show it to you now."

He gave a short bow. "Lead the way."

As he followed me to the counter, I said, "There may be more yet. I'm in the process of organizing the storeroom. My father left it in quite a state."

How smoothly you lie, Lizzy.

I picked up *Ireland's Merrow* and placed it in his hands, reserving no pity for myself over the pang it caused me.

"Ah yes, the Irish merfolk," he said, rubbing a gloved thumb against the green cover. "The illustrations in this one are particularly charming. Now if memory serves . . ." He reached into his pocket and produced another sovereign, holding it out to me.

"Thank you, sir."

"Thank *you*, Miss Grimm." Tucking the volume under his arm, he said, "I'll buy any of the books you find, of course, but I'm particularly interested in *Doorways* and *Ghosts & Spirits*." I felt the heat in my cheeks. "My favorites of the set when I was a boy, you see. If you find one or both, I will gladly pay double for *each*."

A *month's* rent this time, for a single book! I supposed the well-to-do could afford to be sentimental about such things, but I couldn't help feeling a little resentful. I realized I was staring while he awaited my response and blurted, "Of course, sir. If I find them, I will certainly set them aside."

He smiled and replaced his hat. Before taking his leave, he said, "By the way, I understand we have a mutual acquaintance in Mr. Antony Carlisle."

Another flush rose. How could he know this? Had Mr. Carlisle mentioned me to him?

"I met Mr. Carlisle just a few days ago," I replied. "He was in the shop to buy a gift for his sister." Though I was certainly more acquainted with the baron's son than my reply suggested, it was none of his business. Still, I wondered at my reluctance to mention our friendship.

"Ah yes," he said in a more somber tone, "it's a shame about Miss Sophia. Despite their troubles, it seems the family has decided to go on with the annual charity ball at Carlisle House. Perhaps you've heard?"

I frowned, recalling Mr. Carlisle had business at the printer yesterday. Odd he hadn't mentioned the ball when we spoke. "I had not, sir."

"I understand Lord Carlisle decided it should be kept up in honor of the baroness, rest her soul."

"I see." There was little else for me to say, as this was not a sphere in which I moved.

"Apparently the baron has tasked his son and my niece, Miss Isabel Stoke, with all the planning and preparation. My father—Isabel's grandfather—and Lord Carlisle were old friends, since their Eton days. This is of course a great boon and great responsibility for my brother's family, and I'm off to see if I can be of any use, if an old bachelor ever can."

I had frozen, and a colossal effort was required to make my mouth form the words, "I'm sure they will appreciate that, Mr. Stoke. I wish you luck."

"Thank you, Miss Grimm. Good morning."

Mr. Carlisle and a young lady were planning a ball together. I didn't know why it should have surprised, much less *bothered*, me. Perhaps because he hadn't told me. I well knew the Carlisle House Christmas ball was nothing to concern the likes of me, but I think what I didn't like was him knowing it, too. Which was foolish. I also couldn't help wondering whether Mr. Carlisle and Miss Stoke were well acquainted. *More foolish yet.*

Before I could talk myself out of my pique, the shop bells jingled, and another gentleman walked in—or rather, not a gentleman, but Miss Croft.

"I have found you," she said, joining me at the counter.

"Good morning, Miss Croft," I said, surprised. "It's nice to see you again."

"I don't normally make deliveries," she replied, "but I've discovered something I thought you might like to know sooner rather than later, and it's not a thing I'd want to trust to an indifferent messenger."

"Indeed?" I said, heart jumping.

She nodded, eyeing me appraisingly. "I think this information will be unexpected, to say the least. Are you the sort to be taken by fits?"

I stared. Whatever could this be? "I'm not. At least not so far."

"I'll get right to it then. The author A. A., according to a contract I found in my grandfather's records, was Herbert Grimm."

Papa!

Secrets

I'm afraid my vision did swim, and I braced myself with a hand against the counter. "*Herbert Grimm*, Miss Croft?"

She watched me closely. Likely my face had blanched, and she suspected a faint was coming on. "Your father, was he not?"

I tried to swallow, but my mouth had gone dry. "He certainly was."

She took a folded paper from her coat and smoothed it on the counter. I read over it quickly.

An agreement between Croft & Croft and A. A.—signed by my father.

Heart pounding, I read it again more carefully, touching a fingertip to one line. "This says that beyond the first two sets of the books, 'Croft & Croft Printers, doing business as Ginnel Press, is granted the right to publish any books A. A. wishes to offer for public sale.'"

"Which probably explains all the secrecy," said Miss Croft. "My grandfather may have worried about getting crossways with the publishers for eating into their side of the business. But as far as I can tell, no more books were ever printed."

Taking a deep breath, I moved slowly from behind the counter, Miss Croft's gaze following me as I headed for an armchair near the door. A look of relief crossed her face as I sat down.

"I should have guessed it," I said. "How could I not have?"

His note about the books, the ghostly activity. His interest in folk-lore and love of storytelling. The fact that he himself had once led me to that very shop!

And I'd just sold another of the books to Mr. Stoke.

"It didn't fit with the picture you had of your father, I imagine," replied Miss Croft. "It always shocks a family to discover one of them has been living a double life."

I looked at her, and she raised an eyebrow and straightened. "And you're sure only two sets were printed?"

"Sure as I can be, without any of the involved parties still alive to be asked. My grandfather was a stickler about documents, though, and there are no invoices for future printings."

So again the question of how Lady Stoke had come by the books— made even more mysterious by the fact *Papa* had written and printed them. He had never once mentioned any of the Stokes in my hearing. Of course that didn't mean they weren't customers, but why would he sell Lady Stoke the only other copies of his books?

"If you feel all right, Miss Grimm, I should be getting back to the shop." I glanced up at Miss Croft, and she offered a wry grin. "I don't trust those devils not to loiter in my absence."

I rose from the chair, smoothing my skirt. "Of course. It was very kind of you to interrupt your day to bring me this information, Miss Croft. I'll admit it has come as a shock, but I assure you it is a great help to me." My gratitude was heartfelt, yet I wasn't sure what difference this knowledge had made other than to increase my regret over selling the books—and cause me to wonder what else Papa had kept from me.

Miss Croft touched her hat brim. "Glad to hear it. I hope to see you again, Miss Grimm. But if it's not soon, a merry Christmas to you."

"Merry Christmas to you, too."

I was still staring after her, thoughts in a spin, when the door opened again and admitted the landlady.

Back to the present, Lizzy.

Somberly I went to the cashbox for Mr. Stoke's two sovereigns. (The one from Mr. Carlisle had for some reason traveled upstairs in my apron pocket and been placed on my bedside table.) I cobbled together another pound from smaller coins to cover this week and next, so I wouldn't have to see the woman again before Christmas. Aside from a spare shilling and sixpence, Mr. Carlisle's sovereign was all the liquidity we possessed. Indeed some of *that* was owed for consignment items we'd sold over the weekend.

Mrs. Schofield kept up a steady stream of one-sided conversation, apologizing for the necessity of calling for some of what we owed before the new year, as we'd originally agreed, and I held my tongue, annoyed at her, even though really I had no right to be. Increases to our rent had been infrequent over the years, and she had indeed been patient with us since Papa died.

I could see her surprised relief as I produced the three pounds.

"I'm so glad to see your fortunes reversing, Miss Grimm," she said as she was leaving the shop. "Happy Christmas!" But she stopped on the threshold and glanced back. "We'll look forward to accounts being fully settled on the first of January, then."

I froze, responding woodenly, "Of course, Mrs. Schofield."

Three more pounds due in just over two weeks! Above and beyond an additional week's rent that would come due by then, not to mention food and other expenses. Foolishly, I'd assumed her original deadline of "the new year" meant after Epiphany. Short of a miracle, there would be no possibility of paying the rest without selling more of Papa's books.

My mood was not much helped by the rest of the morning, which saw not a single customer enter the shop. Only another person to whom I owed money—a delivery man for a local cider company. He supplied us with animal skulls and bones when he found them on his journeys to the estates around York. Since his last visit, we'd sold a shrew skull. He was an old associate of Papa's who didn't care who was paying him, so I put on a smile, handed over the shilling, and wished him a happy Christmas.

Not even Mr. Carlisle's upcoming visit had managed to lift my spirits. Still reeling from Miss Croft's revelation, I did indeed believe I was in a kind of shock. The idea of selling any more of Papa's books gave me a sick feeling—to say nothing of retrieving the ones I'd already sold—yet I couldn't see how I'd avoid it.

The small part of my mind not occupied with this problem still fretted over what Mr. Stoke had told me about the ball (and what Mr. Carlisle hadn't). I had somehow allowed myself to look on Mr. Carlisle as a friend, when of course he was nothing of the kind. He was the heir to a barony, and I was essentially a shopgirl. A vast societal chasm stretched between us. There were pointy things at the bottom of it, and if anyone was going to be impaled upon them, it would certainly be me. He and I had decided to put our heads together over Mama's and Miss Carlisle's affliction, but that was the limit of our connection. I was angry with myself for thinking it could be otherwise.

All in all, I found myself in a perfectly unreasonable state of mind.

Yet everything fell away upon his arrival. He entered my shop smiling, an adolescent girl on his arm.

"Good afternoon, Miss Grimm."

"Good afternoon," I said, laughing, for he was laden with burdens. "Let me help you."

"No need," he countered. "Perhaps help Sophia with her pelisse. Sophia, this is my friend Miss Grimm."

The girl's blank expression and vacant brown eyes were all too familiar.

"I'm delighted to meet you, Miss Carlisle. If you'll allow me . . ." I reached slowly to untie her pelisse, her brother's words echoing in my thoughts . . . *my friend Miss Grimm.*

Her gaze never lifted, but she allowed me to remove both pelisse and bonnet.

"Sophia," said Mr. Carlisle. "Follow Miss Grimm up the stairs. I'll be right behind you."

I started for the stairs, glancing behind to make sure she was following. When we reached the landing, I turned and gently lifted her hand, placing it on the rail.

"She'll be all right?" I asked, uneasy. I never worried about Mama on the rickety old things, but she'd been navigating them for more than twenty years.

"I'll follow closely just in case," replied her brother.

Together the three of us slowly ascended.

"We have guests, Mama," I called as we reached the top. "You know your way around, Mr. Carlisle. Please make yourselves at home. I'll fetch Mama from the other room, and then I'll put on water for tea."

I seated Mama on the sofa until we could get organized. Mr. Carlisle busied himself with unpacking and laying out the contents of a large basket.

Watching him in wonder, I said, "This was very kind of you."

"It's nothing, truly," he replied with a grin. "Our cook has done it all."

I laughed. "Well, then it is very kind of *her*."

Downstairs, I put the water on and then loaded up a tray of dishes. Glasses, too, as I'd seen my guest place a bottle of sherry on the table.

I returned to a *feast*. On one platter rested slices of cold roasted pork artfully surrounded by boiled potatoes, beetroot, and boiled eggs. Another platter held sausages and wedges of cheese. There was a basket of bread and a thick slab of golden butter, and he was just removing from its box an iced ginger cake decorated with a ring of gingerbread figures.

"Good heavens, Mr. Carlisle! I think it must be Christmas."

His face scrunched, and he scratched his chin as he surveyed the table. "My mother always said Cook never does anything in half measures. But the cake came from one of your neighbors, Finch's Bakery across the way. Cook said they're the best."

"It's all very beautiful as well as generous, and I thank you."

"You're quite welcome, Miss Grimm. Thank you for hosting us."

I went down for the tea and returned only to realize there was no place to put it. Mr. Carlisle picked up the table near the window chair and brought it over close to the dining table.

"There," he said. "Shall we sit?"

Miss Carlisle was already seated in Papa's place, and her brother went to offer Mama his hand. "Time for tea, Mama," I said. "Mr. Carlisle will assist you."

Her eyes moved to his hand and she took it, rising from the sofa.

"Why don't you seat her in her regular place," I said, "the same as before, and then you take my place, so you both can sit next to your sister."

When that was all arranged, Mr. Carlisle poured us each a small glass of sherry. Raising his, he said, "To new friends."

There was that word again, the one I had chided myself over. I held up my glass. "To new friends."

Toast concluded, he said, "Now let us eat. I worked up quite an appetite between Carlisle House and your shop."

"I'm not surprised," I said, laughing. "I can't understand how you managed it all."

We were a cozy party, four people around our small table for the first time in three years. I kept an eye on Mama and Miss Carlisle, but they had taken no more notice of one another than they did of us. For a while there was no sound but the clink of cutlery. The meal was delicious, and as I'd grown more used to Mr. Carlisle now, I found I had an appetite. I could almost forget what an upending day I'd had.

"How has your day been thus far?" asked my guest, like he'd read my thoughts. Papa had always asked this same question of Mama when we sat down to tea. His days in the shop tended to be more eventful than hers abovestairs, but he enjoyed the break from talking to customers, so Mama always tried to inject some drama as she recounted mundane housekeeping details. *Herbert, dear, you wouldn't believe what an industrious mouse we have living in the broom closet.*

I met Mr. Carlisle's gaze. "I believe it's customary to answer such questions in one or two words. But today . . . I'll just say it has been strange and rather trying."

He set down his fork and studied me more closely, drawing my awareness to the quick pace of my heart. "I assure you that I asked the question in earnest, and I hope that you'll use as many words as you require to answer. Unless it's none of my business, in which case you'll not offend me."

I had vowed to stop thinking of this gentleman as my friend, yet he made it quite difficult. "Well, I have learned something startling about the books." I set down my fork, too. "In truth, *startling* hardly does it justice."

"Oh, indeed? Miss Croft found something?"

"She did, and made a special trip here to share her information."

One eyebrow lifted. "That strikes me as uncharacteristic."

I nodded. "She said so herself, but she felt it was too important to leave to a messenger."

"You certainly have me in suspense."

"It's not my intention. I think I'm still trying to take the news in myself. According to Croft & Croft's records"—I glanced at Mama—"*my father* wrote the books."

"Your father!"

I waited a moment to see if Mama would react to this revelation—had she known? She studied her sherry glass, then lifted it to her lips.

Gaze returning to Mr. Carlisle, I said, "It seems Papa hired Croft & Croft—or Ginnel Press—to print them. They had an agreement that made it sound as if more would be printed, but only the two sets ever were. How Lady Stoke ended up with one of them is something I would very much like to know."

"Do you think Mr. Stoke knows about this?"

"I would say not, as he went to Miss Croft looking for the same information."

Shaking his head, he said, "Why would your father have kept such a secret?"

"I confess that is the hardest bit to swallow. Papa and I read those books together *many times*. I can't help wondering what other secrets he might have kept."

My throat tightened, and I rose from my chair and began slicing up the ginger cake to have something to do. I felt Mr. Carlisle's sympathetic gaze and fought back tears. The ache I was feeling was an old pain. Papa and I had spent happy hours together when I was a child, yet I had always felt that he half lived in another world. I thought it was just that he gave *so* much of himself to the shop and his curiosities, but now it seemed there might have been more to it.

As I served us each a slice of cake and refilled our teacups, I began to feel steadier. I managed to answer Mr. Carlisle's searching gaze with a smile.

"Your sister must be twelve or thirteen?" I said, guessing by the length of her skirt.

"Twelve," he replied, mercifully accepting my bid to change the subject.

"She's very pretty."

"I think so, too." His smile was wistful. "She favors our mother."

We watched her lift a gingerbread figure from the top of her cake and nibble it. A dark corkscrew curl had freed itself from her hair arrangement and rested fetchingly alongside her forehead.

"She's always been very busy and happy," he continued, "though you wouldn't know it now. I wish that I could have spent more time with her when she was growing up. I was away at school by the time she was born. If we'd been closer, it might have been easier for her when Mother . . ."

"It's not your fault, Mr. Carlisle."

His eyes came to my face, and I saw his darkened brow and unshed tears. "Is it not?"

"No more than it's my fault what happened to Mama, though I blamed myself for encouraging her in her work as a medium."

He nodded. "You have given me hope, Miss Grimm. You have made me feel less alone."

My heart skipped. "I feel exactly the same."

He cut into his cake, a soft smile resting on his lips. My fingers trembled as I reached for my teacup. *Take care, Lizzy!*

My guest cleared his throat, and in a lighter tone he said, "I presume now your indecision about Mr. Stoke is at an end?"

I gave a weary laugh. "I'm afraid the drama continues. Before Miss Croft arrived with her news this morning, I sold him another of the books."

"Oh dear! But perhaps if you told him what you've learned, he would be willing to sell them both back to you."

"Passionate as he is about the books, I honestly don't know that it would make a difference. The question is moot, however, as the money from the sales is already spent." I took a bite of cake to cover the humiliation I felt admitting this. A silence stretched between us, and I grew even more uncomfortable.

"Miss Grimm," he said finally. The soft way he spoke my name sent a pleasant shiver through me.

I met his gaze.

"Allow me to help. Let me speak to him. I'm sure there's some offer he will accept."

"It's very kind of you, but even if he agreed, I could not afford it." I managed to keep my gaze raised this time, and my tone even.

"But I can."

I stared, wondering if I'd heard him correctly. "You, sir?"

"We are friends, are we not? I would like to help you if I can."

Opposing feelings warred inside me. Gratitude for his generosity. Happiness at hearing him speak again of me as his friend. Fear of that societal chasm, and the sharp rocks that awaited.

I took a deep breath. "I think we must be careful of considering ourselves friends, Mr. Carlisle. We are bonded by circumstances, certainly. By a shared desire to help our families. I am grateful for that, incredibly so, but friends?" He'd grown somber, and I feared I had offended him. Yet one of us must say it. "Only think what your father might say if he knew you were here."

His gaze dipped.

"I'm correct in thinking he doesn't know?"

My guest sat straighter, flattening his palms on either side of his plate. "You are correct. And painfully plainspoken."

"I hope you won't be angry with me for it."

He smiled thinly. "No indeed. I'm only sorry I forced you to remind me of reality. It was thoughtless of me, proposing such a thing."

"I know your offer was genuine, and kindly meant."

The mood of our little engagement had been dampened considerably, and I wondered whether there was any recovering.

"I don't believe there's anything unnatural or wrong in wanting to help our fellows," he said. "It's a failing of society that we should ever feel there is."

"Well," I began carefully, "there are avenues that society condones, such as your mother's foundation, and church collections for the poor. And these are only books, after all. The fact my father wrote them and Mr. Stoke values them—so much that I could probably increase the price without him blinking—might just allow us to hold on to our family business. That is a cause for celebration rather than grief."

He sighed. "Plainspoken *and* clear-sighted. You put me to shame, Miss Grimm."

"Don't praise me too highly, sir. If only you'd seen me earlier! I spent the day in a childish sulk. Everything vexed me. But now you and your sister have come and lifted my spirits, helping me to see things in a better light."

He shook his head. "And now you have managed to give *me* credit for your clear-sightedness. At any rate, I'm glad you're feeling better.

Though I do feel curious about what a vexed Miss Grimm might look like."

The fondness in his tone brought another warm shiver. "For both our sakes, let us hope your curiosity may go unsatisfied."

He laughed, and I was relieved that we seemed to have recovered.

"I'm so glad you were able to bring Miss Carlisle," I said. Noticing her dessert plate was empty, her gaze resting on the remaining cake, I reached for the server and gave her another slice. Mama watched the movements of my hands, so I served her one as well. "Mr. Carlisle?"

"No, thank you." He watched as the two of them ate. "They don't seem to have noticed each other at all, do they?"

"No, they don't. I suppose it was worth a try."

"Where do we go from here, do you think?"

I let out a breath. "I confess I'm not sure, though I'm not ready to give up." As I thought back over the last couple of days, I recalled something. "I wonder if there is some significance in Mama having had a strong reaction to me asking her about Mr. Stoke and Mr. Stoke having owned the only other set of Papa's books?"

Mr. Carlisle's brows lifted. "I would by no means call that a reach. Do you think your mother knew your father wrote the books?"

"I have been wondering about that. I feel like she would have told me after he died, if not before. Yet how he could have kept them from her, I don't know." I recalled Miss Croft's phrasing: *a double life*. "Miss Croft said her grandfather's files on the transaction were four decades old. Papa married Mama rather late, when he was forty."

"So she may *not* have known."

"The more I think about it, the more likely it seems."

He nodded. "Which book did you sell today?"

I felt another pang. "*Ireland's Merrow.*"

"And the first day Stoke came in?"

"That was *Glamour*. He found it on a bookcase in the shop. Somehow it got separated from the others."

"Forgive my ignorance, but what are the subjects of those books?"

"A merrow is an Irish fairy—part human and part fish."

"Like a mermaid?"

"Exactly, yes."

"What made you choose it?"

I recalled my desperation—and determination—after reading the landlady's note. "I didn't deliberately. I was digging through the books, talking to Papa all the while, and—"

"I'm sorry—you were talking to your father?"

"Yes," I said sheepishly. "There was more strangeness with the books after you left the other night, and I started to think it could be Papa trying to save his treasures from beyond the grave. I was explaining to him that I had no choice, yet feeling stricken and guilty, and finally I just grabbed the topmost book. I thought I might find it back in the box this morning, but it wasn't, and I sold it."

Mr. Carlisle sat with furrowed brow considering this, and I was sure he *would* now be wondering about the state of my mind, after our adventure in the ginnel. Yet our first meeting had come about because of his interest in contacting his mother's spirit.

At last he said, "It hardly seems an unreasonable conclusion to draw after what you learned today." I sipped my sherry, relieved, and he continued, "And the other book you sold, what was its subject?"

"It's been years since I read *Glamour*, but it also relates to fairies. Glamour is used to make people see things that aren't there, or to make them *not* see things that *are* there, such as fairies themselves. It can also be used to trick someone into going to Fairy, or to prevent them from talking about Fairy when they come out."

"And you don't know why it was on the bookcase?"

"I do—I put it there. I discovered it on the counter one morning after I opened. But I don't know how it came to be *there*."

"So if your father's the one moving the books around . . ."

I stared at him. "He may have moved that one too! But why move it to the shop, where it was likely to be sold?"

He frowned. "Maybe it's not about selling the books at all. I mean, his note would naturally make you think so. But maybe there's something else he's trying to tell you."

My eyes widened. "Remember I mentioned that I hadn't chosen *Ireland's Merrow*? That it had just been on top of the stack? And that night after you left, I found *The Krampus* on the stairs. Could it be that he knows I need to sell the books, and some of them are less important to him than others?"

Mr. Carlisle nodded slowly. "That sounds plausible. Though it still leaves unanswered the question of Stoke and his connection to the books and your mother."

My gaze drifted to Mama, and I saw that we'd missed something while we'd been talking.

"Look, Mr. Carlisle," I whispered.

He did, gasping quietly.

One of Mama's hands and one of Miss Carlisle's were clasped together, resting on the table.

A Disconcerting Thought

For several moments we could only stare at their clasped hands, until finally we exchanged looks of astonishment.

Then the spell seemed to break, their arms sinking back down to their sides.

"Mama?"

Both of them still wore flat expressions, but the importance of this could not be denied.

"There *is* some connection between them," said Mr. Carlisle, elated. "And not likely based on previous acquaintance."

"I agree with you! I think we might go so far as to say they have suffered the same fate. And they seem to know it somehow."

"At the risk of jumping to appealing conclusions, I think so, too."

In the hopeful moments that followed, the clock downstairs began striking the hour. Four o'clock.

"Heavens, how the time has flown," I said, rising from my seat. "Forgive me for being so abrupt, but I'm afraid I will have to clear up and go down to the shop."

"Of course," said Mr. Carlisle, also rising. "Only let me do the clearing up. You go on down."

"I cannot permit you to do that, sir," I protested.

"I will not allow any argument, Miss Grimm. I can stack dishes on a tray as well as anyone else—or at least well enough, I'm sure—and beyond that I only need pack up our things."

"I wish we had more time," I said, going around the table to help Mama to her room. "I feel we've finally been getting somewhere."

"I agree. But perhaps we can reconvene soon."

Some of the elation had gone from his voice, and I looked at him.

"You must be very busy, sir," I ventured. "Mr. Stoke mentioned your mother's charity ball is to go on after all."

His eyes darted to my face; I had taken him by surprise. "So it is. I had meant to tell you last night. It's the reason I was at the printer—for the invitations. The ball is to be held Saturday."

"I will certainly understand if you need to put off other engagements until after. We all have our responsibilities." I said this earnestly, though my heart was not in it. Our time was already so short.

He shook his head. "There is indeed much to do between now and then, but the ball isn't the only thing going forward. Father had said we would not be going to Gilling Hall, our family estate, on Christmas Eve as we usually do, but he has changed his mind. And from there, Sophia and I go with him to London. That leaves us only the eight days between now and Christmas Eve."

Eight days. This was unwelcome news indeed, but I didn't want to increase his distress. "Well, we need not fix on any date now. Outside of my working hours, I am at your disposal. And we need no longer stand on ceremony. You may drop by at teatime, whenever convenient, with no prior notification."

He offered a subdued smile. "You are very kind, Miss Grimm."

I waited a moment, wondering if he'd mention Isabel Stoke, his partner in ball planning. There was of course no reason why he should—though it ate at me when he didn't, instead turning his attention to stacking dishes. Was there some reason he did not wish me to know?

When Mama was settled, I went down to the shop. No sooner had I unlocked the door than an old gentleman came in. He was talkative and kept me so busy with questions about our collection of snail shells—which ranged from marble-size to one from Australia that was bigger than my head—that I was not able to properly take my leave of Mr. Carlisle and his sister.

The gentleman bought a shell with candylike swirls from the island of Cuba, and it was the last sale I made that day, though a few other people came in to browse.

After closing, I went to the kitchen to do the washing up and was touched to see that Mr. Carlisle had left the uneaten sausages, cheese, and cake. We wouldn't need supper after the heavy tea, but it would simplify meal preparation tomorrow.

When I checked on Mama after, I found her nodding in her window seat. There had been more stimulation in these last days than was usual for her. I readied her for bed, and I, too, put on my nightdress. But rather than going to my own bed, I lit the candles on the dining table and picked up the books I'd left in the chair by the sitting room window—*The Krampus*, *Doorways*, and *Ghosts & Spirits*.

I recalled my last conversation with Mr. Stoke. He'd said he was particularly interested in *Doorways* and *Ghosts & Spirits*. I'd found those two books on the storeroom floor last night, when I first began to suspect Papa's involvement. Was it coincidence? *That seems unlikely.* I thought about the five books that had, to varying degrees, behaved oddly—*Glamour*, *The Krampus*, *Doorways*, *Ghosts & Spirits*, and *Ireland's Merrow*. I could see no obvious way they might relate to each other beyond all being books on folklore.

I turned a few pages of *Doorways*, running my fingers over the fine illustrations. Were they Papa's? They all appeared to have been done by the same hand, and no credit had been given to another person, not even an anonymous one.

How had Papa collected these stories? I picked up *The Krampus*. This particular one was no mystery, as Opa had loved telling stories about the cruel old beast of Yule. But Irish mermaids? Welsh witches and Icelandic hidden folk? It must have been all the old books he'd bought and sold over the years. He had a particular passion for folklore, and those books tended to permanently find their way upstairs. Yet such detail in these Ginnel volumes! Perhaps much of it had come from his own imagination.

And then a disconcerting thought came to me. Papa had written a book on ghosts and spirits, and ghosts and spirits I knew to be *real*.

My breathing grew shallow as I pulled *Doorways* closer, studying the drawing of the wardrobe with the ruins of a stone fort inside, white-capped waves lapping at the base of its clifftop perch.

Closing the book, I rose from the table and made my way down to the shop, ignoring the anxious beating of my heart. I hadn't bothered to put on my slippers, and the worn stair treads felt smooth and cold under my feet. Each time a creak erupted from the old wood, I felt it in my soles.

Slowly I approached the big cabinet that had frightened me as a child. Resting the lamp on a table, I stood before the black-lacquered doors, digging my toes into the carpet. It had been a fixture in the shop for as far back as I could remember. A gentleman had made an offer to buy it once, and Papa had told him it was a family heirloom. I found out later it had come with Opa and Oma all the way from Bavaria.

There was a dark beauty to the strange relic, with evergreen cones carved along the framing above the doors. Raven heads peeked through the jagged lines of fir trees that decorated the doors themselves, and a scaled bird claw reached toward the large iron pull at the inner edge of each door. Hunched and gnarled men wearing conical hats marched across the bottom third of the cabinet, each bearing a burden of some kind—lumpy sacks of toys, platters of cakes and other treats, and bound bundles of sticks. Now that I really allowed myself to study it, the scene reminded me very much of the illustrations in my father's book on Krampus.

I tried to think what was stored in the cabinet. I couldn't remember ever seeing my father open it, and perhaps that was why it had so frightened me. The mystery of it allowed my imagination to conjure up nightmares.

Stepping closer, I reached out and touched one of the pulls. The door was ajar, and I felt cool air against the tips of my fingers. How long had it been like that? I never touched the cabinet except with a dusting cloth.

Get on with it, Lizzy.

Hooking a finger through the pull, I tugged open the door so quickly air breezed into my face—air scented by fir boughs and spice. I wondered what kind of wood had been used in its manufacture. Though the inside had not been lacquered, the wood had aged to a color almost as dark, like treacle.

While I found no other world awaiting me inside the cavernous thing, neither was it quite empty. I retrieved the lamp and examined the contents more closely—a fur-trimmed greatcoat on a hook, a pair of sturdy boots underneath, a crooked walking stick that still had the look of a tree branch, and resting on the floor, a lidded box. In the center of the cabinet's back panel, another evergreen tree had been carved, this one decorated with candles. *A Christmas tree.*

Setting the lamp on the carpet in front of the cabinet, I lifted the box out and removed the lid. I sat down beside it and pulled out a sheaf of papers. They were covered in my father's handwriting.

Perhaps on a cold midwinter night, huddled close to the fire, you've heard tales of the werewolf. In fact, you stand the best chance of seeing one on Christmas night, when they run in packs and prefer to satisfy their hunger on human victims—and their thirst on whatever they find in their victims' cellars. Those unlucky enough to be born on Christmas may themselves succumb to the lupine curse.

The papers appeared to be Papa's manuscript drafts, and the original illustrations were there among them. I paused at a sheet covered with a drawing I recognized—the cave from *The Krampus*. As I was setting it aside, I noticed something scribbled in one corner and brought it close to the lamp.

Astonishingly accurate, M!

The note was also Papa's handwriting, but who was "M"? Did this suggest someone other than him had done the illustrations?

I studied the drawing again—the scattered bones, even a human skull that had rolled into one corner, and the broken toys. A doll had her head turned all the way backward, and a missing limb. A sailboat's mast had been broken. A box lying on its side had a tatty clown falling out of it. There were also a few objects that looked like toys but that I could not imagine anyone actually giving to a child—a goblin-like figure with a windup mechanism, a doll with snakes for hair, and a handful of miniature soldiers that, when you looked closer, had devil horns and tails. These all appeared in the foreground, along with some rustic furnishings. In the background was the cave mouth with a view of snowcapped mountain peaks. Near the opening lurked a shaggy blur, only the eyes and great curved horns distinct.

"M" had a dark turn of mind.

I got up and went for a look at the other items in the cabinet. The greatcoat was nothing I'd ever seen Papa wear, nor had he carried the walking stick. These were things you might use for fell-walking on a very cold day, something Papa had never done to my knowledge. Of course by now it was obvious I hadn't known Papa as well as I thought.

Noticing another item, on the shelf in the top of the cabinet, I reached up and brushed something soft, but only managed to push it farther inside. Carefully, I stepped up into the cabinet and reached again, pulling out a gray flatcap. As I turned halfway and dropped the cap next to the box, a wave of vertigo swept over me. I braced myself with a hand against the cabinet back, ridges of the Christmas tree carving pressing into my palm.

Then the solid surface beneath my hand was suddenly *gone*. I stumbled forward. The light instantly changed, and my knees landed in something powdery.

I knelt, frozen in shock, fear, and actual cold, limbs resting in snow, breath puffing out as a cloud in front of my face. The cabinet had taken me somewhere else, and it wasn't the snowy streets of York.

My eyes beheld a winter scene at twilight—bruised-looking sky over a spotless blanket of white. Beyond the snowfield was a tight line of sharply pointed treetops, green-black and forbidding, and behind *them* a jagged line of mountain peaks, fully black in the distance. Perhaps it was the stark palette that caused my attention to be drawn to a tiny spot of contrasting color—crimson like a drop of blood. Bending closer, I saw it was a holly berry. A couple of feet away, there was another one, and by slight depressions in the otherwise trackless snow, I could make out a line of them leading toward the forest.

I had absorbed all this in the space of a few heartbeats, and now, panic surging, I rose to my feet and turned in search of the cabinet. But the quick motion caused me to slip in the slush beneath me, and with a yelp of surprise, I fell again. Though I hadn't seen anything but bare snow behind me, I found myself once again inside the cabinet. Lightning-quick, I jumped out onto the floor of the shop.

My breaths came hard and fast. I couldn't feel my feet, and I worked to warm them with my hands. As I rubbed sensation back into my toes, I eyed the cabinet with a justifiable new terror. If not for the tangible evidence in my hands, I would have believed the eerie winter scene a product of my imagination inspired by my choice of bedtime reading.

But it was just as I'd guessed: *Doorways are real, too.*

And judging by the coat and walking stick, Papa had made a habit of going through this one. Had there been others, too?

Then I recalled speculating about how A. A. had come by his knowledge.

The author was educated. A folklorist or professor. A traveler, even.

Had Papa *seen* all the things he'd written about? Had he traveled through doorways such as this one to do his research? It was almost too much to take in.

Where exactly had the cabinet taken me? It was a world that the carvings on the cabinet's facade would neatly fit into, reminiscent of those dark old Bavarian folktales Opa had loved to tell.

I thought then about Mr. Stoke. Did he *know* the things A. A. wrote about were real? Might that explain his fever to possess the books?

How tempting it was to jump to conclusions.

The lamp guttered, and the clock began marking the hour. *Eleven.* Gateways to other worlds notwithstanding, I still had to open the shop in the morning. I wasn't going to find answers to my questions tonight.

But what a story I would have to share with Mr. Carlisle the next time I saw him.

If there is indeed a next time.

The thought weighed on my heart like a stone.

"That Will Not Lessen Your Responsibility"

Antony

Damn you, Stoke.

Hours had passed since I'd left Grimm Curiosities, and I found myself fuming still. Worse, my anger at the fellow was entirely misdirected. I should have told Miss Grimm about the ball myself, as I'd intended.

Really, I ought to be thanking rather than cursing him. She needed to know that I had unexpected (and unwished-for) demands on my time and attention that might affect our plans. I'd been too much of a coward to do it, and he'd made it quite easy for me.

Yet it continued to grate. How was Stoke on such intimate terms with Miss Grimm that he felt comfortable telling her my business? I supposed his enthusiasm was understandable, as his niece was helping to plan the ball.

"Antony?"

I turned from the hearth in the front parlor to find my father had come into the room, which only heaped coals on my annoyance. "Good evening, sir." I could feel the hard set of my expression and took a deep breath, hoping to loosen it. I had vowed not to quarrel with my father so soon after my mother's death, no matter how I might resent his painfully obvious attempt to push me at Miss Stoke.

"Where were you this afternoon?" He had dined at his club, and his deeply lined face was ruddy from drink—and drawn in disapproval. "You missed Miss Stoke. She had a list of purchases for you to approve for this ball that is bearing down upon us even as we speak. I told her to spend what she liked, of course, but I've asked *you* to oversee this matter."

"I didn't know she was coming, or certainly I would have been here, sir."

"Bah." He drew out the word, shaking his head. "I expect you to be available when she is. She's doing us a great kindness, and you don't seem to realize how short on time we are."

"I do indeed realize. Which is why I wonder at your change of heart about the event this year."

The baron was acquiring a stoop, and he endeavored to straighten now, I imagined because he wanted to look more intimidating. It was entirely unnecessary. His temper had always had an edge that frightened me, even now that I was many years past my boyhood. The threat of disinheritance, even if never spoken aloud, was quite an effective tool of correction.

"Have I not already explained it is out of respect for your mother?"

While I believed my father had loved my mother, I didn't for a second believe this resurrected ball had anything to do with her or "her charities," as he called them. And with Sophia's illness still unresolved, my heart simply wasn't in it.

"So you have."

"And have you given up the idea of continuing her legacy?"

I could do nothing to stop the heat of anger flashing over my face at his disingenuousness. My father had given not a farthing for my mother's causes *or* her ball, beyond the esteem they conveyed to the family and the fact they kept her content. I was certain we'd have seen the end of the Christmas ball had my father not suddenly found it useful.

"You know I haven't," I said with some bitterness. I had made it clear to him I felt the foundation should be kept up, even volunteering to see to it myself. He had put off answering me for weeks, finally hinting that he would consider—*if* I married and gave my wife the running of it.

"And have I not found an agreeable accomplice for you?" he said. "Many a young man would jump at the chance to spend so much time with such a refined, accomplished, and, if I may say so, beautiful young lady."

I was beginning to seethe inside. Of course Isabel Stoke was an eligible lady, not to mention the granddaughter of one of his oldest friends. It wasn't unreasonable for him to wish me to marry her. But how I resented his meddling. It hardly helped matters that Isabel was the niece of Ambrose Stoke.

Yet lashing out at my father could in no way help the situation. "I'm sure you're right," I said as placidly as I could manage.

He huffed and looked dissatisfied, but he gave a short nod.

"I would feel easier about it, sir," I continued, "if Sophia were recovered."

His frown deepened, and I realized my misstep. Rather than hearing the genuine feeling behind my words, he would view this as a judgment on him for being callous about his daughter's condition. And obviously as another failing of *mine* that I should be so affected by it.

"Sophia may *not* recover, Antony," he said coldly. "That will not lessen your responsibility to this family."

He turned and stalked out of the parlor, and I sank into a chair.

What was I to do? I couldn't possibly give up my collaboration with Miss Grimm. Not when we were finally making progress. But this collaboration with Miss Stoke . . . my father wasn't going to give *it* up, and neither was she. I had told her in a most complimentary way that her competence had rendered me redundant, but she had continued to doggedly pursue my opinion about ice flavors and flower arrangements.

Not one of our conversations had held the warmth or interest of the ones I'd had with Miss Grimm.

It was indeed my duty and responsibility to marry one day, but was it too much to ask that it might be to a woman whose company I enjoyed?

I let out a sigh.

Best that I appease the baron by going to see Miss Stoke at the earliest appropriate hour the following day. Hopefully looking over columns of figures with her would leave me free to see Miss Grimm again by afternoon. I must give him no more reason to suspect my lack of commitment to his cause, or I might find myself even more closely managed. I couldn't help feeling that Miss Grimm was my last, best hope for saving Sophia.

Proposition

Morning saw the return of fog, damp, and quiet streets, which left me plenty of time to think over the previous night's events. As I adjusted displays and lit additional candles to make the shop more inviting, I gave the cabinet an even wider berth than before.

At the same time, my curiosity had been greatly aroused. Was the place I had visited a real earthly location? Or was it a kind of other-world like Fairy, or like the ghostly realm Mama said she visited in spirit when she did her medium work? What had Papa done while he was there? What was the meaning of the trail of holly berries, and who had left it? Eager as I was for answers, I couldn't see myself going back through the old cabinet to look for them. My real world offered enough uncertainties.

I was reordering books in the reading nook and thinking about an early tea when the door bells jingled. My heart gave a leap, but I turned to find Mr. Stoke rather than Mr. Carlisle.

"Good day, Miss Grimm," he said with a smile.

"Good day, Mr. Stoke," I replied, hoping I'd managed to conceal my disappointment. I feared he'd come about the books again. I also feared I'd have no choice but to sell him another one soon and had already been considering which I would be least sorrowful to part with. *Paracelsian Elementals? The Beast of Loch Ness? Tintagel Castle?*

But as he came into the shop, he said, "For once I have come to bring *you* something."

"Indeed?"

Tucking that strange wand of his under one arm, he removed a stiff bit of paper from a coat pocket. "You recall I told you the baroness's ball was to go on?"

Something wrenched in my stomach. "I do, sir."

"Well, I have procured an invitation for you and Mrs. Grimm, and I would like to offer myself as your escort."

This struck me speechless. Mama and I were invited to Carlisle House for a society ball?

When I'd unstuck my tongue, I said, "How can this be, sir?"

"It was my special wish that you be invited, and Isabel—my niece, who's planning the ball with Mr. Carlisle and will accompany us there— agreed with me. It seems she knows you; she made purchases in your shop a few days ago."

Dashed was any slight hope that Mr. Carlisle had been the one who wished us to attend. If Mr. Stoke could invite us, certainly Mr. Carlisle could also have? He and I were more acquainted, and it was *his* family's ball.

Preoccupation with these thoughts prevented Mr. Stoke's last comment from fully sinking in. *Isabel* Stoke. His niece, the granddaughter of Lord Carlisle's friend Sir Arthur Stoke—if I wasn't mistaken, one of the three ladies who'd discussed Mr. Carlisle in my shop the day I met him. She was the lady who, when one of her companions referred to Mr. Carlisle as "devastatingly handsome," replied that he seemed morose.

Apparently she had warmed to him, either naturally or with encouragement from others.

Mr. Stoke's countenance had lost some of its brilliancy, and I quickly said, "How incredibly kind of you to think of us, sir. And your niece as well. But truly I don't feel I could . . . I mean, your circle of friends and associates is not . . . and the shop is quite busy this time of year, so I—"

"Ah, now don't turn me down, Miss Grimm. You and Mr. Carlisle are friends, after all. He will be very happy to see you and Mrs. Grimm,

I'm sure of it." This gave me a start. Had the two of them discussed this? I couldn't imagine Mr. Carlisle confiding so much in him. They were recent acquaintances, were they not?

Mr. Stoke continued, "If you'll forgive me for putting it in such terms, it will also be an excellent opportunity for introductions to people who might be interested in doing business with Grimm Curiosities. It seems that everyone is a collector these days, yet I can imagine it has been harder for you to make your way since your father passed."

My feelings about all this were bewildering to say the least. Besides his familiarity with my relationship to Mr. Carlisle, I had to wonder why he would want to attend such an important social event with Mama and me, going so far as to appeal to my pragmatic side as a further carrot to tempt me. I supposed it might be his respect for my father, and possibly even tied up in some way with his hopes about the books. But beyond all that, there was the thought of walking into Carlisle House on his arm, among my betters, and coming face-to-face with Mr. Carlisle while playing the part of someone who belonged there—when both of us knew that I did not.

Of course there was no question of us going.

"Don't say no," said Mr. Stoke, perhaps seeing something of these doubts written on my face. "Not yet, at any rate. Just give it some thought; that's all I ask."

He held out the paper and I took it—an invitation for Mrs. Herbert Grimm and Miss Eliza Grimm to join The Rt. Hon. Lord Carlisle and his family for a Christmas charity ball in honor of The Rt. Hon. Lady Carlisle on Saturday, the twentieth of December, at nine o'clock in the evening.

"Promise me you'll take a day to consider," he pleaded.

He appeared so earnest I didn't have the heart to tell him I *had* considered, and further consideration was unlikely to make any difference. Whatever his motivation, it was a very kind offer, and I had no wish to offend him.

"Very well, Mr. Stoke."

He smiled. "I'll call again tomorrow."

The moment the door closed behind him, I found myself second-guessing. The possibility of expanding our business connections was nothing to sneeze at. When was another opportunity to meet the wealthiest members of York society likely to ever fall in my lap? I would never attempt such a thing on my own, for I would certainly be shunned. But with Mr. Stoke there to make introductions?

As I turned it all over in my mind, the ticking of the grandfather clock seemed to grow louder. Then a sudden thumping noise made me jump. My first thought was Mama, and I had already started for the stairs when the hairs on the back of my neck stood up and I stopped. The noise had not come from above.

It had come from the cabinet.

Turning slowly, I half expected to find the doors open. But it looked no different than it had earlier. Then came another thump—the whole thing vibrated with it. I let out a cry of surprise and faltered back a few steps.

The next disturbance came from behind me—the sudden ringing of the shop bells—and I spun around, one hand pressed to my chest.

Mr. Carlisle stood in the doorway. *Thank heaven.* His smile evaporated as he took in my state.

"Are you all right, Miss Grimm?"

I took a deep breath. "I'm not entirely sure."

He reached toward the sign in the window. "Shall I . . . ?"

I gave a decisive nod. "Please do."

The immense relief I felt at his arrival was concerning, yet I could not wish him gone. There was no one else I would want to see right now.

His face etched with concern, he hurried over, not taking the time to remove his hat or coat. "Tell me."

I gave a desperate-sounding laugh, realizing how my story was going to sound. "I'm afraid I hardly know how."

"It's all right," he said earnestly, holding my gaze. "I will believe you."

Gratitude swelled, accompanied by a lovely feathery sensation in my chest. *He is my friend, and I'm starting to not care who knows it.*

"It's this old cabinet," I said. "I believe it has been in my family quite a long time. I haven't thought of this in ages, but I recall my grandfather referring to it as his legacy from his father. I assumed that meant it was valuable. It has frightened me since I was a child, though, and I've always avoided touching or even going near it."

He frowned. "I'm guessing that has changed."

Nodding, I continued, "It seems my fears were not wholly unjustified. Last night I was looking through a few of Papa's books. There are two in particular that Mr. Stoke has said he would pay double my asking price for. One of them is all about doorways to other worlds, and in one illustration, a wardrobe opens to reveal an ancient stone fort."

"Which gave you the idea to open this one." His expression managed to mingle resignation and dread.

"I'm afraid it did."

He eyed the cabinet with distrust. "And what did you find?"

"A number of very interesting things, including my father's manuscripts and possible evidence he worked on them with another person. Also a winter coat and hat and walking stick I'd never seen him use. But these are nothing compared to the last thing I found." His gaze came back to my face. "I had to climb into the cabinet to reach something on the top shelf. I lost my balance and steadied myself against the back wall. Then suddenly I found myself in another world."

His eyes opened wide with shock.

"There was deep snow and dark woods, and I saw high, lonely peaks in the distance. It was a hauntingly dramatic landscape, like nothing in Yorkshire." His expression seemed frozen, and I said, "I can imagine what you're thinking."

"I very much doubt that, but please go on."

By his tone, I began to think he was *angry*. "Well, I know it was all real because I had gone in without my shoes, and when I came back, I had to rub the feeling back into my feet. They were numb from the snow."

In that same strangely even tone, he said, "I don't doubt it was real. It's no wonder you're frightened. Were you able to sleep?"

"Not very well, but that's not what has disturbed me today. Just a moment ago, I heard *thumping* inside the cabinet."

His gaze jerked back to the thing. He walked toward it, and I held my breath as he reached for the pulls and yanked it open. There was nothing inside but what had been there the first time I opened it, though the coat had fallen off its hook.

Mr. Carlisle looked at me. "It seems to me this investigation of ours has become dangerous, Miss Grimm."

I couldn't argue. My sudden trip to the other world could have ended quite badly. I had only by accident (literally) found my way back home. But was I ready to halt the investigation because of it? I had a sinking feeling he was going to suggest exactly that.

Before either of us could speak, the front door rattled, and voices drifted from outside: "It's closed, Charles. We'll have to come back."

A gentleman brought his face close to the window and our gazes met. Then his eyes moved to Mr. Carlisle.

A sudden self-consciousness possessed me, and I walked to the door. The man and woman waited as I opened it.

"Good afternoon," I said, smiling. "I'm just closing for tea, but we'll open again this evening, and I will be happy to help you then."

"Very good," said the gentleman with a bob of his head. His wife glanced around me to where Mr. Carlisle waited. Then finally they left. I thought they'd likely recognized him, and I worried what the implications might be.

Mr. Carlisle seemed to have grown even more serious. "Perhaps we should go out and take the air, Miss Grimm. We can continue our conversation there. If you think Mrs. Grimm will be up to it, that is."

"Yes, I agree." Walking would expose us to even more curious gazes, but Mama would be with us, and it seemed best not to appear to have something to hide.

When I had Mama bundled against the cold, the three of us stepped out into the foggy street. My eye followed the curve of Goodramgate until the houses and shop fronts disappeared into the vapor. The lamplighters would be out before long. On these midwinter days it was hard to even remember the summer, when the sun remained in the sky until bedtime. It felt like two entirely different worlds. For someone living even farther north, say in Iceland, I supposed it must seem even more so. I thought about Papa's book on elves, with its illustrations of both fur-clad warriors and gossamer-gowned maidens, and wondered, Had Papa *been* to Iceland? Had some doorway taken him there? How many worlds had he visited?

When we reached the intersection at Deangate, I was called back to the present reality. We met a chestnut costermonger, and I recalled Mama had not yet had her tea. I stopped and opened my coin purse, but Mr. Carlisle drew a penny from his pocket and paid the man before I could.

When I'd thanked him and given the bag to Mama, he said, "Shall we walk to the Minster?"

The jewel of York, the Minster was a magnificent fifteenth-century cathedral. The gothic structure had replaced a much older Norman one. You could find your way around the city by keeping an eye on the towers reaching high above the other buildings. The cathedral's recent history had been troubled, with two fires causing significant damage— one intentionally set by a religious fanatic and one set accidentally by a clock repairman who left a tallow candle burning. The first fire took place the year before I was born and the second when I was ten years old, destroying the roof and vault of the nave and gutting the tower to the right of the entrance. Our house on Goodramgate was just east of the Minster, and I remembered seeing the smoke and showers of sparks above the buildings on the opposite side of the street.

Papa had taken me inside the cathedral many times, both before the 1840 fire and after the repairs were completed. It remained the most spectacular building I'd ever seen—or probably would ever see.

Though it wasn't much warmer inside the cavernous place, at least we were out of the damp and fog, and the calming scent of frankincense hung in the air. With evensong still more than an hour away, the nave was mostly empty. Not even the officiant or choir members had arrived yet, though an acolyte had begun lighting candles. It had been an excellent suggestion, affording us some privacy.

Glancing up at the nave's soaring ribbed and vaulted ceiling, I remembered doing the same thing as a child and feeling tiny. The years of growth since then had not lessened that impression. The airy, upsweeping pillars and many beautiful stained glass windows made the cathedral feel otherworldly. Exploring with my father, holding his warm hand tightly, I had pretended to be a fairy princess walking the corridors of my palace with the king. I imagined that the great heart-shaped window above the entrance had been constructed in my honor on the day I was born. There was even a magical beast on guard—a gilded dragon head hung high above the north side of the nave. Papa had told me it was part of the original architecture, and no one knew its purpose.

For one reason or another, Mama had never joined us on these excursions. She was always busy with cooking, cleaning, going to market, and one hundred other unromantic things I took for granted. She'd also once told me that "the ghosts of Goodramgate" were quite enough for her, which I took to mean that she often encountered new ones when she wandered beyond the places her routines took her. Recalling this, I felt a fresh stab of guilt over agreeing to her medium work. *It was only ever going to end badly.*

Now Mama held my arm as we strolled the length of the nave toward the choir, oblivious to everything around her, Mr. Carlisle matching our pace. If I'd still been a child, I might have imagined my poor mother the victim of a magic spell and Mr. Carlisle a prince visiting from another kingdom.

As if he'd caught an echo of this thought, he glanced at me. His smile felt tentative, and I worried he would revive the topic of our investigation, and its increasing peril. I attempted a diversion, saying, "Something quite unexpected happened today."

His eyebrows lifted. "Something *else?*"

Nicely done, Lizzy. I let out a nervous laugh. "Mr. Stoke brought me an invitation to your Christmas ball. He offered to escort Mama and me."

Mr. Carlisle halted midstride, an expression of pained surprise on his face. I felt a stone slowly sinking from my chest to my stomach. Not only unexpected, apparently, but also unwelcome.

Connections

"Mr. Stoke," he said in a dry tone, glancing at the distant ceiling.

"Of course we have no intention of going," I said quickly. It had been presumption on Mr. Stoke's part to invite us, and on my part for even considering it. But Mr. Carlisle's disapproval stung.

His gaze drifted back down, coming to rest on my face as my heart missed a beat. "Why not? I only wish I'd been the one to extend the invitation."

I bit the inside of my lip and glanced away. "I would never have expected you to, Mr. Carlisle. It struck me as quite odd that Mr. Stoke did, and I feel he shouldn't have without consulting you. I really can't imagine why he did."

"Can you not?"

A stiffness in his tone confused me. "Have I done something to annoy you, sir? If I have, I assure you—"

"Lizzy—" My eyes popped wide, and so did his. "Forgive me," he continued. "Miss Grimm, the idea that you could annoy me is nonsensical, though I do find myself greatly annoyed. I wish you to know that I would be very happy for you to come to the ball, though I'm not sure how I feel about Mr. Stoke as your escort after all this business with the books. Nevertheless, since I cannot escort you myself, I am grateful that he has stepped into the breach so that I may have the pleasure of seeing you there. You would do me a great honor."

This pretty speech was the last thing I had been expecting, and it left me staring.

"I hope now that is settled," he continued. "But there's something else I think we must discuss. Shall we walk on?"

"If you like," I managed.

My heart grew a little frenzied as we crossed in front of the gilded choir screen, with its statues of fifteen English kings and the great organ pipes above. Then we continued down the south aisle of the nave.

"I must tell you," he said, "I'm very worried for you. I fear we may have ventured too far in our search for answers."

"You are perfectly justified in saying so," I admitted. "A number of very strange things have happened since we began."

"I don't like to think of giving up just when we seem to be getting somewhere, yet each time you probe deeper into these books, something even more alarming happens. I'm not comfortable with the risks you're taking at least partly on my behalf. Up to now, only the barest thread seems to be tying the books to the affliction shared by my sister and your mother, but I can't help feeling there may be some real threat that's related to them, and that you are square in its path."

We paused in front of the beautiful arched window depicting the life of St. Nicholas, and Mr. Carlisle turned to me, awaiting my thoughts.

Nothing he'd said was untrue, or even an exaggeration. Though I was frightened, I couldn't help taking these strange occurrences as hopeful, like I was drawing ever nearer the answers I sought. Which could of course be delusion, but hope had been my only friend over the last long year.

Beyond that, now that I'd uncovered this hidden life of my father's, I knew I wouldn't be able to stop until I knew everything.

"Have you had a chance to look at any of the books?" I asked. "I know you had this ball sprung on you and have probably been quite busy."

He laughed dryly. "Indeed, that describes it perfectly. But I have looked through all of the ones you gave me, and I read as much as I could. Your father was incredibly knowledgeable."

"Even more so than I realized. I've begun to wonder whether his knowledge may have been the result of traveling through doorways."

"You mean like the cabinet in your shop?"

"Exactly. Some of what he wrote was clearly informed by my grandfather's stories, but the rest, and the level of detail . . . He might have learned it all from books, but now that I've been through the cabinet, I can't help wondering."

"Do you know much about his life before he married your mother? Had he gone to school?"

I shook my head. "Papa's head was full of history, but he disliked talking about his own. I know that my grandparents were originally from Bavaria. They immigrated here when Papa was very small. My grandmother had a small inheritance—her father was a successful woodworker—and they used it to open the shop, which originally sold old books and furniture along with my Oma's paintings. When they grew too old to run the shop, Papa made the business his own."

"Your grandparents are gone now?"

"Opa died when I was twelve, and Oma soon after."

"How about your mother and her family?"

Mama was staring at the colorful glass before her with a placid expression. Papa had often referred to her as his "Yorkshire sunshine," and she was lovely still, despite the lines in her face and golden hair now faded to white.

"Mama was a butcher's daughter," I said softly. "She grew up in the Shambles. Her family was well respected, and as I understand it, once the engagement had been announced, Grimm's experienced an increase in patronage. I think Papa was considered a step up in the world for her, and her father wasn't shy about telling his customers. Mama had two brothers, but they died in the first cholera epidemic. When Grandfather died, the son of a neighboring shop owner took over the business in exchange for allowing Grandmother to live out the rest of her years above it. She died shortly before Papa."

I'd been watching Mama, but I felt Mr. Carlisle's eyes on me and looked at him.

"This is how you find yourself so alone in the world," he said.

The sympathy in his gaze moistened my eyes, but I smiled. "Yes. As I mentioned, my parents married rather late. Even Mama was more than thirty."

Mr. Carlisle's brow furrowed in thought as he, too, turned to study the beautiful window, now lit more by candlelight than daylight. Studying the lines of his handsome profile, I felt strangely at peace—there in my fairy palace, in the company of Mama, my memories of Papa, and my newest and only friend.

"Have there been any more visits from your father?" asked Mr. Carlisle. "Any more ambulatory books?"

Reaching to adjust one of Mama's gloves, I replied, "There haven't been, though I don't know what was responsible for the thumping in the cabinet. I rather hope it was Papa as opposed to any alternative I can think of. As for the books, no more unbooklike behavior."

"Remind me," he said, turning, "which were the ones you had trouble with previously?"

"Well, there was *The Krampus*, left on the stairs the first night you came to us."

"And what is its subject?"

"It's a folktale from my grandparents' homeland. A kind of Yule monster who lives somewhere in the mountainous north of continental Europe. Krampus punishes naughty children. Despite Mama's protestations, Opa told me the story every year, and every year it gave me nightmares." I smiled. "I loved it."

"Of course you did," he grumbled, but rather fondly, and I felt a tickle of warmth in my belly. "Go on with your list."

"*Doorways* escaped from the box one night, along with *Ghosts & Spirits.*"

He frowned. "In light of last night's adventure, that seems rather significant."

My heart bounced. "Indeed it does! Reading through *Doorways* is what led me to open the cabinet. Now I wonder if that's exactly what Papa intended. Maybe he wanted me to know the truth about him!" Hot tears stung my eyes. I'd believed that Papa and I had been close; in that moment I realized just how much his secrecy had hurt me.

"I think it's a reasonable assumption," my companion said softly. "Didn't you also say the book on doorways was one Stoke is keen on?"

"That's right. He specifically mentioned *Doorways*—and also *Ghosts & Spirits.*"

Our eyes met. "Interesting," he said.

"Very! Though I'm not sure what it means."

"It means Mr. Stoke is even more of a mystery than before. But let's come back to that. Is that all of the books that need mentioning?"

I felt greatly relieved that our investigation appeared to be continuing. A few minutes ago, I'd feared he was about to suggest calling it off. While I knew that I must continue even without him, the prospect was a gloomy one.

"There was also *Ireland's Merrow*," I said. "I'm not sure that one really counts, though it did seem to offer itself up as a sacrifice. And I almost forgot—*Glamour*. That was the first one to behave strangely, making its way onto the counter in the shop."

"I believe you said 'glamour' is a kind of fairy magic?"

"That's right, and—"

I froze as it came to me.

If I'd still been a child, I might have imagined my poor mother the victim of a magic spell . . .

"Oh, Mr. Carlisle!"

"What is it?"

I glanced at Mama and discovered her staring at me. Her expression was blank as usual, but her eyes were open wide.

"What if it's *glamour*, and Papa was trying to tell me?"

"What if *what's* . . ." I watched the change in his face as understanding dawned. "You think your father wanted you to know that your mother's affliction is glamour!" He blinked a few times, staring at empty air as his mind worked. "You've found it, Miss Grimm."

"Sorry?"

His eyes settled back on my face. "A connection between the books and our afflicted loved ones."

I nodded, trying to moderate my excitement.

"Not only that," he continued, "*Glamour* was the first book you sold to Stoke."

"Yes, that's true."

"Could that be a hint about the connection between Stoke and your mama?"

I thought about this. Though certainly tempting to grab on to, it wasn't quite there. "I think that may have just been a coincidence. *Glamour* was the only one of the books on the shelf, so he didn't specifically choose it."

Mr. Carlisle nodded, though I could see he was still turning it over. "So what do we do with this information? If glamour is the affliction, what then is the cure?"

My memory of this book was foggy. The subject matter had perhaps not been as easy for a child to grasp as some of the others. What I mostly recalled was illustrations of fairies.

"I think we must discover who, or what, is responsible for the glamour," I said. "If memory serves, that's the first step. I haven't read the book in years; it's unfortunate we no longer have it." I looked at him. "What if I asked Mr. Stoke if I could borrow it? I could even tell him I believe it might help Mama. He recently told me if there was ever anything he could do for us, I should ask."

Mr. Carlisle's frown was nearly a scowl. "I must confess, Miss Grimm, I don't fully trust Mr. Stoke. Perhaps it's unfair of me. I know he's eccentric and has a personal connection to the books. But he wasn't very forthcoming in your first meeting, and we don't know why your mama reacted strongly to him."

"Well," I said, considering, "generally, Mr. Stoke has been respectful and kind to me. And Mama's reaction to him was very similar to her reaction to *you*, so I'm not sure we can hold that against him."

"That is fair. Although it does make him escorting the two of you to the ball something of an experiment."

I took a deep breath. "In truth, Mr. Carlisle, I don't feel Mama and I can very well attend the ball, though it was kind of you to express your desire to see us there. For one thing, you're right—I've never had an opportunity to observe her with Mr. Stoke, and I wouldn't want to risk an awkward scene in your home. But more than that, I'm not eager to put her and her affliction on display."

Mr. Carlisle didn't bother to hide his disappointment, though he said, "Of course I understand. But allow me to think about this. There may be a solution."

"You're very busy," I protested. "I'd rather you not—"

I broke off, noting a rapid movement out of the corner of my eye. Glancing to my left, back down the length of the nave's south aisle, I saw a figure approaching—a man with a *sword* raised in one hand and some kind of standard in the other. Plates of armor clanked as he strode forward, the pointed toes of his sabbatons striking the floor with force.

Gasping, I said, "What on *earth*?" I pressed Mama closer to the wall and out of his path.

Mr. Carlisle moved closer to us, staring down the aisle. "What do you see, Miss Grimm?"

"He . . . he's right *there* . . ." As the figure bore down on us, I noticed he wore a bloodstained tunic over his armor. Head bare but for a flimsy-looking crown, his dark hair streamed out behind him. There was a hungry, wild light in his eyes. Richard of York came into my mind; he had tried for the crown of England during the War of the Roses. Instead, his enemies gave him a paper one and hung his head on Micklegate Bar.

The swordsman drew near, and though I now suspected this was no living person, I called "Take care!" to Mr. Carlisle, who had stepped directly into his path in an effort to see better.

But at the last moment, the swordsman adjusted course so he was headed for *me*. I thrust my arms before my face as cold air blasted into, then *through* my body.

I staggered and would have fallen, but an arm wrapped around my waist.

Slumping against Mr. Carlisle, I watched the swordsman stalking away from us down the aisle, finally vanishing into the cathedral wall.

Time seemed to stand still as I recovered my mental faculties enough to notice I was in a gentleman's arms. For the space of a sigh, I felt all the places our bodies touched. His hands pressed securely against my back; my forearms rested against his chest.

His eyes searched mine. "Are you injured?"

"No, sir," I breathed.

Then he slowly released me, breaking the spell.

Straightening my bonnet, I glanced at Mama. "They could at least have the decency to *look* like ghosts." She gave no sign of having seen the apparition, but I had a new appreciation for what her "gift" had put her through.

"Another spirit?" asked Mr. Carlisle, still inspecting me for damage.

"I believe so. A swordsman this time, quite lifelike. He came straight down the aisle and walked through me."

He eyed me with alarm. "*Through* you?"

Realizing I was quite cold and shivering, I hugged my arms over my chest. "Yes, and I felt it, too. As I'd imagine falling through a hole in the ice on a pond."

"Let us get you home."

We stood not far from the entrance to the cathedral, and I noticed a small group of robed choristers had come in and gathered there. Several of them kept glancing our direction.

"Yes," I agreed.

Cold had permeated the shop in our absence, and Mr. Carlisle insisted on tending to the fires both upstairs and down while I put the kettle on for tea. I still wore my cape and had draped a shawl over that. The layers hardly seemed to make a difference, like the cold was coming from *inside* my body.

As I came out with the tray, Mr. Carlisle drew a cane from a porcelain Japanese umbrella stand next to Opa's cabinet. He slid the cane through the cabinet's pulls and looked at me.

"I know I'm not your keeper," he said, "but I beg that you won't have any more dealings with this cabinet until I'm with you again. Let's take some time to think over what we've learned and talk again as soon as we can."

"All right," I agreed. Snowy landscapes held no temptation at the moment.

"Thank you," he said, obviously relieved. "You won't be frightened here, just the two of you?"

"Mama and I will be fine," I assured him. "I'm so grateful for your kindness." I hardly felt as calm as I sounded, but I didn't want to keep him from his responsibilities. I couldn't help imagining us all going upstairs together for supper, safe and warm by the fire. The vision brought acute longing.

"If you're sure," he said, and I could see he was reluctant to go.

"I am, sir. Will you have a cup of tea before you go? You must be chilled."

He shook his head. "I've grown warm working on the fire, and if you don't need me, I really should be on my way."

If you don't need me. I almost sighed aloud. "Goodbye for now, then, sir."

"Goodbye for now, Miss Grimm."

As Mama and I drank our tea, my spirits sagged, reminding me how much Mr. Carlisle's visits cheered me. I think I'd actually been dispirited for some time but hadn't fully recognized it before now. I hadn't the *time* to recognize it. Life had been a struggle since Papa's death. I found it so much easier to bear when I had someone to talk to.

Perhaps I should marry. The thought crept up and startled me. It wasn't something I'd considered beyond romantic girlhood notions that came from too much reading of fairy tales. Once well-meaning people had begun to suggest it as a way out of my troubles, I'd set myself against it. Now I saw that there were other advantages.

But *who?* I didn't exactly have suitors falling at my feet. I recalled the self-important old antique dealer who'd taken offense when I'd ignored his hints about marriage.

I'd sooner die an old maid.

Sighing, I cleared up after our tea and went back down to the shop. Despite all the newly discovered wonders in my life, I wasn't likely to manifest a suitor out of thin air. But I could resolve not to be closed to the idea anymore. If someone suitable presented themselves, I could give it serious consideration. (And in truth, I owed it to Mama.) If I did eventually marry, I would owe it to Mr. Carlisle for giving me a glimpse of how much easier life could be with an agreeable partner.

It was hard to imagine a partner more agreeable than Mr. Carlisle.

Who would *he* marry? I wondered. His family would certainly expect it of him. Would he be allowed to marry for love? I hoped that he would, but as he was the future Lord Carlisle, I imagined his father would have much to say about his choice of bride.

Then it occurred to me he likely already had. I thought again over Mr. Stoke's words in telling me about the ball.

Apparently the baron has tasked his son and my niece, Miss Isabel Stoke, with all the planning and preparation. My father—Isabel's grandfather—and Lord Carlisle were old friends . . .

Perhaps it was for the best I'd not be attending.

Get Used to This

By the time I went upstairs for the night, my heart had lightened. Mr. Carlisle and I had finally made real progress. Mama was not ill; she was glamoured. It made perfect sense! Of course the physicians wouldn't be able to diagnose such a thing. Now we must simply find a way to undo the spell.

The true puzzle in all this was who would do such a thing to Mama and Miss Carlisle. Was some mischievous sprite on the loose in York? Why had it chosen them? Could it be related to the fact they'd both been communicating with spirits, as we'd theorized? Were there other victims?

Fatigued by the drama of the day, it seemed best to leave these questions for the morning, when my mind was fresh. The ghostly chill was still with me, so I added coal to the fire and went down to make a cup of weak tea with milk. I took the tea along with Papa's book on spirits and set them on my bedside table before bundling up in an extra blanket and crawling into bed.

How I regretted that I had come into my gift at a time when I couldn't discuss it with Mama. But I had Papa's book at least.

The first thing I learned from *Ghosts & Spirits* was that there were different types of "manifestations." Some spirits could be seen and heard, some only one or the other, and one type—which Papa referred to as a *poltergeist*—was only detectable by the pranks it played on the living. If Papa's spirit was with us, it was behaving most like this latter variety.

Though I believed in Papa's case there was some intention behind it, where it seemed a poltergeist simply enjoyed devilment.

The book also mentioned a type of spirit that was like a *genius loci*. They were so strongly associated with locations—such as churches, graveyards, and old family estates—that they behaved like protectors of the living beings belonging to those places. Ireland had a type of *fairy* that behaved like a spirit and was usually associated with specific families—the banshee, whose keening foretold death.

According to Papa, spirits that were visible might take different forms. They might have a hazy or vaporish appearance, as they always seemed to in stories, or they might look no different from the living. The spirit I'd encountered in the ginnel had been lurking in the shadows, but the one in the cathedral I had seen clearly, and he was as real as Mr. Carlisle.

All but the weakest manifestations could touch and move objects in the living world, or they could be completely unaffected by them, which allowed them to walk through walls. *Or people.* I shivered and pulled my blanket tighter.

There was an explanation, too, about who could see spirits. According to Papa, one could be born with the ability whether a parent had the gift or not, but inheritance was more common. People who suffered head injuries sometimes developed the ability. Some people might see a spirit only once in their lives, oftentimes a family member or a particularly assertive ghost. And some of those born with the ability simply closed themselves off to it out of fear. Papa also believed one could *develop* the ability through a practice of remaining open to communication from the other world—which made me wonder if he had seen them, too. He wrote that people who could see spirits were also attractive to them.

I also couldn't help wondering if I might be one of those who had been blocking out spirits for most of my life. I'd seen how Mama's gift had affected her, trapping her in her routines, occasionally giving her severe frights, and turning her hair white when I was still a girl. As an adolescent, I'd thought of her as frail, which she most certainly was not. I saw what sturdy stuff she was made of as she fought with me to save the family business, eventually turning the gift that had been such a burden into a profitable line of work. If I managed to save her from this spell, I wouldn't let her go back to that. We'd find another way.

I was just about to set the book aside and blow out the candle when the first sentence in the next section caught my attention.

> Spirits are sometimes made to do the bidding of others. One example of this is The Wild Hunt, where Woden, or Odin in Old Norse, compels the souls of the dead to follow him on a harrowing ride in the skies at midwinter. (For more information, I refer you to my book *The Wild Hunt*.) There are other arcane rites, sometimes referred to as necromancy, whereby a spirit may be drawn into a skull or corpse and used for divination or darker purposes. In modern times, a rather gentler form of this practice has been turned into a cottage industry, whereby a person who styles themselves a medium will make contact with the dead at the request of a loved one. While I do believe that some such practitioners are genuine, I leave it to the reader to decide how often these services are worth the shillings shelled out for them.

I wondered how long after meeting Mama it had taken him to discover her gift. He must have been in ecstasies over his find. I could honestly imagine him marrying her for that reason alone, though I believed he did love her. I wouldn't have called their marriage passionate—but then, I wasn't sure what an unmarried woman with no prospects could really know about such things.

A yawn forced its way out, and I realized I was struggling to keep my eyes focused on the text. I closed the book and blew out the candle.

The next morning saw the fog replaced by another gentle snowfall, and business picked up. I sold a set of bones in a small leather pouch that Papa had labeled "divination bones from Anglesey." The sale gave me almost exactly the funds I'd need to have both our silk gowns properly cleaned and repaired—had I been planning to accept Mr. Stoke's proposal.

I dreaded his arrival this morning and having to refuse his offer. Mr. Carlisle had made a comment yesterday that I'd almost entirely forgotten in the excitement that followed. When I told him I couldn't imagine why Mr. Stoke had made the offer, he replied, *Can you not?*—suggesting not only did he have an idea of Mr. Stoke's reason, he wasn't particularly happy about it. Perhaps he thought Mr. Stoke was only interested in getting his hands on the books. Which wasn't very complimentary of either of us, but might indeed be the truth.

Mr. Stoke had not appeared by teatime, and I began to wonder whether he might have thought better of his offer. This should have eased my mind but somehow didn't.

Before I closed the shop, the door opened, admitting not Mr. Stoke, but a woman in spotless servant's garb.

"Miss Grimm?" she inquired, brows lifted. She was older than me, I thought, but no more than thirty.

"That's right. May I help you?"

She came over and handed me a note sealed with red wax. I took it, eyeing her curiously.

"From Mr. Carlisle, miss."

My breath caught. I slipped my finger between the paper edges and broke the seal.

> My Dear Miss Grimm,
> The bearer of this message is Sally Danby. She is a maid of all work, and I am sending her to assist you through Epiphany. I beg of you not to refuse this gift. Our collaboration has taken up much of your time, and I can see what a toll it takes on you. It has also placed you in danger, and I will feel better knowing someone else is with you. In fact, I cannot in good conscience continue our collaboration unless you accept my gift. It will have the added benefit, I hope, of allowing you to attend the ball at Carlisle House, as you would not have to leave your mother unattended for the evening.
> Yours sincerely,
> AC

I stared at the paper. This was incredibly generous, and of course preposterous. Mr. Carlisle? Hire a *maid*? To help *me*, a shopkeeper with no status and no official connection to him? It was to be temporary, but still. I couldn't possibly accept.

"Is everything all right, miss?"

I looked at her. "Yes, only . . . I'm sorry, this is unexpected. Mr. Carlisle did not discuss this with me beforehand."

Her expression dimmed. "Am I not wanted, Miss Grimm?"

Oh dear. "It's not that. And please, it's just Lizzy. I only meant that as I had no prior notification about this, I've had no time to consider whether it's proper for me to agree to such an arrangement, and I . . ."

The more words I strung together, the more worried she looked. Perhaps she needed the work as much as I needed paying customers walking through my door.

Speaking of which, the door then opened again, and Mr. Stoke came in with a young lady I'd seen in my shop before.

For heaven's sake.

"Why don't you go to the kitchen, Sally? It's just through there." I pointed. "You can start water for tea, and I'll be there shortly."

She smiled, clearly relieved, and gave a quick curtsy. "Yes, miss."

Then I pasted on a smile for Mr. Stoke. "Good afternoon, sir."

"Good afternoon, Miss Grimm. You may remember my niece, Miss Isabel Stoke?"

The lady smiled, rather stiffly, but I wouldn't have characterized it as unfriendly. *Efficient* was the word. She had dark hair and light eyes, and her day dress was more elegant than anything I owned. "Pleased to formally meet you, Miss Grimm. You have a most interesting shop."

"I thank you, Miss Stoke," I replied, inclining my head. "I'm pleased to make your acquaintance."

"I have brought Isabel in case you're inclined to refuse my invitation," said Mr. Stoke. "She can be very persuasive."

Studying her expression, I thought it likely he meant in a wear-you-down sort of way rather than a softness-and-smiles sort of way.

"Do agree," said the lady. "My uncle will be so disappointed if you don't. He's been talking of it for days."

Bewildered, I looked at Mr. Stoke.

He laughed. "It's your own fault. Each time I've come into your shop, though I know you must find my inquiries tedious, you've been patient and kind, and I'm afraid I've grown fond of you. We have like interests, after all, and I flatter myself that I'm in a position to broaden your circle. I would like to see you and your mother succeed, Miss Grimm."

His gallantry continued to baffle me. He seemed to have taken a genuine interest in my welfare, though I couldn't help recalling Mr. Carlisle's uneasiness about him.

Yet if I were willing to accept Mr. Carlisle's "gift"—and I had a sinking feeling I wasn't going to have the heart to refuse—no obstacle remained to my attending the ball. Would it not be foolish to miss this opportunity? And I would see Mr. Carlisle and his home in the bargain.

"Uncle," said Miss Stoke as my internal deliberations went on a jot too long, "there's a pipe I have been regretting not purchasing for Papa. I'm off to have another look, but do call if you need reinforcements."

"Thank you, my dear."

Miss Stoke gave me a nod and moved toward the case with the pipes, the fabric of her dress swishing audibly. Despite the stiffness of the lady's figure and manner, I had to admit she was refined and very pretty. Her uncle's eyes followed her, an affectionate smile on his lips, and I thought it looked well on him. His gaze then seemed to rest on Opa's cabinet, with the cane through its pulls.

"Mr. Stoke," I began, lest he question me about it, "I must confess something to you."

His eyes came back to my face. "I'm intrigued."

I took a deep breath. *It's the right thing to do.* Besides, I hoped we could trade honesty for honesty.

"I haven't been entirely honest with you about the Ginnel books," I said. "I do, in fact, have the entire set save the two I've already sold you. There is no other way to say it—I've been holding out on you. I believe the books were important to Papa, and he and I had a connection through them." Enough said about *that* for the time being. "So as you might imagine, I've been reluctant to sell them, though certainly we could use the money. The truth is I still haven't made up my mind whether I will sell the rest. Does this change *yours* about wishing to take me to the Carlisles' ball?"

I watched him closely through this for signs of anger or annoyance, but his features remained composed.

"Miss Grimm," he said gently, "*I* must confess that I have guessed some of this. And I have experienced some twinges of guilt over pressing you about the books. I'm an old bachelor, somewhat set in his ways, and it may not surprise you to hear that I have at times been accused of being insensitive. When I find something I want, I do have a tendency to fix on it. It would delight me to take you to the Carlisles' ball, but if my previous behavior has offended you, or even in any way made you uncomfortable, I shall take your refusal in good grace."

His response was humble and more than satisfactory, and I was now put in a difficult position. I wished I had more time to think, but he had come here explicitly for my answer. What the decision really came down to was Mr. Carlisle's gift of the maid. Dare I accept *that*?

"I think this is the perfect thing for Papa, don't you, Uncle?"

Miss Stoke had returned holding a lovely meerschaum pipe with a hare carved into the bowl.

"I do indeed," replied Mr. Stoke.

She looked at me. "Do forgive me for helping myself, Miss Grimm. I will take it."

Pleased, I wrapped the pipe for her.

"Isabel," said Mr. Stoke, "Miss Grimm and I have not quite concluded our business. If you'll wait for me at the bakery, I'll reward your patience with whatever your heart desires there."

She smiled. "You spoil me, Uncle."

"Whom else should I spoil, niece?"

Miss Stoke glanced at me before leaving with her purchase. "I look forward to seeing you on Saturday, Miss Grimm."

Though the question wasn't yet settled, I replied, "Thank you, Miss Stoke. Good day to you."

When she was gone, Mr. Stoke's eyes came to rest on me. His soft smile reminded me that he was quite handsome still. He wasn't exactly the "old bachelor" he claimed to be—more than two decades younger than Papa.

"Have you an answer for me, Miss Grimm?"

Mr. Stoke wished me to go. The two ball planners wished me to go. Thanks to Mr. Carlisle, I had someone to look after Mama. I had sufficient funds to freshen up my rose silk, so I need not embarrass myself. And I had Mr. Stoke's promise to introduce me to his connections. There was really no longer any question.

"I accept, Mr. Stoke. Thank you."

His smile broadened. "You make me very happy, Miss Grimm. We shall call for you and Mrs. Grimm in the carriage at eight thirty if that will suit."

"Ah," I said, "Mama will be unable to attend, I'm afraid. She suffered a setback in health some time ago and never fully recovered. I fear a ball might be too much for her."

He frowned but nodded. "I had heard something of this, and I'm very sorry for it. But I'm glad you're able to get away. Isabel and I will take good care of you."

"I thank you, sir." All this had gone so well, it emboldened me to add, "There's something I'd meant to ask you earlier, when we were talking about the books."

His brows lifted. "Yes?"

"I was wondering"—*since we're friends now*—"would you consider letting me borrow *Glamour* from you for a brief time? There is something I'd like to look up. It would be a day or two, at most."

If he was put off by this, he didn't show it. "Of course, Miss Grimm. Shall we say after the ball? I can bring it round to the shop."

I tried not to let my disappointment show. After the ball, Mr. Carlisle and I would have only a few days left to continue our investigation before the family traveled to their estate for Christmas.

"That is very kind of you, sir."

"Happy to do it." He smiled and put on his hat. "Until Saturday, Miss Grimm."

"Until Saturday."

He left the shop, and I locked up behind him. Sally met me outside the kitchen with a tray. "Tea is ready, miss."

I saw that she'd managed to find tea, cups, saucers, bread, and jam without any direction from me.

I could get used to this.

A Fine Line

After tea, I gave Sally my rose silk to take to the laundress. The ball was only three days away, but *my new maid* said she could manage the small repairs the dress needed after the cleaning. Though not a ball gown by any stretch, the dress was becoming, and finer than one for daily wear. More importantly, it was what I could afford. In the shop's jewelry case, we had a red garnet brooch and matching ear drops that might brighten things up a bit. I could only imagine the panic the Carlisles had caused with this last-minute invitation. The modistes would be working round the clock.

Sally's arrival had a profound effect on our household, including one unanticipated consequence: with fewer responsibilities, I had more time to fret about the ball. Would I be expected to dance? I believed ladies generally were, particularly unmarried ones. Though I wasn't sure about ladies who were not considered gentlemen's daughters. Since I wouldn't be dressed as finely as the others, I might be overlooked. Which would suit me. I hoped to spend the time meeting Mr. Stoke's associates and satisfying my curiosity about Carlisle House.

As for Antony, he would be busy with his guests, and I doubted I'd have much of an opportunity to speak with him. But I would enjoy seeing him in his element.

Antony.

I recalled how, at the Minster, he'd slipped and called me Lizzy. It had caught me by surprise, yet it had felt natural. What felt *un*natural was spending so much time with another person—especially one close to your own age—and continuing to address them as if they were a stranger.

I wondered whether Miss Stoke, too, thought of him as Antony. I wondered whether she would play hostess at the ball. Perhaps not, with no public engagement between them.

A ball is a perfect place to announce an engagement.

It might be exactly what Lord Carlisle had in mind. In fact, it might be the true reason for Saturday's event. Were that to happen, it could very well spell the end of our collaboration. Of our *friendship*. My heart gave a throb of protest. If things had progressed that far between them, would Antony not have mentioned it?

When Sally returned from the laundress and shopping, she started supper. I climbed the stairs to the attic and made up the narrow bed that Iris (our maid before Papa died) had used. Since Papa's death, Mama and I had sold most of the room's furnishings, leaving it quite spare, but Sally's sojourn with us was to be brief.

I couldn't help wondering what Antony had told Sally about me, Mama, and our shop. Did she think it strange she'd been sent here by Lord Carlisle's son? Had she made any untoward assumptions about my relationship to him? And what of the strange happenings in the shop?

Later, as we were carrying up supper dishes and the beautiful eel pie she'd made, I said lightly, "I hope you don't frighten easily, Sally. We may have a ghost or two in this old building."

"No, miss," she said over her shoulder. "I've heard other servants complain of ghosts, but I've never seen or heard one. I don't think I have the gift."

Sally turned out to be an excellent cook. Mama emptied her plate quickly, and Sally served her more without having to be asked. I tried to induce her to sit down to supper with us, but she refused, saying she'd eat in the kitchen after she cleared up. And she continued to call me *miss* despite my urging her not to.

The day had been so full of interesting events I'd scarcely thought about the books, the cabinet, or any of the other questions that had filled my mind in the days since I'd met Antony. But I turned my thoughts to it all again that night after retiring to my room. I sat at my small writing desk in front of the window, watching the snow collect in soft piles under the lamps.

I had *Ghosts & Spirits*, *Doorways*, and *The Krampus* before me. *Should I spend time on the other titles?* I wondered. At this point, it really seemed *Glamour* was the key; without it I felt helpless and stuck. I couldn't even make a guess at who might have glamoured Mama and Sophia, or why. While I hated waiting until after the ball to get a look at the book, at least it would come into my hands before Christmas.

Ghosts & Spirits was clearly important for a whole host of reasons. *The Krampus*, however, puzzled me exceedingly. If Papa had indeed called it to my attention, why? What possible connection could there be between Krampus and Mama? Was it a suggestion that her affliction was some kind of punishment? Whatever for?

I touched the medallion picturing a Roman arch on the cover of *Doorways*. This book now both fascinated and frightened me. I wanted to know more about Papa's travels. I wanted to know where exactly the old cabinet had taken me, and how many other doorways might be hidden in York. But my collaboration with Antony would soon come to an end. There would be time for uncovering more of Papa's secrets when the Carlisles had gone to their family estate. *And certainly once Antony married.*

I considered the significance of me knowing our connection must end once he married. Did it mean I also knew that what we were doing bordered on impropriety?

With that troubling thought to haunt my dreams, I blew out the candle and went to bed.

The next day saw no visits from Stokes or Carlisles. No surprise invitations or gifts. Just me working in the shop and Mama watching at the window upstairs, as we'd done for nearly a year now.

Yet it was hardly a typical day at Grimm's. Sally had taken over many of my tasks—going to market, preparing our meals, and tidying up. When she had nothing else to do, she sat mending in Mama's room to give her some company. I was free to wait upon customers, continue anticipating the ball, and look up each time the bells jingled in case Antony might appear.

As I was about to close the shop for the night, he did.

"Is it too late, Miss Grimm?"

"No indeed," I said, a happy flutter in my chest. "I was just closing."

He reached up and turned the sign, and I felt a twist of worry. *How familiar we've become.*

"I won't stay long," he said. "I know you have supper at this time." I noticed he had a Ginnel book in one hand and a bottle of sherry in the other.

"Will you join us?"

"I . . . No, that's not necessary."

I heard Sally's footsteps descending the stairs and turned. "Sally, Mr. Carlisle will be joining Mama and me for supper."

"Yes, miss," she said with a quick nod and disappeared into the kitchen. I hoped I'd not caused her anxiety. But there had typically been more than we needed at mealtimes. She told me Antony had given her a small sum to cover her portion of our meals, and beyond that she apparently drove a hard bargain at the market.

"It's kind of you," he said, "but truly unnecessary." He raised the bottle. "Perhaps I'll just have a glass of sherry while you eat."

Smiling, I inclined my head. "As you like."

"You've had no more trouble from the cabinet, I hope?" he asked as we started upstairs.

"None that I'm aware of."

"I'm glad to hear it."

I'd respected his wishes and left the cane where he placed it, though it looked a little odd there. No one but Mr. Stoke seemed to have noticed.

Upstairs, I fetched Mama to the dining table. Sally appeared shortly after with three sherry glasses.

"This is the last opportunity I'll have to get away before the ball, and I thought there might be a few things we should discuss."

I felt a shiver down my back, but said, "Such as your gift. I've had no opportunity to tell you how wrong it was of you, or to thank you."

He laughed, uncorking the sherry and pouring some into our glasses. "I apologize, and you're welcome. It's working out well?"

"Sally is a dream. I can't imagine where you found her. I hope she'll be able to get another place once she leaves here."

"You need not worry. She was a favorite of my mother's, so of course we've kept her on, but we can't keep her as busy as the baroness did, and she's not content to be idle. Sally assisted Mother in some of her charity work. She has cheerfully served in some very rough circumstances."

"Indeed? Well, it doesn't surprise me. I've been very impressed with her in her short time here."

"I thought the two of you might get on." He raised his glass. "To progress in our endeavor."

"Yes," I agreed, "to progress."

We sipped our sherry, and he picked up the book he'd brought. I saw it was *The Wild Hunt* by the medallion with the stag's head on the cover.

"I read this last night," he said.

"I loved that one as a child. My grandfather used to tell me stories about the Wild Hunt during yuletide."

"It's most interesting, and rather harrowing. It doesn't surprise me in the least that it was a favorite of yours."

I laughed. "What an impression you've taken of me, Mr. Carlisle. I think I must mend my ways."

"Don't you dare, Miss Grimm." Mischief glinted in his eyes, and a warm wave swept through me. The fond way he teased me left me feeling pleasantly fuddled.

He glanced back down at the book, opening the cover. "The ghosts in particular caught my attention—the spirits of the dead that took part in the Wild Hunt. Your mother and Sophia seem to share a connection to spirits. You've been seeing them, too." He frowned and slowly shook his head. "I'm not sure what I'm getting at, only that it seemed somehow important in the small hours of last night." He smiled. "Perhaps it was merely an excuse to visit."

"Mama and I are happy to see you here as often as you like, sir."

His eyes met mine, but before I could consider whether I'd said a wrong thing, Sally appeared with the cheese and onion pie she'd baked this afternoon.

"Please have some supper, Mr. Carlisle," I said. "There is plenty for all, as you see, and it's your generosity that has made it possible."

"With such a delicious aroma filling the room, I'm not sure I can refuse."

Sally looked pleased and glanced at me. I nodded, and she set the pie down and cut it, placing steaming golden wedges in three shallow bowls.

The meal was simple, unlike our earlier teas together, and we made short work of it. Sally came to clear the dishes, and we sat sipping sherry.

When she'd gone back down, I said, "I don't know whether it's a piece of our puzzle, but I, too, have been reading about spirits, and

Papa's book on that subject mentions the Wild Hunt. It was in the context of spirits being controlled or used for various purposes."

Antony's brows lifted. "You've helped me remember my point in bringing it up. Woden enlisted spirits for his night rides, but sometimes a hapless mortal would fall into their company. I wonder if there might be something in *that* that is relative to our case. Maybe your mother and Sophia have fallen in with spirits somehow and gotten stuck."

"That is an excellent thought."

"Do you think so? I'm not sure it fits with your theory about fairy glamour, and that was most promising."

"Perhaps not, but Papa has drawn my attention to his book on spirits for *some* reason." I frowned. "Though I suppose it might simply have been his way of letting me know he's here with us. Regardless, I feel all of these pieces fit together, and that we're inching closer to figuring out how."

Antony's gaze moved to Mama. She sat staring at the table in front of her, so still and silent she might herself have been a ghost. Finally, he said, "I agree. Now, unfortunately, I'm afraid I must be on my way. My father is watching me closely and seems to expect I'll spend every moment on punch recipes and table linens. But before I go, what is our plan?"

Drawing in a breath, I said, "Well, I know you won't like it, but I've gotten Mr. Stoke to agree to loan me *Glamour* after the ball. I haven't told him anything other than that I wished to look something up."

He smiled wryly. "I wasn't in favor of it, but bravo, Miss Grimm. How did you manage it?"

"I simply asked him. After agreeing to accompany him to the ball."

His smile broadened as he rose from the table. "Well played. And I'm very pleased you've decided to come."

"It's something else your gift has made possible."

Together we went downstairs and made our way through the shop to the door.

Antony picked up his hat and coat. "If Sally is indeed working out well, I was thinking you might like to keep her."

"Keep her?"

"As I mentioned, we are unable to fill her time at Carlisle House. I'm sure that you can here, and I know it would make your life easier."

The cheese pie began to curdle in my stomach. "We did keep a maid when Papa was alive, but I'm afraid Mama and I cannot afford it."

He shook his head. "You misunderstand me. She would continue to be employed by Carlisle House. It would simply be an extension of the loan."

My heart thumped and my stomach knotted. "Mr. Carlisle, I don't think . . . I mean, if it were known that I, that you . . ." I trailed off, bewildered. He must realize how it would look.

Letting out a groan, he plunked his hat on his head. "How we complicate things that are not at all complicated."

I knew his frustration wasn't directed at me. Though I had not known Lady Carlisle, based on what I'd read in the newspapers and what Antony himself had told me, he was every inch his mother's son.

"I understand that you wish to help both Sally and me," I said, "and I am sincerely grateful. I don't believe anyone has ever made me such a kind offer. But we have been down this road before, and I think you know as well as I do that we're already walking quite a fine line."

Both his gaze and his expression were downcast. As I waited for him to recover and bid me good night, he suddenly reached out and took my hand between his.

I let out a quiet gasp as his fingers pressed mine. It was the first time I'd touched his skin beyond a quick brush of fingers as we passed dishes at tea. For a moment the contact transfixed me. I could do nothing but stare at my hand between his, feeling warmth gathering low in my belly.

I remembered what I'd felt on his first visit, as I'd watched him adding coal to the fire. *Protected. Supported. Not Alone.*

Finally, our eyes lifted and met across our joined hands.

"It is not kindness," he said softly. "It is selfishness. And I beg you'll forgive me."

My heart grew heavy as he opened the door and left me, a breath of winter drafting in behind him.

Complicated

Stepping to the window, I watched him turn up his collar as he trod over fresh snow on the abandoned footway. Several inches had accumulated, but the sky had cleared, and a bright sliver of moon hung in the veil of stars above.

I realized my left hand was holding my right—the one *he* had held—in a vain effort to recapture the feeling of a moment ago.

How we complicate things that are not at all complicated.

He had been wrong. Even as he uttered these words, he must have known. *Everything* between us was complicated. The world would not allow us to be friends, and wishing things could be different only caused us both to suffer. I knew I didn't have the strength to give him up until we saw our investigation through, but after that, I would have no choice. There would be no more looking up at the sound of the shop bells and watching him appear. No more enjoying his company at meals abovestairs, or holding his arm as we walked, or the small (and not-so-small) things he did to make my life easier.

I'd certainly not feel his hands pressing mine again.

A painful tug in my throat, I went to help Sally tidy the kitchen before bed. Then I bade her good night.

One day remained until the ball. Sally had finished mending my dress, which regained its shimmer after laundering, and before tea she brought it down for me to look over. The hem had been unraveling, and there were several rents in the lace. Not only had she made the repairs, she'd taken the initiative to add a row of lace around the neckline, assuring me it could be easily removed after the ball if I wished. How pretty it looked against the pink silk! The gowns of the finer ladies at the ball would be in the latest styles, revealing far more flesh, but mine would at least now appear neat and fresh rather than poor and tired.

"Are you excited for the ball, miss?" Sally asked, eyes shining.

"Indeed, and nervous. It's not something I'm accustomed to. Will there be a great mob of people, do you think?"

She picked a tiny snip of thread from the dress's bodice. "In former years there always has been. The baroness's lady's maid once told me it's the biggest house party in York. I can't say about this year, with the late invitations."

"I suppose there will be some who must travel from estates in the country."

"And up from London, too."

"Has Mr. Carlisle ever been involved in the planning before?" I ventured.

"Oh, no. Everyone at the house was surprised. It's really Miss Stoke that's doing it, though. I suspect the baron thought it up as a way to make the two of them more acquainted. I wouldn't be surprised if it's the only reason the ball is going forward."

Suddenly she lowered her gaze. "Forgive me, miss. Lady Carlisle encouraged free speaking, and I'm afraid I haven't yet shed the habit."

"No need to shed it on my account, Sally. I had guessed as much, anyway." Smoothing a nonexistent wrinkle in the fabric, I said lightly, "It sounds as if they haven't known each other long? Mr. Carlisle and Miss Stoke, I mean."

"They have, in fact. Her grandfather was Sir Arthur Stoke, and he and Lord Carlisle were very old friends."

"So they've known each other from childhood."

"Yes. But I think the families were only together on formal occasions. My former mistress, heaven rest her, was not as fond of Sir Arthur's company as her husband was."

"I see." *Do you think they're in love?* Forthcoming as Sally had been, I knew such a question was taking things too far.

"He's a kindhearted gentleman," Sally said, and I looked at her. She offered a timid smile. "Lady Carlisle's son, I mean. Miss Stoke is very fortunate."

"I agree with you, Sally."

The shop door opened, and Sally started upstairs as I turned to greet the new arrival.

A fine gentleman stood hesitantly in front of the door, much as Antony had on his first visit. I didn't think I'd seen him in the shop before. He looked like he might be lost.

"Can I help you, sir?"

His eyes came to my face, and I thought perhaps I'd been wrong because something about him was familiar. He looked me over, too, but in a way that caused a flash of annoyance. "Miss Grimm?"

"That's right. What can I do for you, Mr. . . . ?"

He had a slight stoop to his posture, but now he drew himself up straighter. "I am Lord Carlisle."

My heart froze, along with my tongue. I forced myself into a stiff curtsy and managed, "It's—it's a pleasure to make your acquaintance, my lord."

"Yes, well." His eyes moved around the shop.

What could he want here?

"Is there anything in particular you're looking for, sir?" No stopping the tremor in my voice this time.

His gaze fixed on me again. "I believe I've found it."

He started toward me, and normally at this point I'd step out from behind the counter, but it was clear from his pinched expression this was no friendly call. I could see something of Antony in his face, but the resemblance wasn't a strong one.

Stopping before me on the other side of the counter, he removed his hat. Despite the stoop, I thought he was not much older than my own father would have been. His eyes were leaden rather than the warm brown of his children's. The cold had stung his cheeks red.

"I'd like a word with your mother, Miss Grimm. Is she here?"

I swallowed. "She is, my lord, but she . . ." If he knew his son had been visiting me—and I couldn't imagine any other reason he'd come here—I realized how the truth was going to sound. "She is currently indisposed, sir."

He smiled, but not exactly kindly. "So I've gathered. She's an invalid, in fact, is she not?"

He wasn't wrong, but his manner was ungentlemanly. Had he not been . . . well, who he was, and Antony's father in the bargain, I would have asked him to leave the shop.

"My mother has not been herself for some time now, but her health is sound." The narrowing of his eyes prompted me to add rather saucily, "It is very kind of you to inquire about her."

He gave a grunt of annoyance. "I'm well aware what is going on between you and my son, Miss Grimm, and I want you to know it is finished."

My heart plunged like an anchor. I took a long, slow breath, trying to contain my dread and increasing anger. "I'm not sure what you mean by *going on*, my lord. I met your son last week, when he stopped in to buy a gift for his sister, and he and I have become friends."

"*Friends!* Ridiculous. Don't you toy with me, Miss Grimm." He lifted his grizzled brows and pointed an accusing finger at me. "You are attempting to ensnare my son."

Heart hammering within the furnace of my chest, I said, "With all due respect, my lord, I don't know what you believe gives you the right to say such a thing to me. You never met me before today and couldn't possibly know anything about me."

The red in his cheeks deepened. "I know that he is in love with you! And certainly a young woman of your station would not miss such an opportunity as that."

Again he knocked the breath out of me. With great effort, I reined in my emotion. "You may believe what you like of me, sir; I have nothing to do with that. But I assure you that your son is not in love with me."

"Bah! He has been *taking tea* in your home. He is reading books you have given him. He has bought food for your family and provided you a maidservant. Unless you are his mistress, and he has assured me that you are not, I don't know what else you'd like to call it!"

Stunned, I could do nothing but stare at the very nearly apoplectic gentleman. He knew everything, and apparently he had confronted Antony about it! I was mortified.

"I see you agree with me that there is no more argument to be made. But hear this, Miss Grimm: it will not be. You cannot have him—he will lose his inheritance if he marries against my wishes—and if you're not careful, young woman, you'll render yourself unfit for anyone else."

I found my voice at last, and it came out icy calm. "What can you mean, sir?"

He gave me a smug smile. "You're a clever enough young woman. You know very well what I mean. Your mother is no longer fit to be your guardian, and all of your neighbors—probably many of your customers—are aware of this fact." He spit out the word *customers* like it was grit from an oyster shell. "What do you think they've made of a young gentleman coming and going from a shopgirl's home both day and night?"

I started to protest that Antony never visited us at night, but it was a very minor point by now, and it had probably been nine o'clock by the time he left yesterday. I couldn't imagine that he'd gleaned all these details from Antony. Then I recalled the man and woman who had peeped in at us three days ago after I'd closed for tea. *Had* we become the subject of neighborhood gossip?

Hot with the humiliation of having this discussion of my private affairs thrust upon me by a stranger—by Antony's father, of all people—I again found myself at a loss for words.

"My boy is too much like his mother for his good," said Lord Carlisle in a less fiery tone—more to himself than to me. His gaze sharpening on me again, he continued, "You must understand, Miss Grimm, Antony is not for you. He knows it, and you know it. Whatever has been going on between you is over, and it is the best thing for both of you. I understand Ambrose Stoke intends to escort you to Carlisle House tomorrow evening. I will myself welcome you there in his company. It's a fine opportunity for a young woman like you. I know how you Grimms like to climb. See you make the most of it and leave my son alone. Good day, Miss Grimm."

With that, he stuck his hat on his head and left the shop. I followed him and locked the door, standing with one hand against it, feeling my heart pounding in my chest.

Friends

There came a light tapping on the window, and I nearly jumped out of my skin.

I could think of only one person I wanted to see right now, yet it wasn't likely, was it?

I looked up and found Miss Croft staring at me. My heart finally slowed.

Her smile faded as she studied me through the window. She pointed at the door. I could hardly refuse to admit her after all her help with the books, so I reached down and turned the key.

"Miss Grimm, you look like you've seen a ghost."

I let out a burst of uneasy laughter and opened the door wider to admit her.

"I'm sorry to disturb you," she said. "Is anything the matter?"

"Honestly, I wouldn't know where to begin. Is there something I can do for you, Miss Croft?"

She slipped her hands into her trouser pockets. "Well, maybe you'll find this an odd suggestion, and maybe my timing is poor, but you and I have a few uncommon things in common, and ever since I met you, I find myself thinking we might be good company for each other sometimes."

I was in no state of mind to make out her meaning and waited for her to say more, but she looked uncomfortable. "Yes?" I encouraged. It was the best I could manage with my thoughts so disarranged.

"The truth is I've had few friends, and I'm not sure exactly how this is done," she said with a nervous chuckle, "but would you want to come for tea sometime?"

I blinked at her. "How about now?"

A relieved grin broke free, and she studied me more closely, gold glinting in her brandy-colored eyes. "Maybe a pint is more what's needed."

"Yes, a pint. Just not from Stoke Brewery."

Her brow wrinkled, and her grin turned quizzical. "All right then. We'll go to The Bell. They aren't overly particular about who sits in their back room."

"Miss Grimm?"

I turned to find Sally standing outside the kitchen with the tea tray. I wondered how much she'd heard of my interview with Lord Carlisle. Likely all of it, as the baron had been fairly energetic in his delivery. At least he hadn't made a scene by dragging her out of the shop. How long before he sent for her, I wondered? Would Antony come himself?

Enough, Lizzy.

"Wait one moment, if you will, Miss Croft."

She nodded, and I went to speak to Sally. "I'm going out for a little while. Will you give Mama her tea?"

"Yes, miss." She bobbed her head and started upstairs, respectful as always, though I thought she looked uneasy. She could have walked out right then, back to Carlisle House. No one would have blamed her for it.

I followed her and went to my room for my cape. I glanced at the bedside table, where Antony's sovereign still glinted. I picked it up, feeling the weight in my hand a moment before slipping it into my coin purse.

I met Sally again as I was heading back down. "I will be at The Bell, Sally, if you should need me." *Or should you need to leave before I return.*

"Yes, miss."

"Also, I want to thank you for everything. You've been a great help to Mama and me these past few days."

She offered a subdued smile. "Just doing my job, miss."

"I know, but I'm still grateful. And I know Mr. Carlisle will see to it that you don't suffer for . . . for any decisions of his that Lord Carlisle may disapprove of."

"No, miss," she gently agreed.

Finally I went down and rejoined Miss Croft. Together we stepped out into the winter-gray afternoon.

There had been no new snow this morning, and most of what had accumulated the night before had melted over the course of the day. A few sooty piles remained on surfaces that weren't used for walking or sitting.

I glanced into candlelit shop windows along our way. With less than a week until Christmas, the smell of gingerbread seemed to waft from everywhere, and I saw many festive displays—evergreen branches and trees, holly, mistletoe balls, and baskets of oranges, fir cones, and star anise.

We walked to Colliergate and then on to Fossgate and The Bell, whose sign declared it had been in business since the turn of the century. Papa had gone to pubs with his associates, and sometimes for a solitary pint at the end of the workday, but he'd only taken me, and occasionally Mama, to the tearoom across from the Minster.

"I didn't know a woman could go into a pub alone," I said.

"You aren't alone, are you?"

"Well, no. I meant without a man."

Miss Croft laughed. "I knew what you meant, and you're right. Most respectable establishments—ones not frequented by the ladies of Grape Lane—won't serve a woman on her own."

"The Bell is different?"

She gave a nod. "Old and honest. My grandfather drank with the owner when he was alive, and the same family still runs it. They tolerate me as long as I sit in the back."

"Do you think they'll tolerate *me*?"

She offered a wry smile. "I guess we'll find out."

Hanging on the door of The Bell was a pretty evergreen and holly wreath with a felted white dove nestling in it. Miss Croft pushed the door open and waved me inside.

The cozy front room, containing only the bar and a table in front of the window, was paneled in dark wood. Ruby-red upholstery covered the chairs and barstools. Oil lamps glowed on the table and bar, and candles burned in wall sconces. An armchair rested beside a coal stove, and a gentleman sat there smoking a pipe.

"None of that here," a large, squinting man behind the bar called to me. A customer on a stool turned to stare at me, and I flushed hot.

Miss Croft stepped in front of me. "She's a friend of mine, Sam. Miss Grimm, of Grimm Curiosities on Goodramgate."

He continued to squint at me. "Mr. Grimm used to come in here sometimes. Friendly sort. Never disorderly. Was sorry to hear he passed."

"Thank you, sir," I replied quietly.

"Not sure he'd like to know his daughter was in here."

I was ready to turn back to the door, but he looked at Miss Croft and tossed his head in the direction of a short corridor near where we stood. It appeared to lead behind the bar.

"Go on and sit down at a table in back," she said to me in a low voice. "I'll bring our drinks."

I opened my coin purse and took out the sovereign. "Take this," I said.

But she waved it away. "First time's on me. But promise to come back again with me if they treat us well?"

I smiled. "I promise."

Miss Croft went to the bar, and I walked to the room in back, which was just as cozy and less public. In fact, there were no other patrons at the moment. The room even had its own coal stove, squat and gleaming in the lamplight. I found a snug in one corner and sat down to wait.

Miss Croft soon appeared, carrying two pints filled with golden liquid and an inch of froth on top. "They have spirits if you prefer," she said. "Didn't think to ask you."

"Beer is fine, thank you." I did prefer sherry, but I was doing things differently today.

She sat down across from me and slid one glass over.

The snug was made more private by two narrow wood partition walls with frosted windows, but from my seat, I could still see most of the room. Many old portraits decorated the walls, as well as hunting scenes and still lifes of food and wine. A large chandelier hung from the ceiling.

I glimpsed myself in a gilt mirror on the opposite wall. *She looks like a stranger.*

"How does it feel?"

I pulled my gaze back to my companion. "Feel?"

"To be out on your own."

"Strange. A little scary," I admitted.

And yet . . . I spent so much time behind the shop counter with the world coming at me, often judging me in the bargain. Always trying to be polite and accommodating. Always worrying whether next week's rent would come. Always sitting down to tea and supper in silence with Mama.

I picked up my glass. "It feels good."

Miss Croft grinned. "It does, doesn't it?"

I sipped the beer—cool, slightly sweet, with a biscuity creaminess but a hint of bitterness, too. I wiped foam from my lip with a gloved finger as I set down the glass.

"I'm so glad you came to the shop, Miss Croft," I said, meaning it. "I wasn't at first, and I'm afraid I was rather short. I'd just had an unpleasant encounter when you knocked, and I'd had no time to think through it."

"Sometimes a pause and change of scenery helps. Things don't seem so serious."

I considered that and decided she was right. I was still sore over Lord Carlisle's rudeness, and I hadn't even let myself really think about the loss of my friendship with Antony yet, but I did feel *better*.

"So is it something you want to get off your chest, or would you rather just get in your cups? You'll get no judgment from me either way."

I grinned. "Tempting as the latter is, I don't suppose it would solve anything."

She raised her pint and tipped it slightly toward me. "Ah, but it *will* make you forget."

I rubbed my thumb against the base of my glass, trying to decide how much, if anything, I should reveal about Lord Carlisle's visit. Yet why shouldn't I have someone to confide in? Antony couldn't be that someone, not any longer. The people of York might judge Miss Croft and me, but at least we wouldn't ruin each other's prospects.

So I lifted my gaze and spun out the history of meeting Antony and our developing friendship. I told her everything, including how our acquaintance had begun with Miss Carlisle's and Mama's affliction and our hopes of helping them. Though I did disclose we believed the affliction to be spiritual, I left out some of the more fantastic details, afraid she might start to question whether I wasn't making the whole thing up. I told her about the ball, too, and the unexpected invitation from Mr. Stoke. Finally, I told her about Lord Carlisle.

When I'd finished and picked up my beer glass, a corner of Miss Croft's lips lifted. "If I don't keep an eye on you, you're going to steal my crown as the most talked-about woman in York."

My shoulders hunched. "You're right. I don't care about it at all, at least not for myself. But I must remain respectable to keep the shop going. Otherwise I don't know what will happen to Mama and me."

"Well, I dress like a man and drink alone in pubs, and I still have Croft & Croft."

I brightened. "That's true!"

"I suppose there's been no romantic scandal in my case." She grunted. *"Yet."* She studied me over the rim of her glass, sipped, and set it down. "There are charities, you know. Including the one started by Lady Carlisle. I think you could get money for the asylum. It would be one less burden to carry."

I shook my head. "I couldn't bear it, Miss Croft. I—"

"Charlie. At this point, I think you might as well call me Charlie." I must have looked puzzled, because she glowered and added, "Charlotte. But don't you dare."

I laughed. "All right. I'm Lizzy. As opposed to Eliza."

"Go on then, Lizzy."

"I know it may come to the asylum eventually. At some point I might simply be unable to make ends meet any longer." How close I'd come even just this week. "But until then, I don't think I can bring myself to do it. One hears such awful stories. And also, I feel like it would be giving up hope. I know she's still in there somewhere."

Charlie swished what was left of the beer around in her glass. "I can understand that." Draining the last of it, she set the glass down with a thunk. "If you ever do lose the shop, I want you to promise you'll come to me. I can always use a hard worker who doesn't mind getting her hands dirty."

Touched, I said, "Thank you, Charlie."

She gave a short nod. "So I guess you'll have to go on solving your mystery on your own now?"

I sighed. "Yes. Though if I do manage to figure it out, I may still be able to help Miss Carlisle. I won't jeopardize her brother by trying to see him again, but I'm sure I could get a message to him."

She sat back, folding her arms. "And what do you intend to do about this ball?"

"Oh, I can't possibly go now."

One of her eyebrows lifted. "You're going to tell Mr. Stoke . . . what? You're indisposed?"

"I suppose so, yes. But I'll send him a message this evening, so I don't have to see him. Unfortunately, I'll likely have to keep the shop closed for the day to support my story." She was shaking her head. "What?" I said.

"You should go, Lizzy."

I stared at her. The idea made my stomach hurt. "Have you been listening to me?"

"Closely."

"Charlie, Lord Carlisle was beastly to me! He doesn't want me there, not *really*. I still don't understand why he didn't disinvite me. I won't be able to speak to Ant—to Mr. Carlisle. Why would I go and let them look down their noses at me?"

"That's pride, Lizzy, not sense. You've earned the right to be proud. Look how you've survived without your father! Without help from *anyone*. So you take that pride along with you to the ball and hold your head up. Do just what that old man said: make the most of the opportunity."

I took another small sip from my glass. "You really think so?"

She shrugged. "It's what I would do."

Something else occurred to me then: the ball might present opportunities beyond the ones already discussed. I had resolved to remain open to the idea of marriage, yet I had not a single prospect. Though most of the ball guests would likely be too far above my station, it was at least possible I might meet someone. There would almost certainly be more young men at the ball than ever came through the door of the shop.

And one of them would be Antony.

My thoughts had almost taken a pointless turn toward his anticipated engagement when I noticed Charlie eyeing my mostly full beer glass. "You're not going to drink that, are you?" she said.

I smiled. "I'm not. I *wanted* to like it."

"Well, I like the fact you have an open mind." She switched our glasses and started working on mine.

Suddenly I recalled a comment from my conversation with Lord Carlisle. A particularly insinuating one that had gotten lost among the other awful things he said.

"The baron said something I didn't understand," I told Charlie. "'I know how you Grimms like to climb.' I wonder what that could mean?"

"It means he's a rude old bastard," she muttered into my glass.

"*Mmm.* I feel like Papa must have been friends with the Stokes at one time, or at least acquainted with them. I don't know why else he would have given them a set of his books. Sir Arthur was an old friend of Lord Carlisle's. Do you think the baron might know something about Papa that I don't?"

"He wouldn't be the first."

"No indeed."

She pushed away what was left of my pint. "I should probably get back to the shop before all hell breaks loose."

"Yes, I need to get back, too."

"I enjoyed this, Lizzy," she said with a smile.

I laughed. "All you did was listen to my problems. But you offered some advice that I'm going to give serious thought."

"Well, next time you can listen to my problems and give *me* bad advice."

"Agreed."

We walked together as far as Goodramgate and bade each other good evening.

As I entered the shop, I tried to settle my mind to the task of finishing out the day as if I hadn't lost a friend and been taken to task by a cranky old peer.

"Miss Grimm?" Sally had come partway down the stairs.

"How is Mama, Sally?"

"She's fine, miss, but I wanted to tell you Miss Stoke was here a little while ago and left something for you. I hope you don't mind that I opened the door for her."

"Do you mean Miss Isabel Stoke?" I knew no other Miss Stoke, but I couldn't imagine why she would come by.

"Yes, miss. The package is just there."

She gestured to the counter, where a large rectangular box rested.

Carlisle House

Sally must have been nearly as curious as I was, but to her credit, she immediately started back upstairs.

I went to the counter and opened the box. Whatever was inside hid behind layers of tissue paper, and there was a note on top.

> My Dear Miss Grimm,
>
> I hope you won't take this as rudeness or impertinence, but I thought that due to the scandalous lack of notice about tomorrow evening's ball, you might be without proper attire. My young cousin Cecile, who accompanied me the first day I came into your shop, is still in York and is about your size. She always packs far more than she needs, and she has offered to loan you one of her gowns. Your maid may be able to manage any necessary alteration, but in case not, I have engaged my seamstress, Mrs. Godwin, to pay you a visit tomorrow morning. If she is not needed, simply send her away.
>
> Yours sincerely,
> Isabel Stoke

I spent a few moments in quiet but utter shock before carefully folding back the paper to reveal the bodice of a dark-blue and white satin ball gown.

I drew back my fingers like I'd been burned, as if my mere touch might be enough to damage the expensive garment (if the word *garment* could even be used to describe such a confection of fabric).

"My *goodness*," I muttered.

Had Mr. Stoke put her up to this? Or perhaps Miss Stoke herself, who'd helped to plan the ball and would likely one day be Lady Carlisle, didn't want to be embarrassed by emerging from the carriage with me. I could hardly blame her. Yet the lady had obviously taken pains in her note not to insult me. It could be that both she and her uncle wished to make me more presentable without seeming to be unkind.

Or perhaps it truly was done out of kindness, Lizzy.

The real question, though, was what now? I had all but talked myself out of even going. Could I feign illness after *this*?

I kept thinking about Miss Croft's—Charlie's—advice.

Make the most of the opportunity.

I would certainly draw more notice in this ball gown than in my rose dress.

And Antony, though he might not be able to talk to me, could hardly avoid *seeing* me. Which should have no bearing on my decision whatsoever.

Sighing, I took the bodice carefully in my hands and freed the rest of the dress. The velvet-and-lace-trimmed neckline dipped low in a broad V, and the short, puffed sleeves would rest below the shoulders. The skirt was impossibly full, with frothy flounces. How many such gowns must the young lady possess not to mind risking *this* one? There would be all manner of hazards at a ball—punch, ices, greasy meats, not to mention candles and careless feet (including mine). How did one keep track of so much fabric as they walked? I couldn't even guess at what a dress like this must cost.

I heard a soft gasp behind me and turned. Sally had come back down the stairs.

"I quite agree with you," I said, returning my attention to the gown. "Do you suppose they're afraid I'll embarrass them?"

"It's beautiful, miss," she said reverently. "Will you wear it?"

"I suppose I must or else cause offense. How will I ever endure it?"

There were several ticks of silence, and I turned to find Sally covering her mouth with her hand. I grinned, and she let out a burst of laughter.

"You'd best put it on, miss, and see if it will fit you."

"Oh, indeed. She's sending her seamstress tomorrow in case it's too much for us."

This elicited more laughter, and though I could still feel the ache in my chest, my heart had without a doubt lifted in the last hour.

As soon as I closed for the evening, Sally and I took the dress up to my bedroom. Miss Stoke had a good eye; it turned out only minor adjustments were required. We must, of course, take care that any alteration could be undone before returning the dress. Sally thought she could manage, though she looked nervous. "If I'm over my head, we'll consult the seamstress tomorrow," she said.

In the end she did a fine job, though we found my petticoats weren't up to such a challenge. All I knew to do was ask the advice of the seamstress, but fortunately she arrived the next morning with crinolines. She went up with Sally to inspect the gown while I opened the shop, and though she restitched one row of Sally's handiwork, she was satisfied overall.

Today was the Saturday before Christmas, our busiest day of the year, and I could not have made it through without Sally. She had learned our routines quickly and never had to be directed, and she was well aware of the state of my nerves. She even took the initiative to make the shop festive by baking gingerbread, and when I got behind, she came out from the kitchen in a clean apron to serve tea to the customers who were waiting.

I kept a loose tally in my head throughout the day and thought we would come very close to settling the rest of our debt with the landlady. This was a relief, yet I feared for the weeks after Christmas, our slowest time of year, which we would go into with no savings at all. We had the books, of course, but I dreaded selling any more of them before we'd solved the mystery of Mama's and Sophia's affliction. Even if we *did* sell them, without some radical and unanticipated change in our fortunes, it would really only be a temporary respite.

After the whirlwind of shop activity—I did not even close at tea—the clock finally chimed half past seven, one hour before Mr. Stoke and his niece were to arrive.

Sally helped me with all the various components of my dress. We borrowed some seed pearl combs from the jewelry case, and she arranged my hair neatly behind my ears, using a little pomade to tame my frizz. We finished with a dainty seed pearl necklace, whose focal point was a snowflake pendant made from clear paste gemstones. "Simple and sweet," Sally said. "The gown is the real statement."

"Well?" I said, turning in front of her, miles of fabric shifting as I moved.

She smiled broadly. "Why don't we go downstairs so you can look in the long mirror?"

The candles and lamps in the shop were all still lit, anticipating the Stokes' arrival. Next to the reading nook we did indeed have a long mirror in a gilt frame.

For the second time in as many days, a stranger stared back at me. The one in The Bell had looked like she was in over her head. I supposed this one did, too, but she appeared every inch a fine lady. Despite the miles of fabric, significantly more of my flesh was on display than usual, and I hoped Carlisle House wouldn't turn out to be drafty.

A creaking noise drew my attention, and a shiver ran through me when I saw one of the cabinet doors had swung open. The cane had been placed back in the stand beside it.

"Did you remove the cane from the cabinet pulls, Sally?"

She followed my gaze. "No, miss."

It could simply have been a curious customer, yet goose bumps rose on my arms. I held my breath as I moved to replace the cane. The interior was just as it should be—mostly empty, with my father's coat still hanging there.

Hearing the shop bells, I quickly closed the cabinet and put the cane back through. When I turned, I found Mr. Stoke standing just inside the door.

"My dear Miss Grimm," he said, beaming, "you take my breath away."

His gallantry released a warm rush of gratitude. Making a small curtsy, I said, "Thank you, sir."

"Your carriage awaits, if you're ready."

I glanced at Sally, who was endeavoring to hide her smile. "You know where to find me should there be any trouble with Mama."

"Yes, miss. Carlisle House."

I took a deep breath. "Carlisle House."

Sally had a light-blue wool shawl draped over one arm. We'd found it neatly folded in the box from Miss Stoke, along with a pair of spotless ball gloves. She lifted the shawl and settled it over my bare shoulders.

Mr. Stoke, very handsome in his formal jacket and tie, offered his arm, and together we went out to the carriage that waited in front of the shop. Snow fell lightly against its gleaming black top, and I was glad for the pomade. Though I suspected my hair would rebel and revert to a crinkly cloud before the evening was half-over.

A gloved feminine arm pushed open the carriage door, and Mr. Stoke took my hand as I raised my foot to the step and climbed in.

"Good evening, Miss Grimm," said Miss Stoke with a welcoming smile. "How lovely you look."

"Good evening. If I do, it's thanks to you, Miss Stoke. And I *do* thank you, and your cousin, of course."

"Here, sit across from me so our skirts don't do battle, and Uncle can sit beside me. That dress is perfection on you, if I do say so myself. I'll wager the blue is the same color as your eyes. No, don't thank me again, I was happy to do it. Cecile is such a goose, bringing *five* gowns when we had only two fetes to attend. But then suddenly there were three, and we were able to offer one to you, so I suppose it was all right."

Mr. Stoke looked bewildered by his niece's stream of chatter, which told me he'd known nothing of the dress. I also learned something about Miss Stoke. She wasn't stiff, as I'd thought. Women were expected to take pains to be agreeable at all times, and she didn't. I began to like her for it. Moreover, if she'd caught any whiff of rumor about Antony and me, there was no outward indication she was displeased.

Antony could do worse. Indeed, Isabel Stoke was the proper sort of wife for him.

"Are you well, Miss Grimm?" I glanced up to find Mr. Stoke watching me.

"Oh yes. I suppose I'm a little nervous."

"Of course," he said. "Try not to be, though. I'll be right there with you. I haven't been to a ball in ages myself. We'll muddle through it together."

"But you mustn't monopolize her, Uncle. Just see how I've turned her out. Lots of men will want to dance with her."

I swallowed. "Dance?"

"Certainly! It is a ball, after all."

"Now don't overwhelm her, Isabel," Mr. Stoke chastised gently. "She may not have experienced many waltzes."

He was right. I had never danced with anyone but Papa, and only in our sitting room.

"You may take the first waltz and teach her, Uncle," Miss Stoke conceded regally. "I know she'll be a quick study."

He smiled placidly, but behind it I thought he was turning over something in his mind.

"Your cousin will be attending the ball as well?" I asked Miss Stoke. "I was hoping for an opportunity to thank her in person."

"Yes, she's there already. Papa had some business to discuss with Lord Carlisle and arrived earlier. We sent Cecile with him to keep our carriage ride comfortable. She's a dear girl, but she is *young*."

Miss Stoke, seeming annoyed, began fussing with one of her gloves, and I got the feeling her cousin's visit had perhaps gone on longer than she liked.

There was no great distance between the shop and our destination on Castlegate, and while we'd been talking, our carriage had joined a line of others in front of Carlisle House. We progressed slowly, as each carriage reached the front of the line and released its occupants. I watched the colorful parade through the carriage window.

"Do you know how many guests there will be, Miss Stoke?"

"Eighty-five have accepted."

I drew back from the window. "So many!"

"We could have expected twice that with more notice," she said. "Many families have already gone to their estates for Christmas, though some have returned for the ball."

"The house hardly seems large enough."

"Well, it is the largest town house in York. The ground floor rooms will have had most of their furnishings removed to make enough space for the dancing and refreshments. I find an intimate setting much nicer than the assembly rooms for a Christmas fete, don't you, Uncle?"

"Indeed," he said, though his eyes had been much on *me*, and I wasn't sure he had actually been listening to his niece's explanation.

"It will be quite lively, though," she concluded.

What I took from this was there would be no disappearing into a corner if it all became too much. Not that one could hope to *fit* into a corner in a dress like this.

Turning back to the window, I noticed a woman standing alone on the footway near our carriage. She looked different from the other guests. More subdued, and her gown and coiffure were dated, like a costume for a masquerade. She was very beautiful, but she appeared confused and forlorn.

"Who is that lady, I wonder?" I said.

Miss Stoke leaned closer to the window, looking out. "Which?"

"Just outside the carriage." We were creeping past the woman even as I spoke. When her eye caught mine, I felt the whole of her attention on me. A chill ran through me, and I pulled the shawl tighter.

"She's wearing gold," I continued, my voice trembling slightly, "and an elaborate hair arrangement."

Miss Stoke sat back and said with surprise, "That sounds like Anne Carlisle, does it not, Uncle?"

"Yes, it does."

There was an edge to his voice, and I looked at him, dread stealing over me. "A relative of the Carlisles, then?"

"A long-dead one, Miss Grimm."

My heart lurched. *Not again. Not here.*

"You aren't the first to see her ghost," he said, resuming his kindly tone. "I didn't know you possessed your mother's gift."

I felt the flames in my cheeks. With her work as a medium, Mama's gift was not exactly a secret. Yet as my own was not public knowledge, it made me uneasy to hear him speak of it.

"Neither did I," I replied. "Not until recently."

"How very interesting," said Miss Stoke, studying me closer.

Thankfully the discussion ended as the carriage rolled to a stop, and a footman opened the door. He handed me out first and then Miss Stoke. Mr. Stoke followed, and we found ourselves in a queue of ball guests stretching to the entrance. A covering had been erected over the walk to shield us from the weather. Snow continued falling lightly, and spirits were high, with much laughter and anticipatory chatter. As for me, winged creatures were apparently at war in my stomach. Thankfully I'd been too nervous to eat before leaving home.

Carlisle House was a fine old town house with a redbrick facade and numerous windows looking down onto Castlegate. Unlike many buildings in York, it wasn't centuries old but had been built by the family in the mid-1700s on the site of a much older ruin. In my evening strolls with Mama, I'd gotten peeks at the richly appointed interior through the candlelit windows. It had never occurred to me that one day I might actually enter the building.

Soon enough we found ourselves passing through the front door, joining another queue in the entryway to greet our hosts—Lord Carlisle and his son. My unhappy stomach grew unhappier. My discomfort must have shown, for Miss Stoke leaned close and squeezed my arm.

"Don't be nervous," she said. "You will easily be one of the most breathtaking young ladies in the room."

This was obviously an exaggeration, but it made me like her even more.

As the couple in front of us moved into one of the rooms that branched off the entryway, Antony's eyes came to rest on me. My heart tried to lift and sink at the same time. I could see the same sort of conflict playing out in his expression, with an added note of surprise because obviously *the dress*.

"Miss Grimm, you look—"

"Dear Miss Stoke," gushed the baron, reaching for my companion's hand and drawing her forward. "And Mr. Stoke, it's been too long since I had the pleasure. Come in, come in, and find yourself a glass of something to warm you up."

"Thank you, Lord Carlisle," replied Miss Stoke, "you are very kind. I'm so pleased that you . . ."

Her words faded into the background as Antony moved closer to me, a stricken look in his eyes. "I hope we may find a moment to speak, Miss Grimm," he said quietly.

"I—"

"Allow our guests to move along, Antony," interrupted his father. "We mustn't leave the others out in the snow."

My throat tightening, I made my curtsy to the baron, but he was already looking beyond us to the next guests in the queue. Tears of humiliation and anger blurred my vision as I took Mr. Stoke's arm. I pressed one hand to my chest, feeling my heart race under my fingertips.

Breathe, Lizzy. That was never going to be anything other than dreadful.

A servant took our wraps before Mr. Stoke, oblivious to my distress, led me through a door on the left into a high-ceilinged salon. The room had a large fireplace, and its red-painted walls were made all the more dramatic by the white mantel and ceiling, and the large mirrors reflecting candlelight. Already quite a few guests milled about, some walking between this room and another that adjoined at the back. Through its doorway, I could see a dining table heavily laden with refreshments.

A harpist strummed in one corner of the salon, and at the farther end, half a dozen long tables had been covered in white linen and set for supper. They were decorated with holly, ivy, and numerous candles in gleaming silver stands.

Before one of the windows that overlooked the street, a table held an enormous punch bowl and a thing I had never seen—a great swan sculpted from ice. There was also a bowl of small objects I couldn't identify. We followed Miss Stoke there, and she drew out one of these and offered it to me. It turned out to be a booklet with an engraved metal case. One more thing I had never seen, nor expected to ever see: a dance card.

"This being a charity ball," said Miss Stoke, "each guest has paid a ticket price to attend, therefore you must dance so everyone will feel they've gotten their money's worth." She helped tie the booklet to my wrist with the attached white ribbon. "Now, if a gentleman asks you to dance and you are free, I'm afraid you must put his name on your card or else offer insult."

She could have saved herself all this trouble, as I felt certain no one apart from Mr. Stoke would ask me for a dance.

"Now, please forgive me," she continued, "but I must leave you in my uncle's care and check that all has been properly managed."

With that, she walked across to the room with the refreshments and disappeared inside.

"If I may, Miss Grimm," said Mr. Stoke, "I will claim the first two dances."

I opened the card case. There was a very small pencil inside, and by steadying the booklet against my wrist, I managed to write his name— messily—on the first two lines.

Closing the case, I smiled and said, "I must apologize in advance, sir."

"I forbid you to do so. I've asked you here, and any uneasiness you may feel due to inexperience, we shall address together, as Isabel has suggested."

"I thank you," I replied, bowing my head to cover the fact I was on the verge of tears again. "Both of you have been so very kind to me."

"Stoke, is that you?"

My companion turned to greet an older gentleman who approached—one I immediately recognized. The antique dealer who'd not-so-subtly suggested that if I'd marry him, he would take Grimm Curiosities off my hands.

"Mr. Lumley, it's good to see you. Allow me to introduce you to my friend Miss Grimm, of Grimm Curiosities."

Again I inclined my head. "Mr. Lumley and I are acquainted," I said without warmth but hopefully also without insult.

How in heaven's name had *he* merited an invitation? He'd made it clear to me that he was wealthy, and I supposed that was enough. Especially for a charity ball.

"Indeed, we are," he said, eyeing me curiously—and a little too closely for my comfort. The whole situation had me feeling exposed, and the low neckline of my gown didn't exactly help matters. "I must say I did not expect to have the pleasure of meeting you here. I hope your mother is well."

"She is. I thank you, sir."

Then I saw his gaze land on my dance card. *No, no, no.*

"If your card is not yet full, Miss Grimm, may I claim a dance?"

I forced a smile and opened the case again. "Of course, Mr. Lumley."

When I'd written his name and closed it—counting my blessings that *he* hadn't had the boldness to ask for two dances—he bowed and started toward the refreshment room.

"I predict your first ball will be a great success," said Mr. Stoke with a smile. "Ah, here comes Sir George and Lady Shipley. Sir George recently told me his wife is an amateur collector. Do you know them?"

The gentleman he'd indicated was about his own age, accompanied by a tall woman in a green ball gown. "I don't believe so."

"Come, I'll introduce you."

It seemed Mr. Stoke was a man of his word.

"She Looks Very Pretty, Does She Not?"

Antony

It seemed ages before my father and I left our posts at the door and joined our guests, who'd all gone to mingle in the red salon or sample the refreshments in the dining room.

Having told the baron that I was going in search of Miss Stoke, I instead went in search of Lizzy, hoping for a chance to speak to her before the dancing began. After the first dance, which had already been arranged with Miss Stoke in accordance with our fathers' expectations, it would be my duty to dance with the young ladies the other gentlemen had not asked. I would hardly have a moment to breathe for the duration of the ball.

Yet I couldn't let the night pass without speaking to her. Not after learning that my father had paid a visit to her shop. Judging by my own interview with him, I could only imagine what awful things he must have said to her. What he had perhaps even *accused* her of. And then the way he had snubbed her when she arrived with the Stokes. What must she be thinking of me, allowing such an insult to occur after I put pressure on her to come tonight? I had never in my life been so angry with my father, and the two of us were bound to have it out again once this ill-timed spectacle concluded.

The musicians engaged for the dancing began tuning their instruments in the drawing room—I didn't have long. Finally, I discovered Lizzy and Stoke beside the ice sculpture, sipping punch and talking closely. Now that she wasn't looking at me, I could fully take her in. The sight of her in that gown, which bared her shoulders and perfectly complemented her eyes, literally took my breath away. If anything, my anger simmered hotter. Why should Stoke enjoy such a privilege? A man who until tonight had been so disfavored by my father that he never numbered among our guests? I made straight for them, intending to pry her away from him for however many moments I could steal. But just as Lizzy looked up, I heard our butler calling for the dancers to assemble.

Blast, blast, blast!

Miss Stoke appeared out of nowhere. "Are you ready, Mr. Carlisle?"

"I am," I replied stiffly, offering her my arm. Together we made our way to the drawing room.

As we took our place and the waltz began, I said, "You look radiant this evening." She did in fact, but my heart wasn't in the pleasantry.

I thought her answering smile a little wry, but likely that had more to do with my own state of mind than hers. "I thank you, sir."

Of course I knew I was being both unfair and unkind. Miss Stoke was perfectly agreeable, and she was terrifyingly competent. I had nothing against the lady except the fact my father was threatening to disown me if I didn't marry her.

We swung past Lizzy and Mr. Stoke then, and I almost tripped over my feet. I don't know why it should have come as a surprise to me that she would dance, *or* that she would appear as a lovely vision on my doorstep, swept upon a frothy ocean wave, like a siren in one of her father's books.

"She looks very pretty, does she not, Mr. Carlisle?"

I glanced down at my partner with some surprise, nearly tangling up my feet again. "Beg your pardon?"

"Miss Grimm, dancing with my uncle there. Not everyone can wear that vivid blue, but how it makes her eyes shine. I believe you're acquainted with her?"

If I didn't know Miss Stoke better, I'd suspect she was mocking me.

"I am, in fact," I said, wondering how she knew.

"I believe my uncle is half in love with her."

I felt my eyes popping at this and struggled to compose myself. "Indeed?"

"Well, he's eccentric, so I'm not sure one can ever really know what he's thinking. But he seems awfully fond to me."

I cleared my throat and said nothing.

"You must dance with her, of course."

My brows lifted. "I had thought I might."

"Oh, you *must*. She's not an eligible match, you see, so the other gentlemen may not ask her. It would be very rude not to. I'm sure your father would agree."

My lips formed a genuine smile. "You are correct, Miss Stoke, as always. I'm not sure why I didn't think of it."

She gave me a satisfied nod, and we passed the rest of the waltz in silence.

As soon as the music stopped and I had made my bow, I led Miss Stoke toward the dining room, keeping my eye on her uncle and Lizzy.

Miss Stoke went to greet her young cousin Cecile, who had arrived at Carlisle House with Miss Stoke's father before the ball. He and *my* father had closed themselves up in the baron's study for quite some time. *Not long now until* that *pot boils over.*

I glimpsed Lizzy across the dining room, accepting a glass of lemonade from her partner. I didn't like that he had so taken charge of her, and really it wasn't quite proper. Her mother should have been here, though of course that hadn't been possible. As it was, she had no other friend here but me.

"Miss Grimm?" I said, joining them.

"Good evening, Mr. Carlisle," said Stoke. "You and my niece have worked wonders. It's a delight to be here."

This was stated in a polite tone, in no way offensive, yet at that moment I wished Ambrose Stoke to the moon.

"Thank you, sir," I said. "You're very welcome here, of course." I turned my attention to Lizzy, who watched me with an expression I couldn't quite interpret. Her cheeks were tinged pink, and wispy curls floated about her face, like she'd been out walking on a breezy day. "Miss Grimm, I was hoping if your dance card isn't full already, I might request to be added."

Her expression now was unambiguous: surprise. But she collected herself and opened the silver case. "There are three dances remaining, sir."

Three dances! And so early in the evening. Apparently Miss Stoke's assessment of Lizzy's prospects had, uncharacteristically, quite missed the mark.

"Will you put me down for the last?" Hopefully by then I would figure out exactly what I was going to say to her.

As she took hold of the tiny pencil in her gloved fingers and wrote my name on the last line, something in me shifted. I knew this from the pulse of my heart; the train of my thoughts was left to catch up.

I had at some point come to think of Lizzy as *my own*. Not oafishly, in the sense of wanting to control her. But having some claim to the privilege of hearing her voice. Of knowing her thoughts. Of walking beside her, be it to the dance floor, to the church, or to the ends of the earth.

There's a name for that, man.

Near Collisions

My thoughts churned as Mr. Stoke led me to the ballroom for our second dance. Antony on my dance card was the last thing I'd expected.

My heart had thrummed with delight until my head cowed it with reason. His father would be furious. I didn't want to create any unpleasantness by refusing him, especially after Miss Stoke's admonishment, but I wasn't sure we should actually go through with it. What had caused him to ask me? Perhaps he thought it was the only opportunity we'd have to speak. Perhaps he wished to inform me of his engagement ahead of a public announcement.

The sooner the better, I suppose.

After Antony had claimed his dance, Mr. Stoke solicited a third from me—the second to last. I suspected he was nearly as surprised as I was that my card had filled so quickly. A few associates of his had asked me for dances, but primarily it was younger gentlemen who had approached asking for introductions. Though I knew it was thanks to the borrowed gown—and possible additional kindly interference by Miss Stoke—I couldn't help feeling gratified after the baron's cold reception.

I don't know how I got through the next several hours. Except for the short pauses for refreshment, the dancing never stopped! Thanks to Mr. Stoke's instruction in the first two, I believe I avoided embarrassing myself. He told me that a gentleman who knew what he was doing made it easy for his partner to follow, and that missteps would be blamed on *him*.

My first and most challenging test was Mr. Lumley, who I think must not have danced much, and we had a few near collisions in the quadrille. I felt great sympathy for him until he let out some hints that he still had the idea of marriage in his head. Luckily the quadrille required concentration on both our parts—and provided regular points of interruption—so I was able to shift the conversation to benign topics such as the weather, Christmas, and the coming new year.

As the night wore on, I felt more and more grateful to Mr. Stoke. Not only had he ensured I could perform adequately in the ballroom, he made a point to speak to everyone he knew as either a buyer or seller of antiquities and curiosities, from the serious collectors like himself to the enthusiastic hobbyists. He had made me promises in his effort to lure me here, and he had kept them.

As the clocks struck midnight, we finally sat down at the long tables in the red salon for a supper before the dancing continued. Sustained up to now almost exclusively by excitement and nerves, I found I was famished. We filled our plates with cold meats, cheeses, roasted vegetables, poached pears, and wedges of pie, along with various types of biscuits and cake. How Mama would have enjoyed herself! I couldn't imagine how I was to get through two more hours of dancing, especially after eating so much. But I drank two cups of tea, and they helped to revive me.

Mr. Stoke and I joined Sir George and Lady Shipley and talked with them for much of the meal. I liked them both very much, especially Lady Shipley, who'd promised to visit the shop in the new year. When they finished eating, like many of the other guests they began to drift about, visiting with friends and nibbling on biscuits and candies. I was content to remain quietly seated until required to do otherwise.

"Mr. Stoke," I said to my companion, "I'm afraid I must regain my strength before the dancing begins again, but you need not be chained to me."

He smiled. "Is that a polite way of dismissing me, Miss Grimm?"

"By no means," I replied, laughing. "Only I don't wish you to feel obligated to take care of me all evening."

"On the contrary, I am enjoying your company and hope that *you* feel no obligation to remain in mine."

"I assure you I am perfectly content, sir. In fact, I want to—"

Before I could express my gratitude for all his efforts on my behalf, a sudden movement drew my eye and I gasped. She had appeared again—the "long-dead" Carlisle lady—directly across from me, behind Lady Shipley's empty chair.

"Miss Grimm?" Mr. Stoke followed my gaze. "Is everything all right?"

"You really don't see her?" I said, my voice almost a whisper. Just like outside the carriage, she had fixed her attention on me.

"I'm sorry, I don't," he replied, studying the air before us. "But I believe you *do*. It must be unsettling, to say the least."

I had always thought seeing a vaporish specter would be terrifying and had believed that to be Mama's experience, but this was so much worse. I could have reached out and touched her. She could have reached out and touched *me*. The way she stared . . . I wondered whether she wanted something from me, yet I couldn't imagine what.

"It's the same woman from before?" asked Mr. Stoke.

"It is."

"Fascinating. She seems to have some affinity for you. Perhaps she has a message."

As if on cue, the woman began *speaking*. Or rather attempting to speak. Her lips moved, but no sound escaped them, much like when Mama had met Antony—though the ghost did not seem to realize I couldn't hear her. When she'd finished, she held my gaze a moment before turning and walking toward the entryway. A ball guest in a red gown stood directly in her path, but the ghost never slowed. She kept on walking and passed right through the guest, who let out a squeal.

The lady's hand went to her chest and some of her wine tipped onto the floor.

"Someone's walked on my grave!" she said, laughing.

The gentleman with her gently removed the glass from her hand and said, "Let's have a sit and a cup of tea, my love."

A cold draft caused me to shiver, and I folded my arms over my chest. A footman walked by with a teapot, and Mr. Stoke hailed him.

As I sipped my tea, my companion continued to study me with concern. "I believe you said your Sight had only just come on?"

"Only a few days ago, in fact."

"It interests me, but you must tell me if my questions are unwelcome. What—or whom—have you seen?"

It interests me. I couldn't help thinking of Papa.

How much to reveal? I had grown more comfortable with Mr. Stoke after his many kindnesses, but I wasn't sure I was ready to tell him about Papa and the books.

"There has been some ghostly activity in the shop," I said. "Things have been moved to unexpected places. I also saw a warrior from antiquity near Stonegate, and later a knight at the Minster. The latter wore a flimsy crown and made me think of Richard of York."

Mr. Stoke's eyes gleamed. "Ah, the ambitious Plantagenet who lost his head. Just the sort of fellow who would refuse to move on from this life. And have you spoken with any of these spirits, Miss Grimm?"

I shook my head. "This evening's was the first to—"

My reply was interrupted by the call to return to the ballroom. Mr. Stoke smiled and said, "I believe your dance card is full, madam. But I would love to talk more of this later."

I rose from the table and was met by my next partner—Sir Francis Davies, a middle-aged widower who collected butterflies. As Sir Francis led me to the dance floor, my mind turned over my conversations with Mr. Stoke this evening. It occurred to me he was trying to be my *friend*. While we didn't share the same connection that Antony and I did, he, too, had been generous and attentive. I had gained three friends over the course of the last week, and I still had two of them—Mr. Stoke and Miss Croft.

I found myself dreading the dance with Antony. Up to now, I had always looked forward to talking with him. But this was bound to be a farewell of sorts, wasn't it? I must strive to keep our conversation as light as possible. I would congratulate him on his engagement and promise to relay any new discoveries that might help his sister. I would thank him for the ball and wish him a happy Christmas.

Feeling an ache in my throat, I forced my attention back to the moment and Sir Francis. Fortunately he was one of those men who didn't require more from his conversation partner than the occasional utterance of an attentive noise.

The night—or morning—wore on, and I felt exhaustion truly setting in. I wasn't used to *any* of it. The strenuous physical activity, the endless small talk, the extremely late hour, the never-ending flow of wine and spirits. At supper, Mr. Stoke had told me that I couldn't beg off with one partner by claiming fatigue and then go on to dance with another. So to dance with Antony, I must dance with the rest. And though I feared it would bring more pain than pleasure, I knew I couldn't bring myself to back out.

Somehow I made it to the third from the last dance. Only one partner to go until I was on more familiar ground again with Mr. Stoke, who wouldn't take offense if I hadn't the energy for conversation. This dance had been promised to a Mr. Strickland, eldest son of Sir Clyde Strickland, a baronet from the East Riding. He was about Antony's age, and one of the higher-ranking unmarried men in the room.

As the dance commenced, he smiled and said, "You work in a shop here in York, do you?"

All my partners had immediately posed some question as we got underway, but there was something in Mr. Strickland's tone that caused me to stiffen.

"My family owns an antique and curiosity shop on Goodramgate," I corrected politely.

"*Mmm*, I know the place. I understand your parents have passed. I'm sorry for your loss."

He didn't look sorry. If I had to put a label on his expression, I would have called it calculating.

"I'm not sure who you've had your information from, sir, but my mother is still very much alive." I didn't even try to keep the cool note from my tone.

"Beg your pardon," he said indifferently.

We didn't talk at all for the rest of the waltz, which was awkward. At the end, as he walked me to the refreshment room, he said, "Look, the squire and I are in York for two more days. My sisters stayed at home, so we've no more social obligations." He glanced around quickly and bent slightly closer. "I understand Carlisle has moved on." His eyes followed Miss Stoke as she happened to walk by. "Perhaps I'll drop by your shop tomorrow."

My heart froze, and I leaned away from him. Young women who worked in shops were sometimes exposed to insult. I had been fortunate never to experience it up to now, probably because my father had been a respected member of the community. Had Lord Carlisle been right? This gentleman clearly knew something of my connection with Antony. Could my reputation have *already* suffered?

A brittle smile on my lips, I replied, "Tomorrow is Sunday and we are closed, sir. I hope you and your father enjoy a safe journey home."

I could tell by Mr. Strickland's expression that he had perceived the snub. "Good evening," he said curtly, making a short bow.

My skin felt clammy, and my stomach twisted into multiple knots. None of my dance partners had spoken to me like Mr. Strickland, but I couldn't help wondering whether others had gotten the same idea. Could I expect more of such behavior? I had just warmed to the idea of marriage; had I now damaged my prospects? And more than my marriageability was at stake. Respectable men and women would no longer come into the shop if they believed it tainted by licentious behavior.

Mama and I were already hanging by a thread! If Mrs. Schofield got wind of it, she might very well evict us to avoid the association.

"You've made it." Mr. Stoke joined me with a glass of lemonade. "Only two dances left, both with friends."

I thanked heaven that he, at least, seemed to have no notion of impropriety. But as he studied me, his smile faded. "Are you well? Have you seen your ghostly visitor again?"

I shook my head and tried to put the scene with Mr. Strickland out of my mind. Discussing it with Mr. Stoke was impossible, and there was nothing to be done now. Perhaps later I might consult with Charlie Croft.

"I'm quite well," I said, "and ready for our last dance. I want to thank you for making my evening so enjoyable." I was horrified to hear my voice break on the last word.

"You are *not* well, Miss Grimm. Will you tell me what's happened?"

Swallowing my tears, I smiled and said, "Indeed, I am. It's only fatigue. But I'm determined to soldier on to the last. Shall we?"

I drank half the glass of lemonade and placed it on a nearby tray. Then we returned to the ballroom.

We stepped into the dance, and I was noticing muscles I rarely used had already begun to ache when Mr. Stoke said in a somber tone, "Miss Grimm, there's something I'd like to discuss with you."

The knots in my stomach tightened. Perhaps I'd been wrong to assume no rumors had reached him. "Of course."

"I hope you won't take offense at this"—*oh dear*—"but there's something I'd like to—ah, I already said that, didn't I?" He laughed.

"Get to it, man."

We spun another breathless circle, and my heart rose into my throat as I waited for him to go on.

"Miss Grimm, I wanted to ask whether you could ever think of—of marrying me?"

I lost my footing and almost stumbled, but the hand at my waist supported and steadied me. Had I heard him correctly? *Impossible.*

"I realize I'm two decades your senior," he went on, "and perhaps that's too much. I realize we've only known each other a short time. I never really considered marrying before, but I feel we have much in common, and as I get older, I find my life more lonely than solitary. You're a lovely woman—intelligent and kind—and I feel we would make good partners."

Say something, Lizzy!

But my tongue had frozen in my mouth. Ambrose Stoke had just asked me to marry him. Could he be serious? He hardly seemed a man to joke about such a thing. It was alarmingly sudden, but I thought not out of character. *When I find something I want, I do have a tendency to fix on it.*

As the son of a knight who'd built a lucrative brewing business, he was above my station. Yet *he* no longer had a father to disapprove of me.

"Forgive me, sir," I finally managed. "You've quite taken my breath away."

He let out a nervous laugh. "I imagine so. I hope you'll forgive *me*. I suppose I was caught up in the festive mood, but perhaps I should have waited."

Studying him closely, I said, "You're in earnest."

His features composed. "Never have I been more so."

I had never in a thousand years seen this coming. Yet now that I thought of it—the invitation to the ball, the gallant behavior, *three* dances now, not to mention remaining by my side the entire evening . . . it would likely have been obvious to anyone else.

"I—I hardly know what to say."

He smiled, a glint of mischief in his eyes. I noticed for the first time they were hazel, one slightly darker than the other. "Say yes. Then we need no longer grapple over the Ginnel books."

He was holding it out to me—an answer to *everything*. Marriage to Mr. Stoke would presumably end our money trouble. He was right that we would make good partners. His joining me at the helm of Grimm Curiosities—or perhaps Grimm & Stoke—would make my life easier in so many ways. Not the least of which, I could stop worrying about us being turned out of the place into the street. Perhaps most critically at *this* moment, it would put an end to whispers of impropriety that could ruin Mama and me.

Such an opportunity might never come again.

Ambrose Stoke is no Antony Carlisle.

But perhaps he could be enough.

"Well," he said softly, "I know that I've put you on the spot. Take some time to think of it, if you will, and I—"

"I don't need time, Mr. Stoke."

"I Could Never Have Consented to Marry You"

Antony

Would this waltz never end?

I'd hardly said a word to poor Miss Stoke in our second and final dance of the evening. My attention instead drifted to her uncle and Lizzy spinning around the floor. They were both very serious, and I knew something of importance was passing between them. Lizzy looked shocked, even. If he'd said anything to upset her—anger flared in my chest. But next they were laughing, and I felt like a fool.

"Mr. Carlisle, is everything all right?"

I steered my attention back to my partner. "Perfectly so," I said, smiling. "Congratulations, Miss Stoke, on this triumph."

"Well, I'd hardly call it that. Many things could have been better arranged, had we more time. But I suppose all in all it turned out all right."

"Only because you are a miracle worker."

Most young women of my acquaintance would have basked in this praise for at least a moment or two, allowing me to refocus my attention where it had been before, but Miss Stoke was not like most young women.

"There is something on your mind, Mr. Carlisle," she said. "I believe I have an idea what it is."

Lizzy was now smiling sweetly at Mr. Stoke. It was a smile I'd seen before, full of gratitude and affection. My heart plunged and my blood roiled. What was the man about?

"Mr. Carlisle?"

Once again I forced my eyes back to my partner. *Stop being such an ass, Carlisle. Miss Stoke deserves better.*

In fact, what she deserved was the truth.

A strange calm came over me, and I said, "It's simply this. I cannot ask you to marry me, Miss Stoke. I hold you in the highest regard, but I am not in love with you. You deserve someone who is."

A *smile* played at the corners of Miss Stoke's lips. "And I could never have consented to marry you, Mr. Carlisle."

The lady had my full attention now. "No?"

"No, and if you'll get on with asking the person you really want to, we'll both be out of this business."

"The person I . . . ?"

"Come now, don't tell me that in addition to not admitting it to *me*, you haven't yet admitted it to yourself. You are in love with Lizzy Grimm. It's plain as the nose on my face. Not to mention my uncle puffs up like a thundercloud anytime your name is mentioned."

I stared at her. "Miss Grimm is my friend," was my halfhearted denial. Because of course she was right.

"Oh, indeed. I wonder, then, why you look as if you'd like to strangle my uncle? Now pray don't contradict me, Mr. Carlisle—I am on your side."

I shook my head slowly in bafflement. "Why?"

"Because though I am not in love with you, I do very much like you. And as I said a moment ago, if you would only get on with it, we could both get on with our lives."

I frowned. "You know it's not as simple as that, Miss Stoke."

"Pray call me Isabel," she said. "We were nearly betrothed after all. And yes, I know—our papas, and the threats, and the title, and the inheritance. I can only imagine what unpleasantness may transpire. But my money is on *you*. You'll figure something out. You won't get that chance if my uncle precedes you, however."

"Precedes me! You think Lizzy is in love with your uncle?"

"I do not. At least not yet. But he is a very eligible suitor for her, though no heir to a barony, and he is clearly fond of *her*."

My gaze darted again to Lizzy and Stoke. He was much older, but it was no real obstacle. He was charming and still handsome. How much easier her life would be with someone to help her, not to mention the financial considerations. Isabel's optimism notwithstanding, if I defied my father, I would have nothing but myself to give her.

And I did, very much, want to give myself to Lizzy. I wanted to take away her troubles and protect her, yes, but more than that, I wanted some part of every day to be spent with her in just the ways we had been together over this past week—strolling through the town, enjoying a meal, and talking over our day. Making each other laugh. But instead of bidding each other good night at the end . . . well, I could hardly let my thoughts travel in *that* direction while I was still dancing with Isabel.

The strains of the waltz were at last playing out. Only one dance remained—possibly the most important of my life.

I escorted Isabel to the salon, but before I could look for Lizzy, I was waylaid by Sir Clyde's son, Strickland. We'd been friends at Eton, but I hadn't kept up the relationship afterward. We had run with a pack of wildings and pranksters, and Strickland's schemes often targeted the weak or friendless.

"It's been too long, Carlisle," he said. "Care to join me on the terrace for a smoke?"

"Perhaps later," I replied. "I'm committed for the last dance."

"Certainly." He grinned. "I danced with that little shopgirl of yours earlier, by the way. She's a proud one. I thought I'd have a go, but she snubbed me. Can you believe it? I know I'm no peer, but I suppose my money spends just as well."

Halfway through this disgusting monologue, my gaze swung hard and landed on his face. My fist was about to follow when I felt a hand wrap around my arm. "There's Miss Grimm now," said Isabel, pointing to the dining room. "If you'll excuse Mr. Carlisle," she said to the horse's ass in front of me, "he has host responsibilities yet. Perhaps he can speak to you after the ball."

Or perhaps I can kick in your teeth.

The encounter left me shaken, and not just with rage. My father had tried to warn me of this. That my "visits" with Lizzy—in light of the generally acknowledged fact that there was no possibility of my marrying her—would be more dangerous for her than for me.

Where did we go from here? What was I to say to her? Isabel, one of the more clever and pragmatic people I knew, had just professed great faith in me. Though she had a heretofore unguessed-at motivation. All that was clear in my own mind at this moment was that both Stoke and Strickland were, in very different ways, after a woman I wanted for myself, and I wasn't about to stand aside for either of them.

Lizzy had started toward us, but then noticed who I was talking to and turned on her heel. I shoved past Strickland, who muttered something uncomplimentary, and followed.

"Miss Grimm," I called. She stopped and turned, waiting for me to join her. "Shall we?" I asked.

It wrenched my heart to see the strain in her smile as she took my arm. We made our way to the ballroom and took up our position for the final waltz.

Resting one hand on her waist and taking her hand in the other, I said, "I begin to suspect Mr. Strickland has offered you insult."

Her cheeks flamed, but she shook her head. "Just a misunderstanding, Mr. Carlisle. Don't give it another thought."

I knew exactly what kind of misunderstanding had occurred, and furthermore I knew I was to blame. But I could see I would only make things worse by trying to apologize. Thank heaven for Isabel arriving in time to prevent me from knocking the man down and opening a scandal before all of York's society.

My next impulse was to apologize for my father's horrid behavior, but I was afraid even that would create more awkwardness.

How has this gotten so out of hand?

In the end I simply said, "I'm so pleased you came this evening. I hope you've been enjoying yourself."

To my own ears it had a hollow ring. But the tension in her face eased and she replied, "Very much. Of course, I have nothing to compare it to, but I've heard several people say that you and Miss Stoke have managed it beautifully."

I winced inwardly. I'd never told her that Isabel and I had been planning the ball together, but of course Stoke was bound to have. She would believe I had intentionally kept it from her. And I had.

"There are rumors, Mr. Carlisle, that the two of you are soon to be engaged. Please allow me to congratulate you."

Her words pressed like ice against my heart. She smiled, but there was none of the old warmth or familiarity in it—none of the old Lizzy. She might have been any one of a dozen ladies I'd stood up with tonight.

I shook my head. "It is indeed what my father expects. However, there is no understanding between Miss Stoke and me. At least, no understanding that he will like. She and I have joined in rebellion against the idea."

Her brows shot up, and I glimpsed a little melting of the ice. "Have you? Why?"

"Miss Stoke is not in love, and neither am I. At least not with her."

I watched her delicate throat work as she swallowed. My eyes dipped to the tiny pearls that rested against the lovely, flushed skin at the base of her neck. And lower still, to the snowflake pendant, its gemstones glittering like the flecks in her blue eyes.

"I see," she said, a tremble in her voice.

"Miss Grimm—Lizzy—I—"

"I have some news myself, Mr. Carlisle."

"I . . ." The interruption unbalanced me. "Do you?"

"It will probably come as quite a surprise." Her manner was heated and flustered. "It certainly did to me. But I hope you will be happy for me. Mr. Stoke has asked me to marry him." The room tilted, and the music sounded tinny in my ears. "And I have accepted him."

"That cannot be!"

I realized how loudly I'd spoken as several dancers turned their heads to look at me.

Lizzy looked wounded. "That Mr. Stoke has proposed?"

Lowering my voice, I said, "That you have accepted him!"

The pain in her face tore at my heart. "But why?"

Why indeed? I took a deep breath and attempted to moderate my tone. "There are still so many unanswered questions. About the books. About the Stokes' connection to your father. The truth is you barely know him, and I don't trust him, Lizzy."

Eyes pleading, she replied, "I know you don't. But you have no real grounds for your distrust. While it's true we haven't answered all the questions we hoped to, we've found no reason to suspect Mr. Stoke is anything worse than obsessive about his hobbies." She held my gaze. "He has been very kind to me, Antony. And you must understand—it falls to me to make the best decision for both Mama and me. This will save Grimm Curiosities, and us along with it."

"But Lizzy, I—"

I stopped as her words sank in and the awful reality took hold. What could I possibly say? What had I the *right* to say? Lizzy was the head of her family, and her family was precariously situated. Even more so, thanks to my thoughtless behavior over the last week. What was a declaration of my feelings worth in comparison to an actual offer from an eligible suitor? I could hardly tell her that I loved her and hoped, in time, to persuade my father to accept her. How pathetic it would sound.

She watched me nervously, and though I felt sick, I said the only thing it was right for me to say, mustering as much genuine feeling as

I could. "I congratulate you, Lizzy. I hope Mr. Stoke knows how lucky he is."

Her eyes shone. I couldn't have said whether the sudden pooling of tears resulted from happiness or regret.

We moved as automatons through the remaining steps of the waltz. Occasionally our eyes met, and we shared a pained smile before Lizzy looked away. At one point, while trying to look anywhere but at her, I glimpsed her betrothed. He stood on the edge of the dance floor with my father, the two of them conversing comfortably over a glass of port while they watched us.

Ambrose Stoke had not been welcomed at Carlisle House since he had disappointed Sir Arthur—his father, and *my* father's dear friend—by refusing to take over the brewing business. My father, to whom loyalty and family legacies obviously mattered a great deal, lost all respect for Ambrose. I had assumed the baron agreed to invite him to the ball because he was Isabel's uncle, and I was expected to marry her. I had assumed *Lizzy* was allowed to attend, despite my father's anger over my friendship with her, because she'd been invited as the guest of Isabel and her uncle. While I might have been correct on both counts, neither of these theories explained how or why Stoke and my father had become so cozy.

When at last this infernal ball came to an end, the baron and I were going to have more words about Lizzy Grimm.

Farewell

I longed for an end to the agonizing and unfamiliar awkwardness between Antony and me, yet I knew this final dance was the closest I was likely to get to a private conversation with him. If Antony wasn't to wed Miss Stoke, which would cause us to be related by marriage, I might *never* have another conversation with him, private or otherwise.

Though I felt rather in shock over my sudden change in circumstances, I still believed I'd done the right thing—truly the only thing I *could* do. But that wasn't the same as feeling no regret. There had been a moment—I shouldn't even allow myself to think of it—when I'd thought Antony was about to tell me he *loved* me.

Miss Stoke is not in love, and neither am I. At least not with her.

I was deeply grateful for his restraint. Though my heart sang at the thought of it, such a declaration could do nothing but make us miserable. Antony might avoid marrying Miss Stoke, but he could never marry me.

Tasting salt and iron, I realized I had bitten into my bottom lip so hard I'd broken the skin. The waltz ended at that same moment, and as Antony was making his bow, he frowned and reached out to touch my lip with his thumb, leaving a bright stain on his white glove. I stood frozen, wondering how many people might have observed him. Then I saw him realize what he'd done.

"Congratulations, Lizzy," said Mr. Stoke, joining us, "at last you've made it through. I've taken the liberty of ordering the carriage round, if you're ready. I know you're unused to such hours, and I am certainly feeling my age."

"Yes, thank you," I said, not quite able to bring myself to use his Christian name yet. "I am indeed ready to retire."

I took his arm and glanced once more at Antony. Antony smiled, but I could see the suffering behind it, and it broke my heart. Was this truly the end of our association? I knew he would be thinking about Sophia, as well, and I wished I could reassure him. I was still determined to help her if I could.

"Good evening to the both of you," Antony said in a steady but quiet voice. "We were very happy to see you here."

I feared I would choke on the tears I held back. "It was such a lovely evening."

"It certainly was," said Mr. Stoke warmly, not seeming to notice our discomfort. "I'll always remember it."

Antony gave a subtle flinch, and he looked as if he would reply. I turned quickly, hoping to spare us both the pain of another regretful congratulations. My betrothed took the hint and led me out to the waiting carriage.

This time instead of Miss Stoke we had her cousin, Miss Broadmoor—the Cecile who had visited my shop and questioned me about Antony. She was full of chatter about the ball, and especially about Antony and the other gentlemen she'd danced with. Her discretion no more mature than her person, she let slip that Miss Stoke had remained behind so she and Antony might meet with her father and the baron. Miss Broadmoor could hardly contain her excitement over the engagement, and I was not about to be the one to break the news to her. In my heart, I wished Antony all the strength he was sure to need for this interview. I hoped he wouldn't be risking his inheritance simply by refusing to marry Miss Stoke. Yet I would hate to see him married to someone he didn't love.

I felt eyes on me and glanced away from the window—where I'd sought refuge from Miss Broadmoor's continuing commentary—to find Mr. Stoke looking at me, a soft smile on his lips.

People can learn to love each other, can't they?

At last the carriage drew up to the shop. Mr. Stoke stepped down first, handing me out and walking me to the door.

When I'd unlocked it and stepped inside, he said, "Allow me to express my gratitude to you again, Lizzy."

"And I to you, sir."

The shop's grandfather clock chimed three times.

"Tomorrow you will wish to rest, but may I come again on Monday, so we can discuss the date for our nuptials? My brother and niece may insist on making a fuss, but I'm for keeping things as simple as we may and not drawing it out much past the new year."

"I agree." After the scene with Mr. Strickland—and considering the state of our finances—I couldn't help thinking, *The sooner the better.* "You may come just as soon as you wish."

He took my hand, pressing it between his—reminding me of the night Antony had done the same thing. "You've made me very happy, Lizzy. Farewell until Monday."

"Farewell until Monday."

He raised my hand to his lips and kissed it. Then he stepped back across the snowy footway to the carriage.

I locked the door and started toward the stairs, my emotions like a great shifting mass of storm clouds. Before I got there, a sudden thump followed by a clatter stopped my heart and my footsteps. I knew without looking that it was the cabinet again, the clattering noise the cane sliding to the floor.

I held my breath as I moved toward it. The doors were still closed, and I reached for the pulls. Once again I felt the whoosh of wintry, spiced air, but still there was no snowy landscape. I had guessed that pressing the tree carving at the cabinet's back, which I'd done by accident that first day, was what opened the doorway. But I was no more suitably dressed now than I had been then.

I reached out and grasped the arm of the coat. "Papa?"

"Is it a ghost, miss?"

I jumped at the sudden voice. Sally stood behind me in her night-dress. I closed my eyes, letting out a breath.

"Forgive me for startling you, miss. Thought you would have heard the stairs creaking."

"It's all right, Sally, I think I'm half-asleep. I'm sorry I woke you." I turned and closed the cabinet, sliding the cane back through. "There is something or some*one* trying to get my attention, that seems certain."

"Are you frightened?"

"A little. I don't like not knowing what's causing it." I looked at her. "How about you?"

She frowned. "Doesn't seem to be me it wants."

I shivered. "I suppose not."

"How was the ball, miss?" she asked in a lighter tone.

"Stimulating. Exhausting. Momentous. I'll tell you all about it in the morning. Let's both try to get some sleep."

She nodded. "I'll help you undress."

"I'm sure I can manage, Sally. You go back to bed."

"Begging your pardon, miss, but I'm not sure you *can*. It won't take but a minute or two."

I was too tired to argue and, in truth, happy to be talked into accepting her help. Soon I was curled beneath the bedclothes. I had never been so eager for the oblivion of sleep.

Sally didn't wake me for church, saving me from the decision of whether I should force myself out of bed in time to go. She served me a late breakfast in my room, and I debated about whether to open the shop for a few hours—despite what I'd told Sir Clyde's beastly son. But I recalled that thanks to Mr. Stoke, Mama's and my continued survival need no longer be the primary reason for every decision I made.

After I'd accepted him, my betrothed had made it clear he had the resources to support both Mama and me, even without proceeds from the shop. Happily, he was entirely content for me to continue her care at home—a condition of my acceptance that I would have stuck to. I proposed we add *Stoke* to the shop name, and this seemed to please him. There was some talk of where we would all live after the wedding, and he indicated a preference for his own house near the Shambles, which was more spacious than our rooms above the shop. We'd agreed to continue that discussion at our next meeting.

Finding myself with no pressing responsibilities for the day, I lingered over my tea and toast in bed until my headache went away, just as I imagined all the fine ladies from last night's ball would be doing. When I finally did rise, I stepped to Mama's room. Sally had been sitting with her sometimes, and there was a second chair beside the tea table. I joined her there.

"Good morning, Mama. I have news this morning." I took a deep breath. "I'm going to be married."

Her head turned slightly from the window. Though she was looking more into the corner than at me, I took this as a sign she was listening.

"To a gentleman who's been very kind to me," I continued. "He escorted me to my first ball, and his niece even provided me with a beautiful gown. How you would have enjoyed it, Mama. I've never seen so much food in one place, and the ladies were like tropical birds in their colorful gowns!"

A trace of a smile sat upon her lips. Encouraged, I continued, "Sometime in the new year I will become Mrs. Ambrose Stoke. My betrothed has promised to take care of—"

A teacup suddenly flipped onto the floor; Mama had reached suddenly to grip the tabletop and caught the edge of the saucer. I jumped up, reaching for the tea towel, but her wide-eyed stare stopped me.

"What *is* it, Mama?" I cried. "If there is something you want me to know about him, you must tell me now."

But her face went slack again, and she turned back to the window.

My voice shook as I said, "Every day I get up and do the best I can for us, Mama. And every day I worry it won't be enough. Unless you have something to *say* against Mr. Stoke, you will simply have to trust me."

I bent and mopped up the small puddle before starting downstairs. Guilt flooded me. Mama had not chosen to be as she was now. But the weight of my responsibility to her and the shop had become all but unbearable over this past year. My betrothal was our salvation. But Mama's reaction—and Antony's—had soured the tremendous relief I felt.

In the kitchen, Sally helped me heat pots of water for washing, and sinking into the tub brought some relief to both my sore thoughts and sore limbs.

She was eager to hear about the ball and I obliged, grateful for the distraction. I learned she'd assisted Lady Carlisle with the planning of previous balls, and I found myself describing every dish, decoration, and dance. When finally I'd exhausted her questions, I told her about Mr. Stoke's proposal.

She responded with enthusiasm, congratulating me warmly and wishing me every happiness. *Finally.* It so lifted my spirits. I wondered whether I might persuade Mr. Stoke to hire Sally away from the Carlisles. Antony had made it clear they didn't really need her. I understood why she'd been a favorite of Lady Carlisle's. She was bright and wonderfully competent, and besides that I enjoyed her company.

"Did you have many dealings with the Stokes?" I asked as she poured another pot of hot water into the tub.

She shook her head. "Not many. I believe I mentioned Lady Carlisle did not care for Sir Arthur."

"Yes. Do you know why?"

She set down the pot and handed me a bar of soap. I dipped it in the water and washed my face. "She felt he was too hard on his sons, especially the eldest. She blamed Sir Arthur for the way he turned out."

"You mean my fiancé's brother? Isabel Stoke's father?"

She looked mortified. "Oh heavens! Forgive me, miss! I oughtn't to have said that. Your fiancé *is* the eldest son."

I sat up, the cooler air raising goose bumps on my wet skin. "May I ask what you mean by 'how he turned out'?"

"Only that it caused a great fuss when he refused to take over the family business, hiding himself away in that old place over near the Shambles. Lady Carlisle said it served Sir Arthur right."

I breathed a little easier. Based on this account, Sir Arthur didn't sound so different from Lord Carlisle. Apparently the baron hadn't bothered to take a lesson from his friend when it came to managing his son.

I recalled then what Mr. Stoke had told me about his father and the books.

Consigned to the flames, I'm afraid.

There came a tapping noise in the shop then—someone at the door. Sally looked up and started to go out.

"Wait, Sally," I said, rising from the tub and reaching for the sheet. "I don't want to see anyone. Unless it's Mr. Stoke."

"Yes, miss."

I hurriedly put on the clothes she'd laid out for me.

Low voices reached me, and I thought it must indeed be my fiancé. I checked myself in the glass Sally had brought in. I'd coiled my hair in a low knot before the bath; though mussed, it was at least dry. I wished I'd brought down one of my shop dresses instead of a faded day dress and moth-nibbled shawl, but there was nothing to be done about it now.

Sally bustled in and moved immediately behind me to fasten my buttons. "It's Mr. Carlisle, miss," she said quietly, "asking to see you." I froze, heart vaulting into my throat. "I've told him I'd check, but I believed you were indisposed. Shall I tell him you are?"

Our gazes met in the glass. Her expression was sympathetic, and I recalled that she'd overheard my "conversation" with Lord Carlisle.

"I think that's best, Sally."

She nodded and was going.

"Wait."

She turned.

"Tell him I'm coming."

"Yes, miss."

Heart drumming, I took one more look in the glass and then followed her out to the shop. Antony waited just inside the door, hat in hand.

"Thank you for seeing me," he said.

"I'll just go up and sit with Mrs. Grimm for a while?" said Sally, lifting her eyebrows as she looked at me.

"Yes, thank you."

I watched until she was out of sight and then turned to my visitor. "Mr. Carlisle, the shop is closed today. You shouldn't be here." Yet to have him here again as if nothing had changed and I could invite him up to the sitting room for tea—it wrung my heart and made me want the world to be different.

"I have something urgent to discuss with you," he said.

He was impeccably dressed as always, the brandy brocade waistcoat a complement to his burnt-sugar eyes. But there were hollows under those eyes, and he had a haggard look.

I knew I didn't have it in me to turn him away. "All right. But you must be brief."

To his credit, he didn't ask to be admitted into the shop, or upstairs to our home, but maintained his position just inside the door. "Last night after the ball I told my father that I did not intend to propose to Miss Stoke."

So he had gone through with it. "How was your news received?"

My foolish heart longed to hear that his father had gotten over his objections to me, and he had come here to stop me marrying Mr.

Stoke. But my head had a better grip on reality and was not surprised when Antony frowned and said, "About as well as you might imagine."

What I imagined was very unpleasant, and I was glad I hadn't been a witness. "I'm very sorry," I said earnestly. "But Mr. Carlisle—Antony—we cannot keep meeting here. If your father hears of it . . . if my fiancé hears of it—"

"Lizzy, you cannot marry Ambrose Stoke."

I steadied myself with a breath. "Nothing has changed since last night. I mean to go through with it. I don't know what else you would say to me, but I assure you, there is—" I swallowed. "There is nothing you *can* say that will alter my decision."

His eyes were soft and shining. "Not even that I am in love with you?"

My heart leaped. Danced. Sang. Then plunged. "Please don't do this, Antony," I begged.

"I shouldn't tell you how I feel?"

His voice had gone to velvet, and butterfly wings beat about inside my chest. I shook my head vigorously. "Not now. Not ever. It can only cause us both to suffer."

"I don't see it that way, Lizzy."

I stared at him in bewilderment. How could he so calmly state such ridiculous things? "You and I cannot marry. Your father would disinherit you—I know this for a fact because he *told* me so—and I could never allow that to happen. Your being here jeopardizes everything for me, can you not see that? If you truly love me, you will stay away from me." How it wrenched me inside to speak to him like this. But he'd left me no choice.

"I assure you that my love for you is the sole reason I have come. I learned something last night about your betrothed, and you have a right to hear it before you marry him."

I felt a twinge of anxiety—yet also I was growing angry. I began to wonder whether, because Antony could not be happy, he was bent on destroying *my* potential happiness. And that was not how love behaved.

"Go on," I said coolly.

"My father and I had more heated words after the Stokes left. I was very angry, and I stormed out of the house. I walked several times to the castle tower and back, waiting for my head to clear. Finally, I decided I'd try my father again at breakfast, when we'd both rested and recovered from the ball. I entered the house as quietly as I could, not wanting to rouse any of the servants, who'd finally gone to their beds. But as I was going to my own rooms, I heard my father and his valet talking in his bedchamber, and I stopped to listen."

"It was wrong of you, Antony," I said unhappily.

"Of course it was," he said, "but please hear me out, Lizzy. They were discussing you and Stoke. Earlier, while we were dancing, I had observed Stoke and my father watching us and pleasantly conversing. I had wondered about it because they had not been on friendly terms for some time."

"Sally told me as much," I admitted. "It does seem strange. Though perhaps the reconciliation was due to the anticipated union between your families."

"A reasonable assumption, though unfortunately not the correct one. I learned that my father allowed Stoke to attend the ball—and to bring you, despite his displeasure with you—as both reward and scheme."

My stomach moved uneasily. "What do you mean?"

"Reward, because Stoke is the one who informed my father that we had become friends. He was watching us."

"*Watching* us?"

"He knew about my visits to your home, and about our walks together. He told my father all of it."

That Mr. Stoke had involved himself so deeply in my business, as well as Antony's, indeed came as a surprise, and not a pleasant one. Yet as I turned it over in my mind. . .

"He may have meant well, Antony. He might have known about the expected engagement between you and Miss Stoke." After all, it had been Mr. Stoke who told me Antony and his niece were planning the ball together. "He may have been trying to save us both grief."

"Yes, but Lizzy," replied Antony, "think how dishonest he's been! To *watch* us? And why wouldn't he speak to you or me directly if he was truly concerned for our welfare?"

Though this revelation didn't exactly sit well, I couldn't help feeling Antony's judgment had been clouded by his prejudice against Mr. Stoke. "As for dishonesty," I said, "you concealed our friendship from your father. I don't judge you for it; it's only to say people withhold information when it suits them to do so. Even I kept secret the fact that I had the books Mr. Stoke wanted."

"You *should* judge me for it," he said bitterly. "I judge myself."

"He may not have been watching us," I went on. "He might have easily observed us in his regular course of business. Indeed, he came to the shop several times about the books."

His expression darkened. "I'll admit it's not impossible. But that's not all. Mr. Stoke and my father agreed that Stoke would bring you to the ball and propose to you. They both gained something from it. Stoke, a wife *and* the return of my father's favor, and my father can rest easy knowing that you are out of his way. And Lizzy, perhaps Stoke is fond of you—how could he not be?—but he's a collector, like your father. Perhaps he also wants the shop. *Perhaps* he's found a sure way of getting his hands on those books he wants so badly."

The damned books! Surely not.

I recalled how he'd joked after his proposal. *Say yes. Then we need no longer grapple over the Ginnel books.*

And last night he'd taken an interest in my Sight, too. I thought about how Papa had collected Mama.

I took a step and sank into the chair beside the door, wishing the interview over so my heart could break in private.

Antony dropped down before me. He took hold of my hand, and my spirits were too depressed to stop him.

"Don't marry him, Lizzy. Marry me."

"Antony," I replied, trembling, "you know I cannot."

He squeezed my fingers, his eyes imploring. "I will happily give up everything for you. Title, money, land—I don't need any of it. Let *me* be the one you lean on. I want nothing else."

The tears pooling in my eyes spilled onto my cheeks. *Let me be the one you lean on.*

I recalled the day I realized I was ready to consider marriage. I had lied to myself that day. Yes, it would make my life easier, and more secure. But that wasn't the real reason I wanted it. The real reason was that I was falling in love with Antony. I wanted to share my burdens not with *someone*, but with him. And I wanted to ease *his* burdens.

He leaned toward me. I shivered as he raised his fingers and brushed them across my wet cheek. He leaned closer still, and my heart pounded. I should have gotten up and sent him away. But it was all I could do to keep *breathing*.

"Antony . . ." It came out the weakest protest imaginable, and not surprisingly he took it for encouragement.

"Lizzy," he replied, moving closer.

One heartbeat after I noticed the fullness of his lips, I found myself noticing their softness and warmth. Twice they brushed gently against mine, and flames leaped inside me. The heat triggered a bone-deep longing that had a will of its own. I leaned into him, hands moving to grip his shoulders. His hand slipped along my jaw until his fingers curled around to the back of my neck, pulling me deeper into his kiss. His mouth moved like silk over mine, and a small sound escaped my throat. His lips parted, his tongue caressing my bottom lip.

Setting my hands against his chest, I pushed him away—though it ripped something out of me to do it.

Breathless, I said, "*No*, Antony."

"Lizzy—"

"If you don't value your inheritance, I must value it for you. And what of your family? Only think what might happen to your sister without you there to look out for her interests."

"I assure you I *am* thinking of my sister! And of your mother. We are their best hope. Look how much progress we've already made toward finding an answer. How can we stop now when it feels so close?"

"Do you honestly think I want that? But Antony, we *cannot* help your sister if your father won't let us near her. That is exactly what would happen were we to marry." I took a breath, attempting to cool the fire in my head and voice. "I intend to continue what we've begun. Be assured I will not rest until I have an answer, and I will not abandon Sophia any more than I would abandon Mama. But your father and my engagement have made it impossible for us to continue *together.*"

He sank back on his heels, crestfallen, shoulders slumping. "I don't accept these arguments, Lizzy, but I can see it will be of no use for me to continue. Refuse me if you feel you must. Only promise me you will not marry Stoke."

I looked steadily into his eyes, though it seared my insides. "I cannot promise you, nor do I owe you any such promise."

He stared, incredulous. "After all I've told you?"

I wasn't unaffected by Antony's revelations. While my betrothed didn't appear to have directly lied to me, and I saw no evidence of truly despicable motives, there had certainly been scheming. But to Antony, I simply said, "Mr. Stoke may not be as gallant as I might like, but to my thinking he has done nothing so very wrong. There are few in York who would understand or approve of my friendship with you, and there are some who would use the information to ruin me."

"*Strickland,*" Antony seethed. "If he ever comes near you again—"

"You will do nothing, even should ten Stricklands present themselves, because it will only make things worse. And as for this marriage scheme that has so offended you, it is really no different than the one your father dreamed up to push you and Miss Stoke together."

He gave a huff of disgust. "That scheme, too, was odious."

"Literally no one but you would fault him for it because it is the way things are. Now you must go, Antony. Mr. Stoke may appear. Your father may be watching us. The longer you linger, the greater the risk, especially for me."

Belatedly I glanced at the nearest of the windows. It was not much past midday, and with the shop closed, only one lamp had been lit. We would likely go unnoticed so long as no one stood directly in front of the window.

I rose from the chair, gazing down at him. "I know that with the life you've lived it is difficult for you to understand, but I *need* this marriage to keep Mama and me safe. We are ever on the edge of losing all we have."

Antony slowly stood up, eyes brushing my face. His expression was somber but his tone genuine as he said, "I'm sorry to have disturbed you."

Then he left the shop.

I sank again into the chair, letting my head fall into my hands, choking over the ache in my throat.

You will not cry about this, Lizzy. It cannot in any way help.

I gripped the chair arms, forcing a fragile composure as I breathed slowly in and out. My mind rebelled, trying to revisit the wonder and joy of feeling his lips against mine, but I mercilessly shoved that memory away, much as I had Antony.

Next my betrothed came into my mind. I had held my ground with Antony and his accusations, but what Antony didn't know was that Mama had again reacted to my mentioning Mr. Stoke. With that on the scale, I was no longer so sure of things as I'd been last night.

I pressed my fingers to my temples. My thoughts were sadly, madly jumbled, and I had no hope of sorting them.

Fresh air, Lizzy.

"Sally," I called in a reedy voice.

I heard her walk to the top of the stairs. "Yes, miss?"

"Could you help Mama put on her warm things? She should have a walk today."

"Yes, miss."

I took my cape from the stand near the door. Then I remembered I'd left my bonnet in the sitting room for mending and started up to get it. But I stopped halfway, noticing something on the stairs. A *book*, with a small toy resting on top.

My hands trembled and a chill chased down my spine as I knelt and set the lamp on the step. The Krampus book, which, last I'd seen it, had been upstairs on my bedside table. The toy was a cylinder of brass with a lithographic illustration of a leaping stag on the top panel, along with a serpentine handle. A music box, possibly from the storeroom. I wound the handle several times, and the toy let out a series of tinny notes.

Studying the stag illustration more closely, I saw that an arrow had pierced its side and blood dripped from the wound into a puddle on the ground beneath it. What kind of person gave a child a toy like *this*?

Then I realized—no kind of person. It was a toy you might find in the cave of the Krampus.

I sat down on the step, letting my head rest against the wall.

The Krampus on the stairs twice now. The cabinet that was a doorway that kept demanding my attention. The grisly toy. At last I understood what I must do.

"Unless He Has Something to Hide"

Antony

Lizzy's logic was faultless, and there had been no point in continuing to argue with her. In truth, from the moment I'd felt her lips against mine, her words no longer mattered, because I had resolved to do whatever was necessary to prevent her from marrying Stoke. If she loved him, things would be different. But after that kiss I was certain she loved *me*. A smile came to my lips as I recalled my fingers threading into the silky strands of her hair, and the damp warmth of the skin at the nape of her neck, like she was just out of the bath.

Though Lizzy might explain Stoke's behavior away because it was a marriage that she both needed and could have, I wouldn't do the same. For I believed with all my heart that he was up to something. I had begun to distrust him the first day I'd seen him in her shop.

Even then I was falling in love with her.

No matter what Lizzy might tell herself, Stoke's dealings had been ungentlemanly and underhanded at best. Which made me believe him capable of even worse.

He and these damned books are culpable somehow in what's happened to Sophia and Mrs. Grimm, I'm certain of it.

Evidence was what I needed, and I was determined to find some.

My family's journey to Gilling Hall in three days had me feeling rather desperate. But when I reached Carlisle House, I discovered an opportunity had presented itself. I asked a footman whether my father was at home, and he replied that Lord Carlisle and Mr. Stoke had left the house together. He believed they'd gone to our club. The idea of them toasting their success at the expense of Lizzy and me made my blood boil—which will perhaps offer some excuse for what I did next.

I set out immediately for Parliament Street, then changed my mind and veered into the Shambles, with its close and crooked streets, where I was more likely to pass unnoticed. On Sunday afternoon the meat market would normally be closed, but the upcoming feast day appeared to have altered the usual business hours. I avoided the crowd—and the steaming, sickly-sweet butcher-shop gore that ran down that neighborhood's gutters—and turned quickly onto St. Sampson's Square.

Like Lizzy's shop, Stoke's house was a very old half-timbered building. I'd overheard a gentleman at our club say there was some kind of ancient ruin in the cellar, but Stoke was so private no one had ever seen it.

I walked directly to the front door and knocked. One of the times my father ridiculed Stoke to my mother, he had told her the man didn't even keep a maid. I had no idea whether this was true, but if not, I would have to leave my card like a regular caller and try to come up with some other way to get what I needed. If it *was* true . . . well, what I had planned was both very wrong and very risky.

No one answered, so I knocked again. When there was still no response, I shot my hand out quickly and tried the door. *Locked.* Unsurprising, but at least I'd determined no one was at home.

Circling around the house, I entered a short ginnel that ran behind. Then I strode through a back gate and crossed a courtyard, passing a thick old apple tree whose snow-dusted roots had disrupted many of the flagstones. Beyond that was the back entrance to the house. I went to the door and tried it.

Blast.

I glanced back through the courtyard and into the ginnel. Seeing no one there, I raised a gloved fist and quickly punched through one of the panes of the window next to the door. Heart racing, I carefully picked out the remaining shards and dropped them into the snow that had accumulated against the outer wall. Reaching my arm through, I patted the inside wall until my fingers found the latch.

Too late to turn back now.

I opened the door and slipped inside.

As I composed myself and got my bearings, I considered the potential consequences if I were discovered. I had a vague notion that I could make myself out to be lovesick and jealous (which I most certainly was), apologize profusely for the lapse in judgment, and compensate Stoke for the damage. If the constable became involved . . . Well, as the son of a peer, I could likely expect leniency—a privilege I would most happily take advantage of.

Finally, I moved away from the door and began my search—for what, I did not know. Some evidence that Stoke was up to something he shouldn't be.

I found myself in the kitchen, so neat and clean I thought it must be rarely used. As a bachelor with no servants, Stoke probably enjoyed his meals away from home—at our club, or with his brother's family. Passing through a door on the opposite wall, I reached the dining room. There was no window in this room, and I returned to the kitchen for a lamp and box of matches that had rested on a table next to the back door.

The dining room, too, appeared rather forlorn, though there was a stack of books and a teacup at one end of the table. I went to inspect a curiosity cabinet that loomed against one wall. Inside were animal bones, including a couple of complete skeletons; a collection of shells in all sizes, shapes, and colors; and stuffed birds, their black bead eyes eerily staring, the most striking of them a very lifelike raven.

From the dining room, I stepped into a short corridor lined with portraits, and passing through the first door on my left, I discovered a library. This room was obviously in regular use. I could still feel the heat coming off the fireplace, and the candles were partially burned down. In addition to the shelved books, there were stacks of them all over the room. Many looked quite old.

Another curiosity cabinet, this one fitting neatly into a corner, contained more items like those in the dining room. There was also a collection of primitive-looking statuary—from what cultures I had no idea—and one of dolls crudely constructed of scraps of fabric, ribbons, yarn, and possibly hair. The cabinet's centerpiece was a human skull, and no ordinary one. A square panel affixed to one side, above the ear, appeared to repair a hole.

I supposed I could see the interest in this stuff, but in this gloomy, silent house, much of it gave me a shiver. And I had yet to find anything useful, though I suspected some of these items properly belonged in a museum. When I tried to imagine Lizzy here, mistress of this cold place with its shadows and oddities, a stab of panic urged me onward.

I left the library and walked to the end of the corridor, where I found the entryway, a staircase to the upper floors, and a drawing room with the same air of neglect as the kitchen and dining room. I climbed the stairs, boards creaking under my weight. At the first landing, I found a bedroom on one side and a study on the other. The stairs continued up to two additional bedrooms, sparsely furnished and apparently disused.

Returning to the bedroom across from the study, I found the hearth warm. Stoke's bedroom, as I'd guessed.

The opportunity to nose into this man's most personal space had appeared like a gift, and I'd snatched at it out of fear that no better opportunity would come. At least not in time to save Lizzy from a lifetime tied to a man I didn't trust and she didn't love. But the heat of that moment had cooled now. Still having no idea what I was looking for, I began to fear the risk had been for nothing.

No time to lose heart, Carlisle.

Raising the lamp, I quickly surveyed the room. Heavy-looking, fanciful antiques surrounded me, including an ornately carved and ostentatious wood-canopy bed. It reminded me of the haunted cabinet at Grimm's. I froze as I recalled something Lizzy had said earlier.

I intend to continue what we've begun. Be assured I will not rest until I have an answer.

She would go on, and at some point, if she thought she might learn anything from it, she was going to get back into that cabinet—probably by herself. Sally's presence would make it even easier, as there would be someone to keep an eye on Mrs. Grimm. I'd already been ordered by my father to retrieve Sally, and though I'd planned to stall, maybe it was for the best.

Tick-tock, man.

I nudged myself forward, taking a closer look at the smaller items in the room. Stoke was the sort of person who kept a neatly cluttered house. Clean and dust-free, yet there were reading materials, candles, bric-a-brac, tobacco pipes, and magnifying glasses on every surface. I couldn't understand how he managed it without servants. He hardly struck me as a man who did his own cleaning.

Unless he has something to hide.

I started opening drawers. Handkerchiefs, underclothing, cravats, linens . . . Sighing in frustration, I took a last slow spin. Then I turned to go, thinking I'd try to find the door to the cellar before taking my leave of the place.

Out in the corridor, I cast one backward glance and noticed something I hadn't before. A box end was just visible beneath the foot of the bed. I went back in and crouched beside it. Setting the lamp on the floor, I slid the box out and lifted the lid.

My breath caught.

Dear Mr. Stoke, what have we here?

The box was full of Mr. Grimm's books.

One by one, I drew them out, counting. Twelve books, including one duplicate. There were two copies of *Glamour*—one of which Lizzy had sold him. If memory served, he'd told Lizzy he'd somehow lost his own books. There wasn't a full set here, so perhaps some of them had in fact been lost. But he'd bought one he already owned, and he'd told Lizzy he was particularly interested in *Doorways* and *Ghosts & Spirits*, which were also right here in the box. Why?

Lizzy had thought it mere coincidence that Stoke bought *Glamour*—the one book that seemed to hold an answer about Sophia and Mrs. Grimm. The fact he already possessed a copy seemed to change things. Might he have bought it *to prevent Lizzy from reading it*? If so, wasn't it likely he wanted her copies of *Doorways* and *Ghosts & Spirits* for the same reason?

My hands began to shake.

It really was about the books. Stoke had asked Lizzy to marry him because he'd figured out she was holding on to them, and they exposed him in some way. Might *he* have glamoured Sophia and Mrs. Grimm? If so, and should Lizzy discover it *after* they were married . . . Well, at that point her fate was in his hands. She might tell whomever she liked, and he could tell them she read too many novels or drank too much sherry or even that she'd suffered a nervous collapse.

I tucked both copies of *Glamour* under one arm and slid the box back under the bed. I was prepared to flee the house, evidence in hand, when I remembered the cellar. I believed I had what I needed to stop Lizzy's marriage, but I still didn't really understand what Stoke was up to. If there were any more secrets to be unearthed in this house, the cellar seemed like a good bet. Was it worth the risk?

You won't get another chance.

I went back down to the kitchen, where a cellar door seemed most likely, providing easy access to vegetable storage for a cook or wine and spirits for a butler.

Indeed, I did find a small door tucked at one end of the kitchen. A table rested in front of it, suggesting it wasn't often used. Still, I set the books and lamp on the table and scooted it back. Then I tried the door. Locked, but on impulse I lifted a teacup that had been overturned on the table. A key rested beneath it, and I fitted it into the hole.

The door swung inward with a creak, and I picked up the lamp and ducked through. On the other side was a cramped and crooked staircase. I paused there, again thinking about the risk. It was true I'd not get this opportunity again. With the broken window, Stoke would know immediately that someone had been here, and he'd be more vigilant.

Sighing, I raised the lamp and started down.

The room below was no more dusty or cobweb-filled than any other part of the house. The walls had been plastered and the floor bricked, though it still smelled like a cellar. Wall sconces had been hung and a few plain furnishings brought down. A wine rack ran from floor to ceiling on the wall next to the stairs, and beneath the stairs was a pantry.

The lamplight didn't reach the opposite end of the room, and I made my way there.

Eventually the brick floor gave way to bare ground. This end was divided into two sections. On one side the ground was uneven, like someone had dug it up and tamped it back down. Sticks with lines strung between them marked the perimeter of this section.

Opposite the dug-up area stood something that I had at first taken for a partition screen. Drawing closer, I began to think it might be the rumored ruin—a remnant of wall that appeared, at least to my untrained eyes, even older than the house. The wall contained an arched doorway, and a large fresco flowed over and around it. Despite its age, the artwork was sharp and distinct and had retained its bright coloring. The style reminded me very much of an illuminated manuscript I'd taken Sophia to see at the British Museum.

Moving closer still, I noticed something else familiar about the artwork. Instead of a biblical subject, as was typical in much of the art that had survived from other eras, this illustration depicted a great, frenzied host. There were warriors on horseback and strange woodland spirits astride stags. Women with flowing hair and garments hovered in the air above the party. At the head of the host was a bearded man with a raven on each shoulder. He rode a horse with eight legs.

Woden. An old Germanic deity. Two weeks ago, I would not have known what I was looking at. I had since then been educated by Mr. Grimm's books. This was the Wild Hunt.

Turning from the ruin, I found other objects nearby. A brazier rested on the floor. A console table had been placed against the cellar's back wall, and some ancient-looking metalwork trinkets were arranged on top. My gaze came to rest on an item I recognized, one that Stoke had been carrying the night we went for a drink—a rod about the length of a riding crop with a metal stag figure affixed to a ring on one end. It looked rather like a scepter, but I'd supposed he carried it for self-defense. Next to it a very old manuscript lay open. One page was covered in script that I couldn't read, but the opposite page contained an *illustration* of the scepter, which showed a flame burning inside its iron ring.

On the ground next to the table sat a large, potbellied clay container with a lid. Atop the lid, in fact molded from the same clay, perched a stag figure very like the one at the tip of the scepter.

I crouched next to the vessel, placing my hand on its rounded belly. I felt a buzzing sensation and yanked my hand away. *What the devil?*

After a breath or two, I regained my courage and touched the vessel again—the same vibration, along with some light tapping.

Dare I open it?

Tentatively, I took hold of the stag and tried shifting the lid, but it didn't budge. A second—stronger—attempt produced the same result.

Rising to my feet, I spent a few moments trying to memorize each detail of the strange tableau. I was sure these items all related to each other in some way. Had Lizzy been with me, she might even have been able to guess at their importance.

Had Lizzy been with me, I wouldn't be worrying about what she might be getting up to in my absence.

Time to go.

I crossed the cellar and climbed the stairs. I repositioned the table in front of the door, replaced the key, extinguished the lamp, and secured the books under my arm.

I moved to the back door, and my hand was on the doorknob when I thought to check the window. Two women were talking in the ginnel, just beyond the gate. If I left now, they would see me.

Then I heard the front door open.

My heart heaved. *What now, Carlisle?*

Little used as the kitchen appeared to be, I thought I might be able to wait here until Stoke went upstairs.

Suddenly a large bowl slid across the kitchen worktable and crashed to the floor. My gaze jerked from one end of the room to the other—no one was there.

But someone was *coming*. Quick steps sounded in the dining room, and I yanked open the back door and raced across the courtyard. The women had finally walked on, in the direction of Bootham Bar, and I ran the other way, back toward the Shambles.

Instead of passing through the market and then south again, I headed north on Church Street, toward Goodramgate.

Lizzy must hear me this time.

Footsteps

When we returned from our walk, I asked Sally to take Mama upstairs and give her tea. I went to the shop counter, where I'd left *The Krampus* and the strange toy. I turned the handle again and listened to the chilling, plinking melody.

Ever since I'd begun to associate Papa with these tricks, I had wondered what was important about Krampus. Now I believed I understood. Papa had been to Krampus's lair. He had used Opa's cabinet to get there, and he meant for me to go there, too. I couldn't guess his reason, but I hoped it might somehow be connected with Mama's affliction.

How I wished I could discuss it with Antony! He would think of things I hadn't, and he would insist on going with me. Instead, I would have to go alone, and immediately. Once Sally was gone, it would no longer be an option, and she might any day be fetched back to Carlisle House.

It was perhaps telling that I had no real urge to consult my betrothed about my plan, and in fact my instincts urged me to conduct the business before I saw him again. In part this was due to my rising doubts about him, but also, marriage was a tricky undertaking. As Mrs. Stoke, I would no longer be shunned by Papa's former associates. But Mrs. Stoke would enjoy far less independence than Miss Grimm. With a pang, it occurred to me the same wouldn't likely be true for a future Mrs. Antony Carlisle.

As Mr. Stoke was still my betrothed, he was the one I should have written the note to. Instead I wrote to Antony, explaining where I had gone and why—a much shorter explanation than would have been required in a note to Mr. Stoke or anyone else. I asked him to see that Mama was looked after until I could return. I told him that if Sally must go before then, he could speak to Charlie Croft. I felt sure she would help if she could, and she likely wouldn't balk at the strangeness of it. I told him where to find what money I had, in case it was needed.

After tea, when Sally had settled with her sewing in Mama's room, I put the note into her hands.

"I must go out, Sally. If I haven't returned in a few hours, I want you to get this note to Mr. Carlisle. Will you be able to do that?"

She looked worried, but she took the note. "Yes, miss. Is everything all right?"

I reached out and squeezed her hand. "Yes, only there's something I must look into, and it's complicated to explain. Until I'm back, just do whatever needs doing. You take better care of us than I ever could."

"I hope you'll be careful, miss."

"I will, Sally, thank you."

I went down to the shop and approached the cabinet warily. I had set myself this task and believed it was necessary, but that didn't mean I wasn't frightened. Grasping the cane and sliding it free from the pulls, I replaced it in the stand.

"You must help me, Papa," I said quietly.

Opening the doors, I took the boots out and slipped my feet into them. I wore two layers of stockings, but the boots were still quite loose, so I stuffed some wadded-up rags inside. Then I plopped the flatcap on my head and removed the greatcoat from its hook. It, too, swallowed me, but it was lined and fur-trimmed and should keep me quite warm.

Taking a deep breath, I took hold of the cabinet's sides and stepped up into it. Then I laid my palm against the Christmas tree carving and pressed.

The sudden sensation of my feet sinking into the snow gave me a moment of panic, as did the frigid air against my face. But I was far better prepared this time, and the feeling quickly faded.

Looking around, it seemed no time had passed in this place. The same leaden sky kissed by dark evergreen tips. Same high and jagged mountains in the distance, reminding me of the Tyrolean Alps in Opa's stories. I also noted the same trail of bright, blood-drip holly berries leading away toward the woods.

The stillness was itself otherworldly. Not a twig stirred. Not a bird called. Not a breeze blew. Like I'd stepped into a painting.

Did time exist here? *Doorways* in fact talked about "otherworlds," which didn't appear on any map and couldn't be reached by traditional means. Fairies lived in such places, and elfin folk, too. Otherworlds often followed rules of their own, or none at all.

I thought about Papa's visits to this world. If there was no change here, shouldn't there be tracks? Or perhaps visitors didn't leave tracks. I took a couple of steps and saw that my own feet left them. My gaze fell again on the berry trail. Could Papa have left *that*?

I had a guilty suspicion that answers to all my questions might very well be found in Papa's books, if only my thoughts had been less pre-occupied with Antony and I'd taken the time to read more thoroughly. I did vaguely recall a discussion in *Doorways* about breadcrumbs and finding your way home.

That thought prompted me to look back. The cabinet had vanished! My heart lurched, but I discovered if I squinted just right, I could see the faintest outline. I took off Papa's cap and dropped it in the snow right in front of it.

Then, lifting my skirts, I did the obvious thing: followed the berry trail. My feet sank in the snow with every step, which along with the oversize boots made for slow going. Despite the cold, I was soon per-spiring, my breath coming out in great huffs of vapor.

The trail ended at the forest—uniform, giant conifers growing so close together that little light got through. A narrow path of dark, firmly packed soil ribboned among them. Both the trees and the path were clear of snow.

Sometimes, on a summer Sunday, Papa would take Mama and me to the country for a picnic. I would explore the fields and hedgerows, and even occasionally a shady, green wood alongside a burbling beck. This forest was vast and dark and far beyond anything of my experience. It made me feel tiny, and my instincts urged me to march right back where I came from.

If Papa did this and lived to write a book about it, so can I.

Stepping into the wood, I flinched at a disturbance just overhead. A great owl winged away from me, letting out a single warning trill. At first I felt relief to finally encounter another living thing. But the deeper I moved into the forest, the less light penetrated, and the more sounds I heard. Rustling and scurrying and tiny footfalls, an occasional tweet or chirp or screech.

I walked through a spider's web, sticky threads tickling my cheeks, and stopped to shake and stamp in hopes of dislodging any unwelcome passenger.

Hearing something that sounded very much like quiet, breathy laughter, I froze. The sound ceased, and I wasn't sure I hadn't imagined it.

My eyes darted from shadow to shadow as I went on. I felt as if creatures were watching me. Something broke suddenly from a clump of fern just ahead of me, and I dropped to a crouch. A stag leaped straight over the path and disappeared on the other side.

I remained crouched, letting my heart slow while I considered my position. How deep into this forest would I have to go? Why hadn't I thought to pack any food or water? What if I became trapped here? I began to think I'd been a great fool. Papa had been gone for three years now, and ever since then I'd been trying to fill his shoes. Hold on to the shop. Put food on the table. Take care of Mama. I'd kept doing it all in a world that didn't want me to, until finally I gave up and betrothed myself to a man who was in many ways *like* him.

And here I was *literally* filling his shoes and walking in his footsteps. I chuckled and let my head fall back against a tree. I watched the vapor of my breath rise and dissipate.

When finally I rose to my feet, I almost turned back. But the smell of a wood fire—and, impossibly, gingerbread—drifted from somewhere.

In every story Opa told, every character who reached a point like this soon suffered some horrific misfortune.

But they often came out all right in the end.

So I continued. I imagined telling Antony about this later, and I knew just what he'd say: *Of course you did.*

Then I remembered I wouldn't likely be telling Antony about any more of my adventures, and my heart gave a sorrowful throb.

Soon enough the path opened out into a small glade, where a lodge with a peaked roof nestled in the forest's perpetual gloom. Smoke curled from the stone chimney, and candles burned in the windows. Firewood had been neatly stacked under a shelter to one side of the lodge, and in front of it, the tool that had done the work was embedded in an immense stump. The warm, spiced aroma of gingerbread made my stomach growl.

Caution was the obvious course. Yet somehow it came into my head that my father was waiting for me inside, and I *ran.*

"Papa!" I cried, big boots thudding softly against fallen fir needles.

I yanked open the door, eyes searching the lodge's cozy interior. Plush-seated chairs with high, ornately carved wooden backs rested in front of a blazing fire. Next to the fire were a stack of wood and a large basket of fir cones. A teakettle hung over the flames, spouting steam into the room.

"Hello?" I called, stepping inside.

In a corner near the hearth was a small library—a bookcase that nearly brushed the ceiling, with a chair and tea table beside it. Opposite the fire was a dining table with two chairs. A plate of gingerbread men, a bowl of sugarplums, and a handful of candy canes rested at its center—the best evidence yet that Papa was here somewhere! In front of one chair sat a burning candle and a thick sheaf of papers.

A great rug—rose, green, and gold with a woodland scene at its center—muffled my footsteps as I walked toward the dining table. I slipped out of Papa's coat and hung it over a chair back, still scanning the room for signs another person was here. Then I bent and lifted the top sheet from the sheaf of papers.

If you're reading this, my darling girl, I have left you.

Gasping, I sank into the chair. I set down the sheet, staring at it blankly while I composed myself. I'd found Papa after all. Just not in the way I had expected.

I picked the sheet up again with trembling fingers.

There are things that you should know. Things I couldn't bring myself to tell you or your mother while I was alive. I'm so very sorry.

I paused. How could Papa have known I would find this? He couldn't have known his spirit would return to point the way. Had he intended to give the letter to me, perhaps to read upon his death? None of us had expected it to come so soon.

Which could explain why he came *back*. Mama often spoke of spirits having messages for the living.

I suppose the easiest place to start is, as ever, at the beginning. My story begins the same way as many a fairy tale. When I was a young man, I fell in love with a beautiful girl. She had auburn curls, gray eyes, and laughter that sounded like chimes in the wind. She also had a gift; she drew the most wonderful pictures. She was adventurous and bold, yet also the kindest person I'd ever known. I must now tell you, she was not your mother, for your mother came into my life much later. Her name was Mary Broadmoor.

I paused as the last line sank in. Broadmoor—the name meant something to me . . . Miss Stoke's cousin, who had loaned me the ball gown, was Cecile Broadmoor. Had I at last discovered a connection between Mr. Stoke's family and mine?

I met Mary on a sunny spring morning on the grounds outside the Yorkshire Museum, where she was visiting the ruin of St. Mary's Abbey with her younger brother and his governess. There was no one to provide an introduction, but both her brother and the governess were preoccupied with his climbing over a pile of bricks while Mary sketched the abbey, and we took the opportunity to introduce ourselves.

Thanks to the lad shouting for her attention at one point, I discovered that her Christian name was the same as the abbey. So I pretended to believe the ruin belonged to her, and we amused ourselves in this fashion for a quarter of an hour. As the governess and the boy were returning, Mary handed me a sketch and hurried to join them. She had sketched my face as we talked.

By the time of our first meeting, I had begun to travel through doorways. Will you recall the book about doorways that we read together when you were a child? The first shocking thing I must tell you is that all of the doorways in that book are quite real, and I have been through them. More about that presently.

All of them! No wonder Papa had seemed to half live in another world. He actually *had*, at least at one time in his life.

Mary and I contrived future meetings, in which I spun her tales of my adventures, and she encouraged me to write them down. I had learned things, she said, that ought to be documented. And they would delight the people who read them. I told her I couldn't possibly undertake such a task unless she would agree to be my illustrator. So we began the work together. You will wonder did she travel with me, and a few times she did.

So the books had been this Mary Broadmoor's idea! And not only had she helped him, she had joined him for some of his research. I recalled Papa's margin note on the illustration for his Krampus book: *Astonishingly accurate, M!* The collaboration Papa described reminded me of the investigation Antony and I had undertaken together.

The letter continued on the next page, and I read on, eager to know what had become of Mary.

At any rate, over the course of more than a year of furtive, feverish collaboration, the books were drafted, and the illustrations were made. And in the end, so was a proposal of marriage. But before I could compile our work or speak to our fathers, the two of us were suddenly and forever divided. Mary was the daughter of a successful carriage builder, and she was to have a substantial inheritance. Her father intended to increase his family's status by marrying her to the son of another wealthy businessman. Mary learned of this the same day she opened her heart to her father about me. Mary was promised to Arthur Stoke, of Stoke Brewing.

Papa had fallen in love with the woman who became my betrothed's *mother!* The mysterious connection was explained, and not in a way I could ever have imagined.

I was shattered, and I confess that in a rather boyish fit of passion, I asked Mary to accompany me to Gretna Green. She tearfully refused, unwilling to betray her family—perhaps even be severed from them.

That Papa would propose an elopement, however, did not in the least surprise me.

Something struck me then—might Arthur Stoke have known about Mary and Papa? It would explain why his good friend Lord Carlisle had said what he did about "Grimms." And if he knew about the books, too? Their destruction was easier to understand.

The marriage was accomplished with startling speed. I believe her father suspected I might indeed make off with her, but I later discovered it wasn't the only reason.

After the wedding, I hid the manuscripts away and lost myself in my travels. (You may read more about those, if you like, in the memoir included with this letter.)

When a few years later I'd somewhat recovered, I determined to complete and publish our little books in hopes of bringing a kind of closure to that painful period of my life. I had only two sets printed, one for me and one for Mary. (If you have not already deduced this, dear girl, the books are those by "A. A." that I read with you as a child. You'll find them in a box under a table in the storeroom.) At the time, I believed I would eventually publish the books more widely, but I later found that I couldn't bear the idea of strangers reading them.

I sent a set of the books to Mary without explanation, but I never heard from her again. I don't know what else I should have expected. In hindsight, it was rather selfish of me.

I was heartened to see this introspection. Papa had figuratively and literally lived in his own world, and he did not always give much consideration to those around him. Mama and I (and of course Papa) had paid a price for this when he disregarded his physician's orders.

I suspected his true motive in sending the books to Mary was to reconnect with her, whether he realized it or not. My heart ached for them both.

A decade later, Mary died during the delivery of a stillborn daughter. Sometime before that, she had passed her copies of the books on to her eldest son, Ambrose, who came very soon after her marriage to Arthur Stoke. I learned of this when the young man appeared in my shop, inquiring whether I had come across any of the books in the course of my business. Apparently Mary had never revealed the books' origin to him. He told me he had loved the books growing up, but that his father had gotten hold of many of them and burned them.

Goose bumps pricked my arms, and I sank back in the chair as a wave of vertigo washed over me.

The underscoring of *very soon*, along with an earlier hint in the letter, suggested something for which I was completely unprepared. If I was not mistaken, Papa was revealing that I had come dangerously close *to marrying my own brother.*

I told Ambrose that I did indeed have a set of the books. I got them out, and we discussed them at length. I confess I was delighted by his attachment to them. I said that I was unwilling to sell them—it was all of her that I had left—but I would loan them to him whenever he liked. I did not tell him the history of the books, which you may think strange, as he is the son of a woman I loved very desperately. I felt that if she had not told him, it was not my place.

Ambrose reminds me in many ways of myself.

He never asked to borrow a book, but over the years he continued to press me about selling them.

His zeal for the books began to worry me. An intelligent person and a creative thinker—both of which I believed Ambrose to be—could potentially use things in those books in a way that might harm others. Were that to happen, it would break both my heart and his mother's, on whichever side of the grave we might reside at the time.

Despite his obvious dissatisfaction with my decision, I stuck to it, hiding the books away in the storeroom along with instructions that they were not to be sold, in case you or your mother should come across them.

You now know the history of these books in full, but I unfortunately must end this overlong missive with a note of caution. If Ambrose Stoke ever appears in the shop asking about them, I strongly urge that you will not—except in direst need—sell them to him.

One last thing I will say, dearest Lizzy, is that I love your mother and yourself more than I could ever put into words. By the time I met your mama, Mary was gone, and I had resolved never to marry. But you and your mother brought joy and laughter back into my life. She is the heart of our family, and I thank God every day for the both of you.

Though you and I never visited any far-flung lands together, our little York adventures are the most precious memories I possess. The years that I've been given to be your papa have been the best years of my life.

Yours eternally,
HG, Papa

A sob escaped my lips, and I set down the last page of the letter. I drew a handkerchief from my pocket.

How I wished Papa might have told me all this sooner, though of course I could see how hard it would have been for him. I had always felt he existed somewhat removed from Mama and me. I thought it was his collecting that held the greatest fascination for him. But he had loved us, and he had been happy. It was simply the wall of secrets between us. I'd sensed it somehow, and I suspected Mama had, too.

I collected the pages of the letter and set them aside before picking up the first page of the memoir. A knock at the lodge's front door caused me to drop it back onto the table.

Three Books

The door swung open.

"Lizzy! Thank God."

"Antony!" How my heart lifted to see him. I pushed back the chair and jumped up, not bothering to hide my relief. "What are you doing here?"

"Making sure you're all right." He stepped inside and closed the door. His eyes quickly surveyed the lodge's interior before they came to rest on me. "I've come to help you."

I had fully intended for our earlier meeting to be our last. I'd meant to go on alone. Yet how much had changed in the hours since then! Papa's letter had shaken me in so many ways, and Antony always helped me find my ground again.

"But how did you know where I was?"

"Partly because I went back to the shop, and Sally gave me your note. But mainly because I knew you'd do something like this."

"Sally gave it to you! Is Mama all right?"

"All is well, Lizzy. Sally was worried, though. She said something about being left with orders to do 'whatever needs doing.'"

I smiled. "Dear, clever Sally."

"And thank goodness for her. Anything might have happened to you."

A new kind of tension stretched between us in the wake of Antony's declaration, our argument about Ambrose, and what came *after*. A pleasurable heat spread through me at the memory.

I cleared my throat. "Antony, I've found a *letter* from Papa."

His brows lifted. "Indeed?"

"Yes, come in." He had remained near the door, and I noticed in one hand he carried the physician's bag I'd given him for the books. I motioned to the chair across from me.

He hesitated, looking around again. "Whose lodge is this?"

"I don't really know," I admitted. "Papa's, maybe. It's a bit of a mystery."

"There's a surprise," he murmured, smiling wryly.

He came to the table, and we both sat down. "I hardly know where to begin," I said. "The letter doesn't really help us solve *our* mystery, but it is yet another of Papa's secrets. One I could never have guessed. I'm still feeling the shock of it."

Antony frowned. "Well, ready yourself for another one. But yours first."

Heart skipping, I said, "What's happened?"

"It will keep." He gestured to Papa's stack of papers.

Should I let him read the letter? There were many personal details. I didn't mind—I'd never kept things from Antony—but they were Papa's, and some touched on Mama, too.

Finally I said, "In short, Ambrose's mother, Mary Stoke—Mary Broadmoor at the time—was the illustrator of Papa's books. They were in love!"

His eyes went wide. "Truly?"

I nodded. "Which is why Papa gave her the other set of books, so I suppose that's one question answered. But that's the least of it, Antony. Without going into particulars . . ." Heat bloomed in my cheeks. "Well, I'm quite certain Ambrose is my half brother."

"Your *brother*!"

"Papa doesn't come out with it in those words, but it's very clear from what he *does* say."

Antony stared, shaking his head. "Does Stoke know?"

"I rather doubt it. After all, he did ask me to marry him. And it sounds like both Mary and Papa kept their secrets tightly locked away."

He eyed me with concern. "This must feel very . . . confusing. And unsettling. You seem remarkably calm."

"It doesn't feel real. Not yet. But it's a relief that Papa has been honest with me at last."

Antony nodded. "Well, thank heaven that's an end to your engagement. I don't mean it for selfish reasons, but because I care about you, Lizzy."

"I know," I said softly. "Papa, too, was distrustful of Ambrose. It sounds as if he hounded Papa about the books, and Papa worried about his motives. Papa never revealed to Ambrose that he was the author."

Antony's gaze sharpened. "Did he know *why* Stoke wanted the books?"

"Unfortunately, no. But Papa was concerned about his 'zeal' for them. He believed the books could be dangerous in the hands of too clever a person."

"I fear that worry may have been justified."

I sat up. "Tell me."

He interlaced his fingers on the table and let out a slow breath. For a few moments there was no sound but the crackling of the fire—and the soft hiss of the teakettle, which should have boiled dry long ago.

"You're sure no one is about to burst in on us?" he said. "It doesn't seem to me this lodge is abandoned."

"I don't know what to make of it. But it seems certain Papa has spent time here. There is definitely something off about this whole place, but we'll save that for later."

At last Antony's gaze settled on my face. "Well, I must first tell you that I've done something I'm rather ashamed of, yet I don't at all regret it."

My stomach twisted. "I'm afraid that's just enough information to be alarming. You had better get on with it."

His gaze shifted to the plate of gingerbread men, and he reached out. I was about to caution him against eating anything here, even if this *was* Papa's lodge. Such actions in fairy tales often had disastrous results. But instead he pulled out a slip of paper that I hadn't noticed.

"'K's favorite,'" he read. "Who is K?"

"Antony! If I didn't know better, I'd think you were stalling!"

"All right," he said, dropping the note. "I broke a window of Stoke's house, let myself in, and rummaged through it like a common thief."

I stared. "You did not!"

"On my honor, I did."

"But *why*, Antony? Did anyone see you?"

"I'm almost certain no one saw me. I told you I didn't trust him, and it turns out I had good reason. I found a box under his bed, and inside it were copies of *twelve* of your father's books, including two copies of *Glamour*—one of which you sold to him—along with copies of *Doorways* and *Ghosts & Spirits*—which he told you he particularly wanted."

My eyebrows knit together. "But he said his father burned them. Why would . . . ?" I recalled wording from Papa's letter: *His father had gotten hold of many of them and burned them.* "He might not have lied," I said. "I might have made the assumption they were all destroyed."

"Possibly. Yet why is he so desperate to buy books he already owns?"

Why indeed. Taken together with what Papa had said in his letter, it was worrying.

Antony lifted the bag from the floor and took out three books. "Forgive me—I asked Sally for *Doorways* and *Ghosts & Spirits.*"

He set those two, along with *Glamour*, on the table.

"You took a book from Ambrose's house!" I knew little about the law, but I assumed burglary was a greater crime than window-breaking and trespassing.

"Lizzy, listen to me. I think these three books have to do with what happened to your mother and Sophia. I think Stoke is involved in that somehow, knew these books were in the shop, and didn't want you to get any ideas should you happen to read them. Later, because he was watching us, I think he figured out that's exactly what was happening."

After Papa's letter, not to mention his recent attempts to call my attention to these same books, there was really no arguing with this. Antony and his instincts had been right, as much as I'd needed them to be wrong.

He leaned across the table, reaching for my hand. The warmth and press of his fingers loosened something inside me. "I'm convinced the only interest Stoke had in mending the breach with my father was getting the baron's help with a scheme that would both divide you and me and allow *him* to get his hands on those books."

"But that would be risky, wouldn't it?" I said. "Once we married—once we lived together—there would be even more opportunity for me to discover his secrets."

Antony nodded, lips forming a tight line. "But you would be in his power. Even if you did figure him out, what could you do? He might simply deny it. And if you persisted, he could commit you to an asylum or whatever he liked."

I stared at him, aghast. Not wanting to believe it. Not only had Ambrose been kind to me, he was truly family now. *But he doesn't know that.*

Letting out a sigh, I admitted, "I feel quite foolish. You suspected him all along, and I kept defending him."

"That's because you are kind, and I'm only a jealous horse's ass." I laughed, heat fanning through me as one corner of his lips lifted and his thumb brushed the back of my hand. "But I well understood that his proposal represented safety and salvation for you and your mother. My heart simply wanted things to be different."

Glancing down at our clasped hands, I replied faintly, "I'm familiar with that longing."

The tip of his thumb now traced a circle on my skin, igniting little flames all over my body. I was afraid of these feelings, and of these pleasurable sensations. Where could they lead us? Only to sorrow, I feared.

I looked up, a slight tremor in my voice as I said, "Why would Ambrose do all of this?"

"Indeed. That's the last piece of it. What is he trying so hard to conceal?"

I reached out and touched the cover of *Glamour*. "You think it was Ambrose who glamoured Mama and Sophia?"

"I hate to say it, but I do."

I recalled how I'd asked to borrow the book from Ambrose, and though he consented, he stalled. He had two copies!

"It would explain Mama's reactions to him. I didn't want to tell you this earlier, but when I told her I was to marry Ambrose, it clearly upset her."

He nodded grimly. "At least we now have a copy of the book."

"Thanks to you."

"And the fact I'm a jealous horse's ass."

I smiled. He gave my hand a squeeze and let it go. Then he picked up *Glamour* and began slowly turning pages.

"'To protect from fairy glamour,'" he read, "'clothes may be turned inside out, elf-shot or a nail may be placed in a pocket, or a blackthorn staff may be carried.' It's too late for all this." He flipped a few more pages. "'A glamoured person may sleep at all hours, may be senseless to those around them, or may have strange visions and talk to unseen beings. Once a person has been glamoured, there is no certain cure except to compel the entity that did the glamouring to remove it. Or to kill that entity. Other remedies suggested in the lore—such as casting the afflicted person into frigid seawater, setting a fire at their feet, or causing them to drink an infusion made from a foxglove flower—may cure the spirit at the expense of the body.'"

Decidedly unhelpful. Setting the book down, Antony raised a hand and began to rub his temples.

I pulled the book toward me, scanning the first few pages until I reached an illustration of a hostile-looking hob. "'Glamour is fairy magic,'" I read, "'a regrettably unscientific term. In many cases, glamoured persons exhibit a trancelike state, such as those induced through mesmerism. Glamouring differs from mesmerism in that some subjects actually experience fairy worlds through their physical body.'"

I looked up. "Maybe it's not fairy glamour. Maybe they've been *entranced*."

Antony dropped his hand. "Hypnotism! I've read that it's being used by some physicians as an anesthesia for performing surgery, even amputations."

My hope dimmed. "That would suggest it can be quite powerful. Do you know how the trance is broken?"

"Unfortunately I've just given you the extent of my knowledge on the subject. I know hypnotism is based on mesmerism. There are mesmerism demonstrations in London from time to time, but I've never been to one. They have the reputation of being more showmanship than science. It's something that could be researched—had we more time."

I sighed. "Would it do any good to confront him, I wonder?"

"It could be risky." He winced. "Especially now that I've broken into his house."

Something occurred to me then. "Assuming Ambrose really is going around entrancing people, and setting aside the question of why he would choose Mama and Sophia, why didn't he just do the same to us when he thought we were figuring it out?"

Antony thought for a moment. "I suppose at some point, people begin to notice? Such as when it begins to affect whole families."

"Especially the children of peers."

"Yes," he admitted. "But still he might, if he felt trapped."

"Which he will if we confront him."

I slumped against my chair back, letting out another sigh.

Rubbing at the stubble on his chin, Antony said, "I've been thinking that whatever Stoke is hiding—whatever he's really up to—has somehow to do with spirits."

"What makes you think so?"

"Mainly because he was so interested in obtaining your copy of this book when he already had one." He rested his hand on *Ghosts & Spirits.* "But also, we know he was watching us. Either following us himself or perhaps having us followed. My father specifically mentioned us walking in the Minster and into the ginnel next to Croft & Croft."

"I saw ghosts in both places! You don't think that's a coincidence."

He shrugged. "Maybe Stoke somehow set them to watch us. He probably doesn't know you can see them."

"He does now. I saw another ghost at the ball—Anne Carlisle, according to Ambrose and his niece. And now that you mention it, he was very interested and questioned me about it."

Antony's brows shot up. "Indeed? Anne is family legend. She was executed during the Reformation for hiding priests in her home, which stood on the same spot as Carlisle House."

"That's awful!"

"I believe it was. I'll spare you the details." He hesitated. "You didn't see . . . I mean, I don't suppose you'd know her by sight, but after what the governess said about Sophia and my mother, I wondered whether you might have also seen *her.*"

I recalled that first day he came to our home, when he said he preferred to think of Lady Carlisle peacefully resting. "I saw no other," I assured him. "Though if I'm going to see ghosts, it would be nice if I could at least see ones who might be able to help us."

Antony sat up, fixing his eyes on me. "Lizzy, that's *it.*"

I frowned, waiting for him to go on.

"Stoke's reason for glamouring, or entrancing, Sophia and your mother. They were both communicating with spirits. Maybe they learned something Stoke didn't want them telling anyone."

"Oh!" I said, excited. "Ambrose *asked* me if I'd spoken to any of the ghosts I'd seen. In fact, Anne Carlisle did try to say something to me, though I couldn't hear her."

"I think one was watching me at his house. He came home while I was still there, and a bowl suddenly shattered near where I was standing."

I shuddered. "You're lucky you weren't caught, Antony. You still could be."

He shook his head. "I'm convinced Stoke's up to worse tricks than any I could even contemplate. He won't want the constable in his house. Considering what he's got in his cellar, I doubt he wants *anyone* in there."

"His cellar!"

"Yes, there's still more I must tell you," he went on, taking no notice of my distress. "I believe I may have found answers down there, but I need you to help me understand them. There was a very old ruin, along with some interesting artifacts."

I stared, incredulous. "You went into his cellar, with no idea what you might find, where you could have been trapped had he come home earlier—all while you suspected he might be dangerous. Antony! You might never have come out again, and no one would even know where to look!"

His gaze made a slow pass around the lodge before it came pointedly to rest on me. "Let me understand—I'm being called to account for an ill-considered decision to rush into danger?"

I cleared my throat. "No. I don't know why you would think so."

He pursed his lips, subduing a smile. "My mistake."

"Yes. Well," I said breezily, folding my hands on the table, "in this cellar that might or might not have been a death trap, you found . . . ?"

"A bit of old wall with a well-preserved fresco. I wish you could have seen it, as I've no doubt you'd have had a better idea what you were looking at. But I think the fresco may be Anglo-Saxon. It's a depiction of the Wild Hunt, which I know only because of the illustrations in your father's book on the subject."

"An Anglo-Saxon fresco! While I'm not as knowledgeable as Papa, I think such a thing must be quite rare and probably worth a fortune. Little has been found from Anglo-Saxon culture beyond the beautiful manuscripts."

"That odd scepter of his was down there, too. A larger version of the deer figure on its tip rested on top of a clay vessel that looked a lot like an urn, though an enormous one. And there was an old manuscript that contained an illustration of the scepter. The things were obviously connected, and the way they were arranged, it almost looked like . . ." He broke off, thinking.

"Some kind of ceremonial space?"

He brightened. "Yes. Exactly that. And Lizzy, I touched the side of the urn, and I *felt* something. Like it was full of hornets."

Slowly shaking my head, I said, "It almost sounds like he's a kind of sorcerer."

I stared at the three books resting on the table, considering what I knew about my half brother—his obsessive collecting, his passion for folkloric subjects, his alleged desire to conceal the sources of his knowledge.

"Tell me what you're thinking," said Antony.

There *was* something of a theory bubbling up, though a rather outlandish one. "Do you think Ambrose might be collecting *ghosts*?"

Antony's expression was more disturbed than surprised. "I confess it does sound very Ambrose. Especially after touring his strange old house. Is that something he could have learned from your father's books?"

I shook my head. "Not directly. Papa was an explorer. He documented what he experienced. I think what Ambrose gleaned from Papa's books were his own ideas of what is possible."

Antony folded his arms over his chest, considering. "If you had to guess, how might he do it?"

I thought about each of the items Antony had described. "The scepter—I've rarely seen him without it. And it sounds as if the scepter, the wall, and the manuscript are all Anglo-Saxon, so that feels important. I wonder if he might have found the artifacts in the cellar along with the wall fragment."

Antony nodded. "There was a cordoned-off area in the same part of the cellar, where the ground looked to have been disturbed and smoothed again. My fevered brain at the time conjured visions of exhumed corpses. Maybe he conducted an amateur excavation?"

"That also sounds like something Ambrose would do." Or Papa, for that matter.

Something flashed in Antony's eyes. "In the illustration of the scepter, a flame burned inside the ring at its tip. It's only just occurred to me, but candles can be used for hypnosis."

"He might have used the scepter to entrance Sophia and Mama! Maybe he could use it to control the ghosts as well."

"Maybe it's the scepter's *purpose*. And the manuscript could be a kind of instruction book."

My elation began to temper as I thought through it. "I like the ghost theory. But how could he entrance Sophia and Mama when they were both safe at home?"

Antony's gaze locked with mine. "They were both communicating with ghosts, Lizzy."

Doorways

"That's right!" It was one of the very first facts we'd seized on as likely to be important.

"There's a detail I've left out that it now occurs to me I shouldn't have," said Antony. "The wall with the fresco had an arched opening in it."

I stared at him. "You mean like a *doorway?*"

"It seems that way, in retrospect," he grumbled. "If only I'd thought to step through it and check."

I couldn't help laughing at this, and he shot me a bewildered glance. "That sounds very *Lizzy*," I said. "I'm glad you didn't."

A smile spread over his face and made my heart skip. "Where, then, might a doorway in an Anglo-Saxon wall lead?"

"Well, the carvings on Opa's cabinet give hints of where *it* leads, so the fresco could be a clue. The Wild Hunt isn't a place, though. It's a piece of folklore shared by various—"

"Lizzy! The Wild Hunt—ghosts and spirits!"

My breath caught. "Yes, spirits *ensorcelled* by Woden, in fact."

"Where might Woden—or Ambrose—find spirits?"

Now my eyes popped open. "There is such a place! Mama once told me that to speak with the spirits of the dead, she had to project her own spirit into a kind of in-between place. She called it a 'ghostly realm.'"

"So if Ambrose is using the doorway to go there, he and your mother could have been there at the same time." The furrows in his brow deepened. "Sophia, too, when she spoke with *my* mother."

I reached out and covered his hand with mine. "Which is how they discovered his secret, and he entranced them to keep them from revealing it."

His eyes shone. "I think we may have solved it at last, Lizzy."

"I'm almost afraid to hope."

We sat in a kind of stunned silence until Antony said, "He must have known it was wrong." I looked at him, and he added, "What he was doing."

I gave a weary shrug. "Papa knew that if he continued to eat sweets, he might be taken from Mama and me. But that didn't stop him."

Antony's face softened. "In other words, the temptation was too strong."

"Once Ambrose found the artifacts, he wasn't going to be satisfied with simply adding them to his collection. He had to learn their purpose."

"They seem alike in many ways, Ambrose and your father. I suppose it's not surprising."

I nodded. "The irony is that if it hadn't been for Ambrose's 'zeal' with regard to Papa's books, Papa might even have taken him under his wing and shared his otherworldly knowledge, much as I suspect Opa did with Papa. A bit of fatherly guidance might actually have prevented this." I couldn't help feeling that Papa's fear of disclosing the truth about his past had brought harm to both his children.

Sensing my bitterness over Papa's various choices, Antony said, "Well, it seems your father has somewhat made up for it now. He's told you the truth at last, and he succeeded in steering you toward the answers you need to help your mother."

"Yes. We wouldn't be here now if not for his ghostly tricks."

I looked at Papa's stack of papers. As successful as this adventure had been, I couldn't help feeling the business was yet unfinished.

"I wonder if the letter is the only reason Papa wanted me to come here."

Antony frowned. "It has saved you from marrying your brother *and* served as warning about him. What other reason should there be?"

"I guess after everything Papa has managed to do this past week, I feel like he could have gotten the letter to me without sending me through a doorway into a frozen wilderness."

"Lizzy." The sharpness in Antony's voice drew my gaze. "I know that look. You're plotting something I'm not going to like."

"I'm not!"

He stared, expressionless.

"Maybe a little. But hear me out."

He let out a disgruntled sigh.

"Besides apparently using this lodge as a kind of writing refuge, I believe Papa traveled to this world to visit the cave of the Krampus. He and Mary went there together at least once, and I can't help feeling he means for me to go there, too. He left the book on the stairs *twice*. Last time he even left a toy from Krampus's cave. I'm wondering if maybe Krampus can help us somehow."

Antony *now* wore an expression. One of disbelief. "Didn't you tell me Krampus was a kind of Yule monster?"

I nodded, not really liking the idea any more than he did.

"Lizzy, I don't for a second believe that your father would want . . ."

I saw the moment the thought flitted through his head. It hadn't yet flitted through mine, though, so I said, "What is it?"

"Nothing." He set his eyes on mine. "It's nothing."

I don't know whether our minds worked similarly or if we shared an actual connection, but suddenly it came to me, too. "Krampus punishes naughty children."

"No." Antony's voice was sharp.

My gaze drifted down to the plate of gingerbread figures, and its note. *K's favorite.* Recalling the illustration that showed Krampus gobbling up children, I shuddered.

"Lizzy, no. We'll find another way."

"Ambrose may very well have your mother's spirit closed up in that urn. Who knows who else might be in there? Maybe Krampus can stop him."

Antony shook his head. "I should have tried harder to open the urn. But we still can."

"It might be that easy, but we don't know for sure. And how will we get him to release Mama and Sophia? We have a theory about his scepter, and that is all."

"We could destroy the scepter."

"But we have no idea what that might do to them!"

He sat with arms crossed, staring blankly at the books. Finally, his head sank into his hands, and he groaned. "How would one go about finding Krampus?"

I gnawed my bottom lip. "I'm not sure."

I got up slowly, limbs sore from dancing now stiff from sitting, and walked to the window. I couldn't see the mountains for the tall trees. "I can't imagine Papa walked all that way. It would take weeks, maybe longer. And then he'd have to walk all the way back, unless he found another doorway."

I turned from the window and began to pace around the lodge. Antony sat looking miserable. Mostly I didn't want to go to the cave, either, but the fact Papa had sent me here gave me courage.

Pausing in front of the bookcase in the corner, I read the spines of the books there. They were all on folkloric topics associated with winter and Yule, written by people other than Papa. Books on winter solstice celebrations, the Wild Hunt, Krampus, and St. Nicholas. The lettering on the spine of one slim, red volume was too small to read at a distance, and I leaned closer. *Lair of the Krampus*. Elated, I pinched the spine and pulled. The book slipped partway free and stuck—and then the bookcase began to swing toward me.

"Lizzy!" called Antony as I jumped back.

The bookcase stopped and stood open, revealing an empty closet. A framed drawing of a bundle of switches, like the medallion on the cover of *The Krampus*, hung on the back wall.

"It's another doorway," I breathed.

"What is your plan?" Antony's voice sounded flat.

I turned. He still slumped in the chair, but he'd begun to look resigned.

"I confess I don't have one. All I know is my brother has taken a St. Nicholas Day gift that was lovingly bestowed by his mother and used it as part of a selfish scheme that caused others to suffer. If that's not a case for Krampus, I don't know what is."

"We have no idea what he might do to us."

"We don't," I acknowledged. "But Papa and Mary journeyed there and back again. There's always danger in fairy tales."

Antony's expression darkened. "I'm going to pretend you didn't just say that."

I sighed. "I know this isn't a fairy tale, but you must admit it feels like one. I don't in any sense mean it isn't real. In some ways it feels *more* real than the life I've been living the last year. Perhaps I get that from Papa, and it's something to be wary of." I took a step toward him. "I don't want to see anyone hurt, not even Ambrose, but if I don't do all I can to help Mama, I won't be able to live with myself."

He slowly shook his head as he reached for the physician's bag. He stacked the books and replaced them inside. My heart ached as I watched him, but it would be selfish to persuade him to take this risk with me.

Then he picked up my father's papers and put them inside, too, and one by one he did the same with the gingerbread men.

"I won't pretend I'm in favor of this," he said, "but I would hope by now I've learned to trust your instincts."

His eyes settled on my face—so softly and mournfully that I went to him, feeling equal measures of guilt and relief. I stopped short, uncertain, but he reached out and pulled me into his arms, pressing his cheek into my hair. It was hard to imagine feeling any safer than I did in that moment.

"You are the bravest person I know."

I laughed. "I'm not. Not really. It's just that after the last three years, I'm used to doing what needs to be done, however hard it is and however desperate the situation might seem. I'm scared *all the time*, and I've never faced a fear greater than the possibility of Mama and me out on the street." I drew back and looked at him, and his hand came to my cheek. "I never wanted to marry Ambrose. I didn't know who or what he was, of course—I actually thought he was starting to care for me—but I only agreed to marry him to keep Mama and me safe. And because I was tired of doing it all alone. But I've only ever been in love with one person."

I thought about how similarly situated Antony and I were to Papa and Mary—except I wouldn't allow Antony to give up his life and his family for me. I didn't say that to him now, nor did I stop him as he bent and touched his lips to mine. One hand still cradling my face, the other curled around me, pulling me into him. The sudden press of our bodies caused a hot wave of sensation to surge through me.

Just as I was winding my arms around him—pulling him closer still, until he was all I could smell and feel and taste, giving in to this moment as possibly the last like this that we'd share—he released me and took a step back, muttering an oath under his breath.

"This must stop," he said hoarsely. "Forgive me. I know now that I was selfish to ask you to marry me. The very last thing you need is one more person to be responsible for, and that's all I would be if my father disinherited me." He smiled thinly. "I never learned any kind of practical skill, as you did. I can't earn a living wage with a rapier or a hunting rifle, or with Latin or a waltz. It's just that . . ." He looked away, and I watched his throat work as he swallowed. "Well, I've never known this kind of wanting, Lizzy."

His eyes settled on mine again, and I thought my heart would burst. Was this what love was? Torturing each other? How many people were actually allowed to marry the ones they loved? Despite what Papa had said about Mama, I couldn't help thinking that marriage generally had little to do with love.

"Neither have I," I said faintly, a tremor in my voice. "I wish things could be different."

A fool's wish. And not the first time I'd made it.

He took my hand and raised it to his lips. I felt their silken warmth against my palm for the space of a heartbeat before he closed my fingers over the spot. "Let us at least promise that we'll see this through together. If you went off on your own and I never saw you again . . . I wouldn't survive it, Lizzy."

"Yes," I breathed. "I promise."

He turned, picked up the bag, and put out his arm. "Shall we?"

Then we stepped together into the empty bookcase closet.

Misbehavior

The cave was just the same as Mary's illustration. The strange toys strewn over the floor, the view of the peaks out the entrance, the fire in the great hearth, which had been constructed roughly from stacked river stones. Even the chimney climbing in higgledy-piggledy fashion up the wall to join with a smoke hole.

I noted new details, too, like the row of worn and patched stockings hanging from the crooked mantel. Tallow burned in earthen bowls resting on tables and on great stacks of books. On a table near the fire, there was even a chipped tea service.

The place reeked of unwashed animal and woodsmoke.

I took a slow step, crunching a fir cone underfoot.

"Hallo, wer seid Ihr?"

We jumped, turning to find a figure had entered the room from a back passageway. I recognized him as the subject of another illustration in Papa's Krampus book. Mary had drawn several versions of St. Nicholas—all with a long white beard, and two wearing formal robes and miter and carrying a crosier. This one stood out in my memory because he wore a plain robe belted at the waist like a monk, with a crown of holly resting on his head.

St. Nicholas and Krampus were connected. In Opa's village on St. Nicholas Day, a man dressed as the saint and another as Krampus had gone door-to-door together asking for the household's children so they could reward or punish them accordingly. The saint handed out small toys and treats while Krampus gifted small bundles of switches. But what was St. Nicholas doing in Krampus's lair?

"I'm sorry," I said. "We don't speak German." I had learned a few words and phrases, enough to understand the question he'd asked. "I am Lizzy Grimm, and this is Antony Carlisle."

He stared at us for several seconds and then blinked. "Ah yes. Have you come with Herr Berti?" He moved his head to see behind us.

Glancing back, I couldn't see the doorway we'd come through, but there was a real bundle of switches leaning against the cave wall near the spot. "I don't . . ." *Herr Berti.* Oma and Opa had called Papa "Berti." "Do you mean Herbert Grimm?"

"We had an agreement," the old fellow grumbled. "No one else was ever to be shown the way here. No one else was ever to be told about me." Now he grimaced, transforming from puzzled old man to severe saint. "Herr Berti gave me his word."

"Herr Berti was my father," I explained quickly. "He has passed on now. But he didn't show me the way. I discovered the door myself." While this wasn't *precisely* a lie, it came close enough, and I moved on quickly to the business at hand. "We've come here seeking an audience with Krampus. Is this where he lives?"

A coarse, spiky white brow lifted, and he eyed us suspiciously. "*Der Krampus? Ja,* this is his lair. There are only two ways to gain 'an audience,' and I promise you will not like either of them."

Antony cleared his throat, and the old man's eyes darted to him. "May we inquire what they are?"

"Present yourself as a misbehaved child, or as a tasty morsel. Results are sometimes comparable, depending on the severity of misbehavior."

I shuddered, and Antony's alarm was palpable. "Supposing we *know* a person who has misbehaved gravely," I said, "and we would like to see him stopped, but not harmed? He's not a child now, but of course he was once. In fact, another child of Herbert Grimm's."

The old man's expression was brittle as ice. "I'd say you've come to the wrong place, and you'd best move along before the beast arrives."

"Let us go, Lizzy," urged Antony. "We'll find another way."

I rested my hand on his arm and continued—cautiously. "In the country where my father was born, there are tales about St. Nicholas and Krampus. The tales suggest that St. Nicholas has some authority over Krampus. Perhaps if you spoke to him on our behalf—"

"Authority." He let out a very unsaintlike snort. "Impossible."

The word had the finality of a sealed coffin.

Antony and I exchanged a glance, and I reached into the physician's bag. "We've brought along something he likes. Perhaps a bargain might be struck."

The saint's eyes went wide as saucers as I held out the ginger-bread man.

"Fools!" We staggered back as his voice rumbled out like thunder. He toppled onto his knees, and his body began to sprout *thick, dark hair.*

I stood transfixed, vaguely aware of Antony tugging at my arm.

The saint expanded. His lips parted and then broadened, long fangs spiking both up and down, two pointing toward his broad nostrils and two toward the end of his blunt chin. His old onionskin flesh thickened to burnished leather, wrinkles transforming into extreme ridges and valleys. The irises of his eyes went from glittering ice to smoldering coal, and horns sprang from his shaggy head, sending thin rivulets of blood down his face. He let out a horrific bleat that I felt in my chest.

Leaning forward onto his knuckles, he stretched his neck and head toward me and let out a roar, blasting my face with hot, foul breath.

My hand had hung frozen in the air up to this point, but as Antony dragged me away, the gingerbread figure dropped from my fingers. The massive head snapped forward, jaws snatching the treat before it hit the ground.

Antony plunged his hand into the physician's bag and drew out more gingerbread, tossing it toward the tea table. As the beast's eyes followed the treats, Antony and I dashed at the cave wall and back through the doorway.

We stumbled into Papa's cozy refuge. Antony urged, "Let's keep going! He may follow!"

"Surely he's too large to fit!"

"I don't think we can afford to assume that matters."

Antony's hand gripping mine, we fled the lodge and started back down the woodland path, shattering the relative stillness of the place with our thumping and crashing. We were nearly to the snowfield when we heard a loud crack followed by a splintering sound, then the thunderous roar of the beast.

I gave a panicked cry and Antony called, "Nearly there!"

We charged out into the snow, frantically searching for the cabinet. Our earlier tracks had *vanished*, and belatedly I struggled to pick up the holly berry trail; we'd already obscured some of it in our panic and flailing. Then I saw Papa's cap in the snow.

"There!" I cried, and we scrambled toward it.

"You go on," said Antony. "I'll track up the snow so it can't follow our trail."

"Don't let him see you!" I warned. "And be sure to grab the cap!"

Crossing the last stretch of ground, I could see not even the faintest outline of the cabinet. I rushed at the cap anyhow.

Relief washed over me as I felt the shift from cold to warm—light to dark—but then my head struck something solid, and everything went black.

<hr />

"Lizzy." Antony's voice was low and urgent, and I opened my eyes. Pain shot through the top of my head and I gasped.

"Lizzy! Are you all right?"

"I—I hit my head."

"You did indeed. So did I, but I think you got the worst of it."

It was fully dark, and I was enveloped in something warm. Hearing a rhythmic thump, thump, thump, I realized my head rested against

Sharon Lynn Fisher

Antony's chest. *Enveloped in Antony.* My eyes fluttered closed again. I felt like I could sleep for a week.

"We're inside the cabinet," he said, voice rumbling through his chest and rousing me. "Something is blocking the doors."

I breathed deeply and opened my eyes again. It was in fact *less* than fully dark—a sliver of light gleamed dully between the doors, allowing me to get my bearings. Antony's back rested against one side of the cabinet's interior, and I was folded between his legs.

"Did you just say the doors are blocked?"

"I did."

I raised a hand and shoved at the seam of light; the doors rattled but didn't budge.

How could this be? The cabinet's latch had been missing for as long as I could remember. Someone would have had to deliberately block the doors closed, as we'd done with the cane.

"I think we'd best not move much if we can help it," I said. "If we accidentally open the doorway, we'll be trapped between that beast and these cabinet doors."

"I wholeheartedly agree," muttered Antony.

"Have you tried calling for Sally?"

"I have, and I've tried forcing the—"

Both of us jumped as something struck the front of the cabinet.

"Who's there?" demanded Antony.

Another impact came, and Antony's arms tightened around me.

"Please let us out!" I called. "The doors seem to be stuck." I wasn't sure how we were going to explain this, but at the moment, that was of secondary importance.

"I apologize for the noise," answered a familiar voice in a friendly tone. "For the time being, these doors will require reinforcement."

"Stoke?" Antony said sharply.

Then came several more blows, and I now understood that planks were being nailed across the cabinet's front.

252

"Come, man!" cried Antony. "You can't possibly intend to seal us in here."

"There is no need for you to remain confined," Ambrose replied. "Simply go back to wherever it is you came from."

Aghast, I said, "Ambrose, open the doors and let us talk over all of this. I have much to share with you."

"I'm sorry, my dear. I'm afraid the time for disclosures has passed. You must consider our engagement at an end."

"You've taken leave of your senses," persisted Antony. "Our disappearance will be noted."

"Indeed," said Ambrose casually, as though we weren't having what might very well be a life-and-death discussion through the doors of a cabinet. "It shall be noted and put down to the impetuosity of two young people in love. After all, the whole town will soon know you defied your father and threw over my niece because of your infatuation with my fiancée. I shall simply tell everyone that I discovered you absconded with her. You see, I won't even need to lie."

Antony and I quieted. The lump on my head throbbed. Ambrose was right. Elopement was common in such situations. Confinement in a cabinet was not. While Antony had been wary of Ambrose for some time, I'd never imagined him capable of something like this.

"Tell us what it is you want from us," said Antony.

I pressed my hands over my ears as two more blows to the cabinet landed. Then Ambrose said, "Only that you do what everyone expects. Disappear."

My heart kept up a panicked rhythm, and I could hear Antony's doing the same. Ambrose was banishing us to the Tyrolean winter. And we would have to go soon, as I had lost feeling in both a hand and a foot due to the cramped position. But what of Krampus? We'd very likely find him waiting for us. Possibly tearing around the snowfield like a berserker.

"If you truly wish us to disappear," began Antony, his voice amazingly steady, "why haven't you merely destroyed the cabinet?"

I knew the answer to that. "It's a doorway. He'd never do such a thing, no more than would Papa."

"Very perceptive," replied Ambrose. "Of course there's no need to destroy such an important artifact. But rest assured, it will be guarded around the clock."

"What of my mother and Sally?" I said, the implications of all this finally sinking in. "What have you done with them?"

"Nothing at all, my dear. They are safe and sound in your home. I simply let Sally know that after our impending nuptials, we intended to share my home. That being the case, the cabinet was a family heirloom and you wished it moved here right away. I'm not sure she believed me, but she was hardly going to naysay your fiancé."

"You *stole* the cabinet from the shop," I said in astonishment.

"As Mr. Carlisle stole property from my home. I'm willing to call it even, though I didn't go snooping through anyone's personal effects. Now, you must excuse me—Yule is nearly upon us. I've been a year preparing for the hunt, and there is much yet to be done."

The hunt! We had not quite followed our theory to its most obvious conclusion. This was no mere collector's obsession. "You mean to *lead* the Wild Hunt."

"I'm very sorry that you won't be here to witness it."

How much like our father he was. Though Papa would never have gone to the extremes Ambrose had, the idea of leading the Wild Hunt would have delighted him.

"Lizzy," Antony said urgently, "tell him about the letter."

I carefully wriggled until I was sitting upright. Again pain flared across my brow.

"Ambrose, listen to me. We found a letter from my father in the world we've come from. There are things about him that you should know. He was a traveler between worlds, and *he* was the author of the Ginnel books."

A long silence ensued. Antony's hand curled around mine.

"I've long suspected the traveling," Ambrose said, "and that the cabinet was a doorway to somewhere. But I confess I had no idea about the books. It explains a great deal. Have you known all along?"

"I've known for a few days. But there's more. Your mother and my father . . ." How was he going to react to this? *What choice do we have?* "I learned from my father's letter that they authored the books *together*. He wrote them, and she created the illustrations. They were in love, before she married your—before she married Sir Arthur. They even traveled through doorways together. Ambrose, this will certainly come as a shock, but you and I have the same father."

This silence extended for *days* compared to the first one. At length I heard him move around and set something down. *It's worked!*

"It's an easy enough story to concoct," he said. "With no way of proving it, conveniently. Yet I believe you. It, too, explains a great deal."

Relief washed over me. "I can show you the letter." I wasn't sure whether the bag was in the cabinet with us or out in the snow, but if we could just get him to open the doors . . . "Please let us out so we may talk this through. We have no intention of exposing you. No harm has been done that cannot be remedied. We only wish you to release my mother and Antony's sister from whatever spell they are under."

There was the question of the collected spirits, and whatever other ill-advised schemes he might be involved in, but once we were out of this box, I believed we could make him see reason.

"You must understand," he said, "I never intended to use the scepter on the living. It's not what it was created for, and indeed I'm surprised its effects have held. You might be interested to know it was something in one of your father's books that gave me the idea to try it. But I suppose by now you've figured that out."

He took a couple of steps. When he next spoke, he sounded farther away. "Thank you for the information, but I'm sorry to say I've come too far now to risk exposure."

My heart sank. Perhaps he had spent too much time alone—and too much time obsessively pursuing curious objects and hobbies—to be brought back. I wondered what would have become of Papa had he not married Mama.

Not this. More likely he would have one day simply walked through a doorway and never returned.

Earlier I'd guessed that Sir Arthur might have known Mary and Papa had been in love. If he'd also suspected Ambrose wasn't his son, Ambrose's strange interests, along with his refusal to take over the family business, must have seemed like proof of that suspicion. How fatherless Ambrose must have felt, without ever fully understanding why.

"Stoke," said Antony, voice edged with anger, "Lizzy is your *sister*."

"Yes," Ambrose replied pleasantly. "I shall give our relationship as much consideration as our father did to his and mine."

I closed my eyes. *Oh, Papa.*

"I Trust You Completely"

Antony

"Stoke!" I shouted.

We heard the cellar door close, followed by the key turning in its lock. Footsteps moved along the ceiling over our heads.

I let out a breath and carefully reached down to touch Lizzy, though in the dark I couldn't be sure of where my hand would land. I felt the seam of her bodice where it joined her skirt, just above the curve of her waist. She wasn't wearing her father's coat; she'd left it behind in the lodge. Injured as she was, it would be a long, slow walk back there in the cold.

But could we even go back? The beast had followed us there from the cave. It might no longer be safe.

I chuckled inwardly at the notion of safety.

"How is your head?" I asked.

"I've got a lump, and it hurts, but I'm all right."

"We need to get you out of here. Do you think Stoke really has us guarded? I don't believe he keeps servants."

"Someone must have helped him with the cabinet."

"True." I called out, "Is anyone there?"

No response came.

"I suppose he might've paid laborers," she said. "They may be gone now."

I nodded, though she couldn't see me. "What about the ghost I encountered here, if indeed it *was* a ghost? Could it actually hurt us, or prevent us from leaving?"

I felt her breath against my cheek as she sighed. "Conceivably. You said it broke a bowl, didn't you?"

"*Mm*, I did."

"Regardless, we would need to force open both the cabinet and the door to the cellar and escape the house, all without giving Ambrose the opportunity to entrance us, too. And if we managed it, we'd still have no way of helping Mama and Sophia." Her voice had a tinge of hope-lessness. "We couldn't tell anyone our story. One or both of us would wind up in the asylum."

"You're right, as usual."

She groaned quietly. "It's kind of you to forget that the whole rea-son we're stuck in here is my brilliant idea to visit Krampus. In all the ways I'd imagined that could go wrong, I confess this wasn't one of them."

Reaching my arms around her, I pulled her close. "Don't despair, Lizzy. We're not finished yet."

Thinking through our very limited options for the dozenth time, I tried, in vain, to banish from my mind the story of the lovers locked in the catacombs in *Melmoth the Wanderer*, which a schoolmate had given me to read at Eton.

But we don't have to starve to death. We can opt to be eaten instead.

I stifled a groan of my own. "We're going back out there," I said. "I think it's the only choice we have. Hopefully the creature will have given up by now. On my feet and with a little momentum, I should be able to force the doors open. The commotion will bring Stoke down, and we'll be ready for him. With luck, I'll subdue him before he can subdue us." *And we'll just have to hope there's no one else in the cellar.* "What do you say?"

"Only that I trust you completely."

Anyone might say such a thing in such a moment. Anyone but Lizzy. Since Mr. Grimm's death, she had learned to rely upon herself and trust her own instincts. And it had kept her and her mother out of the workhouse and off the streets.

My hand found her cheek, and I gently lifted her face, lowering my lips to hers. She leaned into me, warm fingers coming to the spot where my neck met my shoulder, slipping inside my shirt collar to touch my skin. I felt the tip of her tongue against my bottom lip and thought my desire for her would reduce me to ash. Heart hammering, I deepened the kiss, letting my tongue sweep into her mouth before finally breaking away and pulling her tightly against me.

Please let me not fail her.

Away They All Flew

With much cramped maneuvering, we managed to more or less right ourselves inside the cabinet.

"Are you ready?" asked Antony, bent near my ear.

"I think so."

"Once we're out, stay close to me."

He pressed a hand against the tree carving, and we staggered back out into the snow, squinting at the sudden brightness. Though the field must have been churned up mightily by Antony and me and the beast that pursued us, all signs of that had now vanished. Once again an unbroken line of holly berries led to the woods.

We stood still a moment, letting the blood flow back into our limbs and listening to the silence. Finally, Antony turned and readied himself for an assault on the cabinet doors. Before he'd begun, we heard another demonic, bleating howl. Krampus came charging at us from the cover of the trees.

This dark, shaggy mass springing deftly across the expanse of white managed to be even more terrifying than in the cave. I had thought he would shamble or run on all fours, but here, out in the open, he could unfold to his full height—easily several feet taller than Antony. He ran like a man, but on massive fur-covered feet. I could feel each impact through the compacted snow beneath my boots. Clouds of breath puffed through his fangs like a dragon, and though his ram horns curved away from us, I had no doubt they'd still be lethal in a charge.

Antony and I stood petrified. We couldn't possibly outrun the fiend in the snow. If we returned to the cabinet, we'd be crushed, as he would see us this time and have no trouble following.

When he was nearly upon us, Antony hooked an arm around me and dived to one side.

We splayed in the snow as Krampus plunged past us to where the doorway stood unseen. The cabinet became visible again as he entered—smashing into, then *through*, its sealed doors.

Antony was up in an instant, reaching out and hauling me to my feet. My head throbbed, and a wave of nausea washed over me.

"Come," he said. "I don't think it's safe for us to remain out here."

He was right. I didn't know what happened to a smashed doorway. We could be trapped. I followed him back in, and he paused only a moment before hopping through the ruptured doors. Then he turned to lift me over the rubble, splintered wood tearing at my skirts.

We watched Krampus dash toward a staircase on the opposite side of the cellar, where my half brother stood, staring wildly. Ambrose gripped the scepter in one hand, extending it before him, and uttered a command that sounded like *"Slap!"* A flame flickered to life in the ring at the scepter's tip.

If Ambrose thought he'd entrance Krampus, he was wrong, because the beast reached the stairs in one final long stride and snatched the artifact right out of his hand. In trying to hold on to it, Ambrose stumbled and fell, rolling down the steps and landing at Krampus's feet.

Scepter held aloft—and looking far less impressive in the huge hand with its sharp bone tips protruding through the fingers—Krampus spun and headed for us again. He let out a couple of deep, goatish grunts, and we scrambled out of his path.

Reaching a great clay pot in one corner—the urn Antony had mentioned, by the stag figure on top—Krampus brought the bottom end of the scepter down hard against the vessel's rounded belly.

The pot shattered, throwing the room into utter confusion.

A cloud of chaotic sound—shouting, crying, screeching, bellowing—expanded around us. Every candle and lamp extinguished. The temperature dropped, and goose bumps crept over my flesh.

"I think he's let them out!" I cried, but my voice was lost in the heaving sound.

Antony's arms came around me, and we huddled against a wall.

Violent thrashing noises at the other end of the room added to the escalating confusion. Then came the sound of splintering wood and falling rubble, like the place was coming down around us.

"He's breaking his way out!" Antony shouted. "Let's go!"

I doubted there could be anything much left of the stairs, but we joined hands and started toward them, choking on the dust and navigating falling debris. What would happen now? I could only imagine the terror struck into the citizens of York by Krampus tearing through the streets. How long would it be before St. Nicholas returned?

A little lamplight had been let in by the complete destruction of the cellar door above us, and I looked for Ambrose at the foot of the stairs. I couldn't see him for the shadows, wood fragments, and loosed rock.

Antony was assessing the stability of the rubble pile, which appeared to be our only escape route, when I felt a strange pulling sensation at my middle. It reminded me of water tugging at my ankles in a stream, only *much* stronger.

"Hold on to me, Lizzy!" cried Antony, grip tightening on my hand.

The current dragged us both abruptly upward, lifting our feet from the ground. I flailed out with my other hand and managed to catch hold of Antony's coat. He reeled me into his arms. The cloud of sound now fully enveloped us, rendering further attempts to speak to each other pointless.

We were whipped up and out of the cellar and then the house itself, Krampus's escape having punched a hole right through the wall. Thanks to the clear night sky, we finally got a look at what was happening—yet I could hardly believe my eyes.

Cloud had been an apt word, for we found ourselves swept up in a kind of cold and vapory train of movement—a sinuous stream of blowing snowflakes filled with all manner of beings. Warriors astride horses galloping into the sky. Knobby, stocky men like the ones carved on Opa's cabinet riding springing stags. Women with loosed hair and trailing garments balanced sidesaddle on brooms arcing upward like great geese. And many regular folk with no mode of transportation who simply flew alongside the others, hair whipped back by the wind.

Out ahead of us charged Krampus astride an enormous stag, scepter held high, its flame burning bright.

We're caught up in the Wild Hunt.

The sleeping city of York spread beneath us, streets all but empty. I saw a man stagger out of a pub, look up at the sky, and hurry back inside. A man on horseback behind the Minster was thrown as his horse took fright at the commotion overhead, and I saw him crawl under the shelter of the trees in the park. We arced round the Minster's great towers and joined the flow of the River Ouse on its course out of the city, starlight gleaming and glinting across the slowly moving black water.

"Mother!"

I pried my eyes from the fields and hills unfolding below us to look into the face of my nearest traveling companion, who still had his arms wrapped securely around me. Following his wide-eyed gaze, I glimpsed a lady a short distance behind us riding a fine-boned mare. The lady leaned over her mount's neck, reins gripped securely and eyes bright with excitement, like she was approaching a fence. As if feeling our eyes on her, she looked up, lips curving in a grin of fond recognition that I had seen before—on Antony.

Our train dipped suddenly, along with my stomach, as we swooped low, racing over the ground. Then the lady got her chance. The front of the train swept over a wall, and the lady and the other mounted spirits jumped it one by one. Yelps of elation went up on all sides, and the riders readied themselves as we approached a hedgerow.

I glanced at Antony and saw relief and joy reflected in his eyes. His gaze met mine for only a moment before it lifted, eyes narrowing. He bobbed his head toward the back of the train. "Look, Lizzy."

A sleigh brought up the rear. Drawn by some stocky breed of deer and driven by one of the knobby, bearded forest men, it bounced along wildly over walls and hedges. A man flailed about in the back, making desperate grabs for the sides and very nearly flying out several times. Periodically he gave a shout of . . . fear? Exhilaration? Impossible to say, but I knew the voice.

Ambrose.

The train was lifting and arcing again, now pointing directly into the cold and distant stars. We climbed and climbed into the glittering sky, frigid air stinging our cheeks and forcing tears from our eyes. Sensing what was coming, I tightened my arms around Antony. Our flight slowed and arced downward. Soon we were plunging toward the earth, and I let out a scream of real terror.

Just short of ploughing into the ground, the train suddenly banked and headed back toward the city, leaving my wretched stomach behind. I prayed it meant the end of this wild ride was in sight. If I could but feel my feet on solid ground again, I hardly cared what came next.

The train plunged right back into the ruined house and down to the half-caved-in cellar, where Antony and I were released without ceremony, tumbling onto the hard floor. The lump on my head pounded anew as I rolled slowly onto my back, catching my breath and checking that Antony was safe and whole beside me. His head rolled toward me, and we shared a look of stunned relief as we sat up.

Overturned lamps and candles began to right themselves and flare to life just in time to illuminate the train of our ghostly companions as they flew through the arched doorway in the Anglo-Saxon wall.

I glimpsed Lady Carlisle among the final riders. Before going through the doorway, she veered away and circled round to make a final pass close by us. She touched her fingers to her lips and raised them in a mother's benediction, and then she, too, disappeared through the wall.

Tears glistened on Antony's cheeks, but before I could speak to him, there came a loud grunt of effort followed by another crash of destruction. I glanced up to find Krampus had knocked down the ancient wall, and it had broken into large, jagged blocks over the floor.

A cry of alarm went up from the opposite end of the cellar. We saw now that Ambrose's sleigh had come to rest on the rubble pile where the stairs had been. He tried to climb out, but the driver muttered something sharp at him and he sank back.

Krampus began stomping the pieces of wall, crushing them to powder. After surveying his handywork, the beast turned, retrieving the scepter from where it rested atop a fallen ceiling beam. Then he fixed his gaze on us.

Antony jumped up, holding out his hand to me but never taking his eyes off Krampus.

Rising, I said on impulse, "St. Nicholas?"

The smoldering dark eyes closed, and the massive shaggy body shrank and receded. The hair that had sprouted all over him reversed direction, and soon a naked old man stood before us, smears of dried blood on his forehead, hands, and various other places. I looked away, and Antony took off his coat and carried it to him.

Despite the saint's frail appearance, he called out in a commanding voice, "Come here, Eliza Grimm."

I swallowed, drew myself up, and obeyed.

"You'll want *this* to put everything to rights again." My breath caught as he held out the scepter. I hesitated, but his gaze sharpened, and I reached and took it from him.

"But how—"

"The command is 'awaken.' Your brother used the Old English, but translation is not required." He frowned. "He carries everything too far."

"What will happen to him?"

The saint's gaze found Ambrose, watching us wide-eyed from the sleigh. "I have long been without a valet."

"You're taking him back to the cave?" I wasn't sure how to feel about this. He had caused a great deal of pain, yet he was still my brother, and it seemed entirely possible he might die in that cave. I didn't think Papa would want that. And to my thinking, Papa and his secrets bore at least some responsibility for what Ambrose had become. "Will it be permanent?" I asked.

"That will depend upon him."

"What of the spirits he imprisoned?" asked Antony. "Have they all returned to . . . wherever they're supposed to be?"

"They have, young sir. Your mother will find peace now, and beyond that, each to what they deserve."

Antony's eyes gleamed, and I reached for his hand.

Then I remembered something. "Several spirits appeared to me in York recently. We thought they might have been watching us for Ambrose. Two of them I would certainly recognize again, and I didn't see them in the hunting party."

"Mm." He frowned. "Place spirits, perhaps. For reasons of their own, they never left the living world. Most of them simply fade away over time. Others become protectors, and your father called those *genius loci*—your brother could have no power over such spirits."

"Maybe they actually meant to *warn* you about Ambrose," said Antony.

I nodded. "Perhaps." Looking again at Nicholas, I said, "What of my papa? I haven't actually seen him, but I feel certain his spirit returned to our shop to help me uncover what Ambrose has been doing."

The saint's brows lifted. "That does indeed sound like Herr Berti."

I waited for him to say more, but instead he turned from us and walked to the sleigh. The hem of Antony's coat reached to his bony knees, and he held it closed as he climbed up to the seat. He gestured for the driver to move and took the reins.

The team of deer had been missing since the spirit train's return, but Nicholas spoke a few words of German and they reappeared. He gave a grunt and snapped the reins, and Antony and I retreated toward the wall again.

Saint, sleigh, deer, and Ambrose lifted from the rubble, and the old man's eyes fixed on what was left of Opa's cabinet—one upright side, the floor, and the back with its carving. The doors lay akimbo in front of it. Off to one side, I was relieved to see the physician's bag with Papa's books and papers resting among the shards of the urn.

Nicholas gave a whistle, and the sleigh heaved toward the cabinet and smashed through, the rest of it splintering and flying apart.

I thought of Papa's lodge and of Ambrose and of whether I'd see either of them again in my lifetime. But as Papa had once written, *any sort of door may take you to any world so long as you believe it will.* Like running curiosity shops and seeing ghosts, I imagined it was a thing a person could eventually learn to do. *Or at least a Grimm.*

Remembering I was gripping the scepter, I held it up and examined it.

"Perhaps we might use it on Father," said Antony.

Our gazes met, and we fell into each other's arms, shaking with laughter.

Awaken

Kissing my forehead, he said, "We should go before anyone grows bold enough to investigate, lest we be swept up in rumor and very perilous questioning."

Antony retrieved the physician's bag, and I gave him the scepter to tuck inside, though it stuck out the top. Then together we scaled the rubble and made our escape.

Clouds had now crowded out the stars, and beautiful powdery flakes were coming down. We tucked our heads, huddled together, and hurried off toward Goodramgate, ducking into shadows or ginnels when we thought we heard voices. Dawn had yet to brighten the sky to the east, but morning came late in these December days. It occurred to me then that today was Yule, the shortest day of the year.

At the shop I produced the key, miraculously still riding in my pocket. Try as we might to keep our voices low, Sally came hurrying down the stairs before we'd made it three steps into the room.

"Mr. Carlisle! Miss Grimm! Thank heaven." Her eyes showed signs of sleeplessness but also great relief.

"Indeed," replied Antony. "I hate to ask at this hour, but we are sorely in need of tea. And brandy, if there is any."

"Yes, sir," she said, nodding and turning for the kitchen. We heard the creaking and clanging of the stove being roused.

I looked at Antony, anticipation roiling my stomach. "I'm not sure I can wait until morning."

"Of course not."

He took the scepter from the bag and handed it to me. Then he lit a lamp, and together we went upstairs.

"Mama," I called softly, tapping her door.

Antony gave me the lamp, and I went to her bedside while he waited outside. Mama rolled toward me, blinking and squinting at the light.

Sitting on the edge of the bed, I set down the lamp and raised the scepter. Her eyes fixed on it with a look of terror.

"Awaken," I said, trying for the tone of command I'd heard Ambrose use.

The flame flared within the iron ring. Mama blinked several more times and then suddenly sat up, gasping like she'd been holding her breath.

"Mama?"

"Oh, child," she answered in a voice rasping from disuse. My heart leaped, and Antony let out an exclamation of surprise and relief.

She reached for me, and I laid down the scepter and fell into her arms. The moment her soft sobs began, my own tears streamed down. I raised my legs to the bed and curled against her, head on her chest, feeling her hand stroking through my hair, which had long since freed itself from its knot.

I heard a soft click as Antony closed the bedroom door between us.

Her arms around me, her breath in my hair—I'd thought I might never feel this again. I was a little girl again, knees bruised from a fall. I squeezed her, nuzzling closer, assuring myself it was real. "Mama is here," she said softly.

When I could speak, I murmured, "How I've missed you."

"Oh, child," she repeated, tremulous, "I'm sorry you've been so alone. It breaks my heart to think of it."

Her voice was still full of gravel. Outside the door, I heard Sally ask Antony whether she should enter.

"Come, Sally," I called.

She carried in the tray, set it on the table by the window, and poured two cups. Keeping her gaze unobtrusively lowered, she carried the cups to the bedside table and set them down.

"Thank you, Sally," said Mama.

A smile spread over Sally's face. She gave a quick nod, replying, "Yes, ma'am," before leaving us.

Mama picked up her cup and drank it quickly. When she spoke again, her voice had steadied. "You and your young man seem to have worked a miracle, Lizzy."

I tilted my head, looking up at her. A smile rested on her lips. "You know of Antony?"

She nodded. "After what happened to me, I mostly wasn't here. But sometimes I was. Though try as I might, I couldn't speak to you."

I sat up, taking her hand in mine. "Where were you when you weren't here, Mama?"

Her eyes drifted to the window, and I felt a stab of dread. But she replied, "Oftentimes simply lost in my head. My thoughts. My memories. But sometimes I was *there*, in the ghostly realm, where it happened."

"Where you met Ambrose Stoke?"

Her gaze came back to me. "I had been speaking to Laura Hollis, whose distraught husband had asked me to contact her—you remember? Mr. Stoke appeared, carrying that stick with him. I knew him because he came into the shop once after your father died, asking about some books. I was still too grief-stricken to do more than make a cursory search for them, and I sent him away disappointed."

So Ambrose had come and tried his chances with Mama after Papa died. Knowing what I did now, it didn't surprise me he'd omitted this detail when he came to me. But I did wonder about him making a point of confessing that he'd come to Papa. Perhaps he thought his honesty might soften me toward him. He'd also told me on that visit the whole sad story about his mother's gift and his father's book-burning.

Mama's eyes moved to the scepter. "He held up the stick and said something, and Laura Hollis . . ." She frowned, thinking. "She was somehow drawn *into* it. He did the same to me, but it was different. It left me . . ." She looked at me. "Well, you know."

"You went to sleep for nearly a year, until one day you tried to speak to Antony—to Mr. Carlisle. Do you remember?"

She nodded. "I do. When I was in the ghostly realm, though I could no longer speak, I was more aware of what was going on around me. At one point I recognized Lady Carlisle, talking with a girl I assumed to be her daughter. Mr. Stoke appeared and took Lady Carlisle, leaving her daughter in the same state he left me. When you introduced Mr. Carlisle to me, it woke me enough to try to speak to him about his sister. Of course it came to nothing."

"No, Mama!" I squeezed her hand. "Because of what you did, Antony and I shared our stories and began working together to solve the mystery of your affliction. I could never have done it without his help."

She smiled. "I like Mr. Carlisle very much, Lizzy."

I smiled, too, but looked down at my hands. "I wish his father felt the same way about *me*."

"Perhaps he may experience a change of heart." She pulled me into her arms, rocking a little, as if I were indeed a child again. I rested my head against her chest, more tears falling.

There was so much more to discuss. Papa and his books and his travels. Mary Broadmoor, and the truth about Ambrose—his scheme, and his fate. Yet in this moment, it seemed that none of it much mattered.

I woke in the gray light of morning. My first thought was that I was late to making breakfast and opening the shop. Then my head throbbed, and the whole of the past week came back to me.

I glanced at the bedside table, where the scepter still rested. Where was Mama? And Antony?

I got up and went to the door, steadying myself against it as vertigo unbalanced me. I took a slow breath and went out.

Antony sat alone at the dining table drinking coffee, and my heart sang to see him there.

He looked up. "There you are."

I smiled. "Here I am."

"Come and sit down."

I joined him at the table. "Where is everyone?"

Filling my cup, he replied, "Mrs. Grimm insisted on opening the shop and letting you sleep, and she and Sally have done so."

Happiness flooded me. "If this is all a dream, I hope it never ends."

His eyes danced. "It's not a dream."

Realizing I was both starving and tremendously thirsty, I added milk to my coffee to cool it and drank the entire cup. We never had coffee in the house since Papa had gone. Sally must have bought some. Antony poured me another cup and buttered a piece of toast, setting it on my plate.

After the second cup, my faculties returned to something like normal. "We must go and wake Sophia." Thinking of my last encounter with his father, I frowned and amended, "Or you must."

"Finish your breakfast," he said. "Then you can tidy up"—he reached out and gently rubbed at something on my cheek, causing my heart to flop over—"and we'll go together."

I eyed him dubiously.

"We must face him, Lizzy. For better or for worse. He must be made to understand that the very thing he closed his mind against has brought him a cure for his daughter. That if I had been more like *him*—which he has wished for as long as I can remember—Sophia would likely have spent the rest of her days in an asylum."

"And if he doesn't see it that way?"

He reached for my hand. "Then you and I will find another way. Because nothing I would gain by losing you could make my life worth living."

Trembling, I nodded, and he leaned forward and caught my lips between his.

Then he murmured against my cheek, "Do you still trust me completely?"

"With my very life."

Antony left for Carlisle House, insisting on sending a fly for Mama and me so we need not walk in the snow. When I'd washed my face, subdued my hair, and donned my newly cleaned and repaired rose silk, I went down to the shop—arriving just as Charlie Croft came through the door.

Going to meet her I passed Mama, who was helping a customer, and I overheard the gentleman mention last night's "ruckus." Mama was replying, "You know, Mr. Grimm's father—he was from Bavaria—used to tell stories of . . ."

"Morning, Lizzy," said Charlie, pinching the brim of her hat. She wore a worried expression.

"It's good to see you," I said. "Is everything all right?"

"I'm all right, but . . ." Her gaze found Mama. "Is that Mrs. Grimm?"

"Indeed it is, Charlie. She has recovered."

Eyebrows lifting, she replied, "So I see. That's wonderful. Will be some consolation after . . ." Her eyes came back to my face, searching. "Could we have a word in private?"

"Certainly," I said. "I'm going out, but I think I have a few minutes. Why don't you follow me."

I led her to the reading nook in the back corner of the shop, where Mama had once done her medium work and I'd first met Mr. Stoke. Two more customers had come in, and Sally was bustling about with tea and biscuits, so the activity would give us a little privacy.

"What can I do for you, Charlie?"

"First off I'll come right out and say that I heard of your engagement to Ambrose Stoke—though I understand it had not yet been publicly announced—through a friend of mine."

Oh dear. "Yes, that's right."

"Well, after last night, I wanted to check on you. But by your look, I'm guessing you haven't yet heard, and I'm sorry for that. Though maybe it comes easier from a friend." She took off her hat, and I held my breath. "Mr. Stoke's house was badly damaged last night, Lizzy. There are signs he was excavating in the cellar, and I believe the constable has blamed that for the collapse. There's also some gossip that Stoke may be responsible for the ghostly shenanigans some folk witnessed last night. But I'm afraid the worst of it is that the man himself is *missing.*"

"I . . ." What could I say? This wasn't something Antony and I had gotten around to discussing.

My friend looked worried I might faint, like the day she'd revealed the truth about the Ginnel books.

"May I ask how you've come by your information, Charlie?"

She shuffled her feet and lowered her gaze. "Well, some is just talk in the street, but also I'm pretty closely acquainted with Isabel Stoke." Her gaze came again to my face, and there was something in her eyes that hadn't been in her words. "That's just between you and me. I don't believe her family would understand our . . . friendship."

"I . . . I see." I thought I did, anyway. "Thank you for trusting that to me. I may not be as good at secrets as Papa, but yours is safe with me." She smiled, inclining her head. I continued, "I like Miss Stoke very much, and I can imagine she is beside herself with worry."

While I hesitated, I realized I didn't have it in me to lie to her. Not after the kindness she'd shown me. "Charlie, the truth is that I know something of last night because of the investigating Mr. Carlisle and I did while trying to uncover the source of Miss Carlisle's and Mama's affliction. It has some to do with Papa's books but mostly to do with Mr. Stoke losing his way and getting in over his head. While I believe Mr. Stoke is well and whole, I don't believe he's likely to be heard from anytime soon. This is not information we intend to share with the constable, because frankly, the fellow would only question our soundness of mind. But you are free to use it as you like."

Charlie chewed on this a long minute, and then her gaze again found Mama, whose smile was lighting up the place. "I know Isabel is fond of her uncle," she said. "The girl has a heart of gold, just maybe isn't as worldly as some of us have had to be. When he was in my shop about the books, he rubbed me wrong. He's a charmer for sure, but I couldn't help feeling it was all shine on a shadow." Her eyes came back to my face. "I thank you for being honest with me, Lizzy. I may tell Isabel something of all this, to give her some relief, but we'll leave the constable out of it."

I reached out and squeezed her hand. "Thank you, Charlie. And I especially want to thank you for your concern for me. You've been a true friend."

The shop bells jingled then, and a man in livery stepped inside. "Mrs. Grimm?"

Mama looked up, and I called, "We're coming." The man gave a nod and stepped back outside.

Charlie smiled, eyeing me speculatively. "If you happen upon any more news worth the telling, come by the shop. I'll give you tea."

I grinned. "I will."

Charlie left us, and as Mama finished the transaction with the customer she was helping, my gaze wandered to the void where Opa's cabinet had been.

And there stood Papa. He wore the coat, and the flatcap, and the great winter boots, an ornately carved pipe between his lips. With a grin he lifted his cap. Then he turned and walked through the wall.

Hearing a quiet gasp, I glanced at Mama. She smiled, closed the cashbox, and wiped a tear from her cheek.

Mama and I bundled up against the cold and climbed into the small carriage that awaited us outside the shop.

"Don't be nervous, Mama," I said as we got underway.

She smiled, wrapping her gloved hand around mine. "I'm not, my love." Her cheeks were pink, and her hair and eyes shone. She looked ten years younger.

I laughed. "I suppose it's me."

"All will be well, you'll see."

I wanted to believe her, but inside I was a mess of twitching nerves.

All too soon, the fly pulled up in front of Carlisle House, and a footman handed us out. The snow continued its soft descent, accumulating in earnest now, though still in its gentle, quiet way. The path to the front door had been recently cleared, and we arrived with dry feet.

"You're here," Antony called, meeting us in the entryway. He kissed Mama's hand. "Welcome to Carlisle House, Mrs. Grimm."

"Thank you, Mr. Carlisle," she replied with the sweetest of smiles.

"Is all well?" I asked quietly.

"All is rather the same," he replied, frowning, and my stomach knotted. "Which is not to be unexpected, considering the rather fantastic nature of the story I've just told him. All will be well now that you're here."

I raised an eyebrow. "People keep saying that, which unfortunately tends to have the opposite effect of the one intended."

He grinned and offered Mama his arm. Sighing, I tucked the scepter—which I'd wrapped in an old shawl—under my arm and followed them to the stairs between the salon and the drawing room.

Upstairs, Antony led us to a beautiful bedroom, all soft surfaces and floral patterns. Sophia sat in a chair by the fireplace, staring into the flames. The baron stood at the mantel, severe as ever. When his eyes came to rest on Mama, they widened slightly.

"Father," said Antony, "this is Mrs. Grimm. *Miss* Grimm you've had the pleasure of meeting already."

Lord Carlisle's grunt was almost, but not quite, under his breath. Yet his tone was civil enough as he said, "I'm happy to see you recovered from your illness, madam. I'm sure it must be a great relief to both of you."

"Thank you, Lord Carlisle," she said graciously. "I'm so grateful to your son and my daughter for bringing me back."

The baron frowned. "Yes, well, I'm sorry to say that what my son has told me, if you'll forgive my language, sounds like a lot of trumped-up nonsense."

Mama's lovely smile remained, but she said, "Indeed, sir, I'm not sure that I *am* comfortable with your language, considering my life would be worth little had it not been for them." She looked at Sophia. "I was exactly as your daughter is now, you see."

Lord Carlisle's frown remained frozen on his lips, but a shine came to his eyes.

Mama looked at me. "Perhaps what Lord Carlisle needs is a demonstration."

Drawing a breath, I unwrapped the scepter.

The baron couldn't refrain from letting out a dubious huff, but I kept my eyes on Sophia.

Antony stepped back so that I could stand before her. I knew he wanted *me* to do this. I knew he believed if I did, his father would accept me. But in that moment, I realized he would never accept me until he accepted his son.

Turning to Lord Carlisle, I said, "I hope that you are proud of your son, sir. From the moment I met him, he has thought of little else but the plight of his sister. He resolved to save her, and he braved great danger to do so. I've never met a man to whom his family mattered more."

I held out the scepter to Antony. He looked conflicted, but he took it from me.

Holding it before Sophia, he commanded, *"Awaken."*

The flame within the ring flickered to life. Sophia's eyes regained their focus. Her lips parted, and she uttered hoarsely, "Papa?"

A quiet sob escaped his lips. Wide-eyed, he dropped down before his daughter and took her hands. Voice quaking, he uttered, "My darling girl, Papa is here."

Her gaze slid past him, and she held out one of her hands to Antony. "Brother?"

He beamed at her, tears sliding down his face, and joined his father on his knees before her.

I took Mama's arm, and together we left the room, closing the door behind us.

We made our way downstairs and were intercepted by a maid, who told us tea and cakes awaited us in the red salon. The grand room where we had supped at the ball felt much cozier with all its plush and elegant furnishings returned. Mama sat down and accepted a teacup, but I walked to one of the windows facing the street, where the swan sculpture had been stationed. As I watched the snow coming down, I began to hear ripples and flutters among the household staff as word traveled round that "Miss Sophia" had woken from her long sleep.

Then I heard a door close upstairs. My heart thumped as footsteps crossed above us and quickly descended.

"Mrs. Grimm?" I turned at the sound of Antony's voice. "My father would like to speak to you in his study. Helen will show you the way."

Mama looked at me, eyes glittering. Then she nodded and rose to her feet, following the maid back to the stairs.

Antony's eyes met mine, and my heart thumped faster as he moved toward me. "How is Sophia?" I asked.

His smile broadened, and he took my hands. "Sophia is fussing in front of the mirror so that she may come down to you."

"Indeed?" I said tremulously.

"Indeed. For I've told her she must properly meet her new sister-in-law. But I'm afraid we've all gotten ahead of ourselves."

"Have we?"

He laughed, pulling me closer and wrapping his arms around me. He kissed my forehead, then my cheek, then murmured in my ear, "You have enchanted me, Lizzy Grimm. Will you help me give this fairy tale its proper ending?"

The low rumble of his voice sent a warm shiver through me.

"Happily," I breathed.

"The Best Gift of All"

Antony

With many preparations to be made for Christmas, we left early for Gilling Hall. The old place might easily have been very dreary that year, our first without Mother. I could see that my father felt it. By the way his fingers trembled as he helped Sophia cut paper angels for the tree. By the way his eyes kept drifting to the place we set for her at dinner each evening. By the tears that threatened as we loaded up the sleigh for starlight rides in the snow—something Mother would have taken great delight in.

Sophia and I missed her, too, but we had something he didn't. We each had been granted our own glimpses of her since her death. And we were secure in the knowledge that she was where she was supposed to be now, wherever that might be.

Though the atmosphere of the house was tinged with this sweet sadness, joy also spread throughout. The servants buzzed with busy excitement in their preparations for the two great occasions. The house was virtually stuffed with evergreen boughs and holly. We woke each morning to icicles at the window and the aroma of warm spice drifting up the stairs. Our days were filled with sledding and snow play. Our evening feasts began with champagne, ending with mulled wine and ghost stories before the blazing fire in the hall.

My favorite moments were those when Lizzy and I stole away to the morning room, whether day or night, to sip tea together—much as we'd done in the early days of our acquaintance—and to talk about the future.

I had told Lizzy I'd never stand between her and her father's business, no matter what *my* father might have to say on the subject. But the old baron was cunning and triumphed in the end, promising to increase his support for Mother's foundation if Lizzy and I would run it. Lizzy accepted graciously, and tearfully. Like me she had admired my mother, and she would now be in a position to help women like herself, who found themselves on the brink of losing everything.

It was agreed that Mrs. Grimm would take over the management of Grimm Curiosities for as long as it pleased her to do so. I couldn't imagine Lizzy ever fully leaving the old place, and it was understood—between the two of us, at least—that she would spend as much time there as she liked, and that we would take tea above the shop as often as we were able.

By Christmas Eve, all of it had been settled, and Papa, Lizzy, Mrs. Grimm, Sophia, and I decorated the Christmas tree while the staff sang carols. On Christmas morning, Lizzy came down the grand staircase, Sally managing her skirts, an angel in snowy white silk.

I don't think a wedding had ever come to pass so quickly, and eyebrows would surely be raised. But with all the gossip among the good people of York surrounding me, Lizzy, and Ambrose, even the baron had agreed that the sooner Lizzy and I settled into Carlisle House as man and wife, the sooner people would grow bored and move on. No one had thought a special license could be obtained in time, but it was the season of miracles—and the archbishop admired my mother's charity work.

When we'd returned from church and the wedding breakfast had been eaten, we all ran out into the fresh snow together, and it was very late that evening before Lizzy and I found ourselves alone in the rooms the servants had prepared for us.

Sally had just left my new wife, whom I found curled on the rug before the fire, a glass of sherry in hand, her cloud of golden curls loose about her shoulders.

Kicking off my shoes, loosening my tie, I went to sit beside her. "Merry Christmas, my love."

She smiled. "Merry Christmas."

"I thought we'd never be alone together again." I bent toward her, rubbing my nose against hers.

She laughed, and I felt her tremble under my hands as they slid up her nightdress to hold her waist. "We've had tea together, haven't we?" she teased.

"So much tea," I agreed, and she laughed harder. "But there were always servants. Or Sophia."

"You don't really mind that. Sophia, I mean."

I leaned forward, touching my lips to hers. "No, I don't," I murmured. "I thank heaven for it every moment."

"She carries that doll you gave her everywhere. The one from Grimm's."

I pressed a line of kisses down her neck, and her trembling increased. Her hand came to the back of my head as she made a soft sound that set my blood racing.

I drew back and looked at her. Snowflakes danced in her eyes, reflecting the firelight.

"Really she was too old for the present," I said. "I knew it even then, though she does seem to love it." I traced her mouth with the tip of a finger, and her lips parted. "But the doll had golden curls and a rose gown, and I bought her because I wanted something to remember you by, though I didn't realize it until later. At one point I wondered how I would ever give it up."

She moved closer to me, fingers slipping into my hair. "But you did."

I took hold of her waist and pulled her into my lap. "Ah, but you see, St. Nicholas has given me the best gift of all."

Acknowledgments

Like the Victorians, I adore a curiosity shop and a good Christmas ghost story, and after setting *Salt & Broom* in the Yorkshire countryside, I was keen to write a story set in a city. All these elements came together in *Grimm Curiosities*.

Before I go on to talk about that, there are some folks I could not do this without whom I need to tell you about.

First of all, at Writers House: my agent, Robin Rue, my champion and sage, along with the indispensable Beth Miller. Also Tom Ishizuka for breaking me in on a new side of the business.

To my Amazon editor, Lauren Plude, and to 47North for believing in me and my stories, and to developmental editor Lindsey Faber for making my stories better. Also to my copyeditor, Sarah E., for patience, enthusiasm, and a sharp eye.

To the cover design team for *Salt & Broom*, who freakin' knocked it out of the park. Thank you for your beautiful work, Colin Verdi. Also the voices of Jane and Rochester in *Salt & Broom*, Elizabeth Bower and Tim Bruce.

To the witches of Instagram, who inspire me every day and who helped to make the launch of *Salt & Broom* successful beyond my dreams!

To Debbi and Jason for always being there.

Now, about *Grimm Curiosities* . . .

I got to visit York, England, in 2023, and it is *made* for storytelling. So much history every way you turn. Goodramgate, where the Grimms live, is a real street, and their house is based on a real one on that street (now a very good Italian restaurant where the owner will sing to you).

Carlisle House is loosely based on Fairfax House, a lovely Georgian town house that belonged to an earl and his family. The ghost Anne Carlisle is loosely based on Margaret Clitherow, a Catholic saint and martyr executed for hiding priests. And the ghost Richard of York was inspired by the real nobleman who tried to be king during the War of the Roses. And if you loved Charlie Croft as much as I loved writing her, you might be interested in reading about Gentleman Jack (a.k.a. Anne Lister), who inspired Charlie. In 1834, Anne Lister married Ann Walker at the Holy Trinity Church on Goodramgate, which is also mentioned in the book.

The ginnels and snickets of York, now often referred to as snickelways, thanks to author Mark W. Jones, really exist, and I walked through as many as I could find. I particularly loved the Barley Hall snickelway where Lizzy sees the Viking ghost (now referred to as the Coffee Yard) because there is a lovely little café with seating in the courtyard. And the red devil above the printshop? He's real, too, as is the lore about him!

Finally, the items used by Ambrose (including the scepter) were inspired by artifacts in the Anglo-Saxon treasure of Sutton Hoo. And his house is based on a real one in York that has ruins of a Roman bath in the cellar.

I did tons of research for this book, and particularly helpful were:

- *The Krampus and the Old, Dark Christmas* by Al Ridenour
- An 1851 map of the city of York by John Rapkin and Henry Winkles
- The incredibly helpful History of York website (www.history-ofyork.org.uk)
- Blog posts too numerous to mention about various aspects of Victorian society but especially currency, courtesy titles, and balls

- My language guy Jeff Lilly, who helped with my German and Anglo-Saxon (and has helped with Irish and Old Norse in my other books)

I strive to get things right every single time—I seriously hate even the tiniest errors—and still, every single time something gets missed (like loons in *Salt & Broom*, which are apparently called *divers* in England). I wish I could blame the printer's devil, but I can't. I apologize in advance for inaccuracies.

About the Author

Sharon Lynn Fisher is the author of *Salt & Broom*, the Faery Rehistory series, *Ghost Planet*, *The Ophelia Prophecy*, and *Echo 8*. She writes smart, twisty, passionate tales—mash-ups of fantasy (or sci-fi) and slow-burn romance set in lush and atmospheric worlds. A city mouse whose country-mouse-aspiring family dragged her to an acreage just outside Seattle, Sharon is mom to two brilliant teens, two ridiculous goats, an orange cat, and a fluctuating number of poultry. When she's not writing, you'll find her wandering the woods looking for mushrooms and fairies. For more information, visit www.sharonlynnfisher.com.